Marina

by Susan K. Downs
and Susan May Warren

Marina

ISBN 1-59310-350-6

This book is a work of fiction. Names, characters, places, and incidents are either products of the author's imagination or used fictitiously. Any similarity to actual people, organizations, and/or events is purely coincidental.

Scripture quotations are taken from the King James Version of the Bible.

Scripture quotations are also taken from the HOLY BIBLE, NEW INTERNATIONAL VERSION®. NIV®. Copyright © 1973, 1978, 1984 by International Bible Society. Used by permission of Zondervan. All rights reserved.

For more information about Susan K. Downs and Susan May Warren, please access the authors' Web sites at the following Internet addresses:
www.susankdowns.com
www.susanmaywarren.com

Acquisitions and Editorial Director: Rebecca Germany
Editorial Consultant: Becky Durost Fish
Art Director: Jason Rovenstine
Layout Design: Anita Cook

Published by Barbour Publishing, Inc., P.O. Box 719, Uhrichsville, Ohio 44683, www.barbourbooks.com

Our mission is to publish and distribute inspirational products offering exceptional value and biblical encouragement to the masses.

Member of the
Evangelical Christian
Publishers Association

SUSAN K. DOWNS

Dedication:
It is for freedom that Christ has set us free.
GALATIANS 5: 1 NIV

Thank You, thank You, thank You, Lord,
for setting my spirit free!

Acknowledgments:

We've taken to calling them "The Greatest Generation"—those who sacrificed and fought for freedom, not only for the sake of Americans, but for citizens of the world. Without the commitment of these brave souls to liberty's cause, our world would wear a much different face.

I hope you will allow *Heirs of Anton: Marina* to serve as both *a reminder. . .*and *a call.* Not all World War II freedom campaigns were publicized in the daily newspaper. Not all who fought received the honor and recognition they deserved. And not all who battled could claim a decisive victory in their war against tyranny. Even so, they remained faithful to the cause of liberty, regardless of the cost.

The struggle for freedom should not be confined to generations past. May we never forget our obligation as children of The Greatest Generation. We who now enjoy the unmerited liberties that our parents and grandparents sacrificed to uphold must continue to fight for all those who seek release from the bonds of evil oppression and domination. The call continues to go forth. We cannot bask in our blessings while souls still cry out from their captivity. " 'From everyone who has been given much, much will be demanded; and from the one who has been entrusted with much, much more will be asked' " (Luke 12:48 NIV).

As precious to us as our civil rights may be, there is a freedom far greater than freedom from earthly tyranny. "For our struggle is not against flesh and blood, but against the rulers, against the authorities, against the powers of this dark world and against the spiritual forces of evil in the heavenly realms" (Ephesians 6:12 NIV).

As you read the story of Edward, Marina, and their partisans, remember that the yearning for independence is not limited to residents of a democracy in the Western hemisphere. The thirst for liberty springs from the heart of every soul.

" 'So if the Son sets you free, you will be free indeed' " (John 8:36 NIV).

I dedicate my efforts on this project to my stepfather, George Williams, and to all those brave men and women of The Greatest Generation. George, you are an inspiration to me.

Thank you, Susie Warren, for sharing my vision of the story of Anton Klassen's family. . .and for putting feet to the dream. We are quite the team!

And, special thanks to David, my beloved husband and best friend. You've given me the freedom to discover who God intended me to be. For that, and so much more, I am forever grateful.

SUSAN MAY WARREN

Dedication:
For Your glory, Lord!

Acknowledgments:
The *Heirs of Anton* series sat in my heart for years before Susan and the Lord's prompting brought it to light. I remember sitting in my neighbor, Totyemilla's apartment, listening

to her tell me the story of when her father returned from war—five years after he'd left. She and her mother were working in their garden and an outline appeared on the horizon. Her mother dropped her spade and sprinted toward the man—her husband and the father of her three children. Totyemilla, then seven or eight, had no recollection of him. I remember thinking—How did people stay sane during the dark years of World War II, when fathers, sons, and brothers (as well as many women!) left for the front, an unknown future before them? How did they cope with the suspicion and fears that permeated their culture during the reign of Stalin? As Susan and I developed this series, one verse seemed to stand out as an answer—Psalm 100:5. The belief that God was faithful from generation to generation and that His love would permeate their lives. Russia is just beginning to see the fruition of years of teeth-clenching faith. And while tomorrow may be uncertain, especially in our current political climate, Christians can trust in the Lord's faithfulness, especially when we don't understand the mess around us.

As an adopted daughter, I was blessed to have incredible parents who cherished me. But I never understood the deep sacrifices of adoption or the trust involved in surrendering your child to the unknown until I had my own children. The Heirs of Anton books have given me an opportunity to experience that sacrifice, as well as the strength that comes from believing in God's promises. Marina is a story of trust. It's a story of looking back and recognizing God's faithfulness and looking forward to believe Him for the future. And, it's a story of the real meaning of love. . .that sometimes it means more than sunsets and holding hands and happily ever after.

I wrote this story twice—once in Russia and once in America. And, as usual, God provided on both sides of the ocean. My deepest gratitude goes to the following blessings:

Dannette (Bell) Lund—yes, this is that book I was telling you about! Your friendship that summer in Russia was a fresh breeze into my life. A reminder that God loves me and cares even about my frazzled emotions. Thank you for your enthusiasm and support for all my projects and for being an iron on iron sister-in-law in my life.

Maya and Daniel Denisiuk—I still can't believe how much you know about Japan. But most importantly, thank you for not laughing too hard at the (former) French guy in Poland and helping me get it right. (I hope!) I'm still amazed at God's timing. . .and so glad I have someone to speak Russian with. You both are a blessing to my life and the life of our small church.

Susan K. Downs—thank you for being excited about this story! I can't believe God has graced me with your friendship. Thank you for believing in this project, for your commitment to getting the details right, and for crying at all the good parts. Your friendship is a gift in my life.

Gene and Luda Khakhaleva and Antonina Fedorovna—your stories still linger in my heart—as do you. I miss you tremendously and thank the Lord for His faithfulness in giving the Warrens a family in Russia.

Vadeem and Sveta and kiddos—we miss the fish! And we'll never forget "nasha vremya na morye!" Thank you for letting us share your lives, your stories, and your family. (I told you your great-aunt would make it into a book!)

David, Sarah, Peter, and Noah—I'm so blessed to be your mom—more than you will ever know. And I'm praising God for Psalm 100:5 in your lives.

Andrew—For the yesterdays, todays, and tomorrows that you are used by God to remind me that He loves me.

PSKOV, RUSSIA 1941

In the quietest, most fragile corner of her heart, Marina knew Dmitri would abandon her—just as her parents had.

Marina Antonovna Klassen Vasileva barely restrained herself from crumpling at her husband's feet as she watched him pack his meager belongings: a comb, his Bible—pieces of his life snatched from hers, leaving gaping, ragged holes in her chest.

It was quite possible she'd never be whole again.

"I can't believe you volunteered." Her voice sounded ghostly, to match her dying spirit. Marina sat at the end of the wooden bed, her knees pulled up to her chest so as to hold in her heart lest it shatter. Her gaze fell away from her new husband, from his movements at the mirror as he adjusted his olive green Russian army uniform. She couldn't bear the expression of anticipation on his face.

"It's not too soon." Dmitri turned, and Marina couldn't ignore the way her pulse notched up a beat when his sweet, honey brown eyes traveled over her. He always had the ability to reduce her to a puddle of kasha with a smile, and now, the sadness on his face stirred away her fury. She bit her trembling lip and blinked back tears, feeling only weak.

He took a step toward her and ran his strong hand over her hair. "The Motherland needs me. Hitler can't be trusted, and our Fearless Leader needs us to guard our new lands."

Marina knew more than loyalty beat in his wide, muscled chest. Dmitri longed to see the world. Taste adventure. She could hardly blame her peasant husband for his enthusiasm. He'd been offered a chance to explore the new land Stalin had annexed for Russia—Lvov, Ukraine. The world outside of Pskov suddenly called to him in volumes he, at twenty, couldn't begin to ignore.

Didn't he hear his bride, their future calling him, as well? Marina pressed her fingertips to her eyelids. "Promise me you'll come back."

His shiny new leather boots—the first pair of new shoes he'd ever owned—squeaked as he knelt beside her. "Of course, *maya dorogaya*. Russia is not fighting a war. We're simply reminding the fascist Nazis that we're here, on the other side of the border, and that they need to stay in their yard. I'll be back before the potato harvest."

Marina opened her eyes, attempting a smile at his humor. She ran a trembling finger along his square jaw, taking in every last detail—the way his dark hair curled around his ears, the scar on his chin from a childhood brawl, the rapscallion curve of his smile. Her chest constricted, and she fought for breath, nearly drowning beneath a cascading sense of loss.

"Oh, Marina," Dmitri said, and the texture of his voice caused tears to flow down her cheeks. He pulled her to his chest. Her cheek rubbed against rough wool, and the smell of mothballs obliterated his masculine, earthy, farmer's scent.

"You're all I have," she whispered.

He leaned away and cupped her face between his hands. His eyes darkened. "That's not true."

Marina looked at her fingers, knitted together on her lap. "Mother isn't my real family. She just took me in because I needed a home." She met his eyes and saw the sadness in them. "But now I belong to you and you to me. I have no one else."

Dmitri dragged his thumb along her cheek. "Dear Marina. You do have someone else. You have God. He's been your Father when you had no earthly father. And He will bind our family together. No matter what happens, He will guard over us and protect our family. You must trust Him for that."

"Will He bring you home?"

Dmitri smiled and kissed her sweetly, gently. "You can count on it."

<hr />

Edward Neumann crouched next to a gnarled oak tree, his eyes trained on a small clearing twenty yards in front of him, and wondered how he'd come to despise spring.

When he was a kid in upstate New York, the thaw and the breaking of the Schoharie River brought the promise of lazy days of fishing and cool dips when the temperature soared. He loved the thick smell of overturned earth as his father and brothers plowed the soil in the fields, and at times, he ached for the feel of cold, rich dirt filling the pores of his hands. Somewhere deep in his farmer's heart, he knew he should love spring.

Unfortunately, spring in this swatch of northern Poland, thirty kilometers from Lodz, meant mud, cold, and a rotting food supply.

A leftover breath of winter wind hissed through the Polish forest and raised the hair on his neck. He shivered despite his leather coat. His fingers felt wooden, and he hoped he still had a grip on the trigger of the US carbine rifle he poised on his shoulder. Mud and grime and cold had long since soaked through his worn wool pants and found the hole in his leather boots.

But the cold that saturated his bones emanated from within. A cold that on inky-dark, frigid nights weakened his tenuous hold on faith and nudged him further into despair.

At the moment, however, he clutched a death grip on the only thing that mattered—hope.

For you, Katrina.

Around him, an eerie quiet pervaded the forest. No birds chirping. No branches cracked. The low sun boiled crimson along the treetops and turned the birch trees blood red. Edward glanced behind him and easily made out Marek, the upper-class Pole who had, some six months prior, escaped the net around Warszawa and joined the Farmer's National Army. His cool demeanor while he assessed the clearing betrayed a nobleman's posture, as if he were watching a performance of *Swan Lake* at Teatr Norodowy.

Edward held up a hand to Marek, then pointed to Raina, who'd taken a position across the forest. He could barely make out the blond's face, but her quick wave settled relief in his heart. Her team was in place.

The song of a mockingbird brought his gaze left, to Simon, the RAF Hurricane pilot who'd barely escaped a fiery landing on the border of Estonia. Fleeing from Estonians loyal to Germany, Simon joined the Polish resistance. The two-way radio he'd secreted with him sent Edward to his knees in gratitude, and even more so when he discovered the Brit was a fellow believer. Edward had to admit, even after crawling through sodden leaves and cold snow, Simon still looked the Englishman—clean-shaven, tidy. Bringing a touch of class to their ragtag partisan unit.

Marek signaled all clear—his scouts had scoured the south end of the forest and come up clean. Edward nodded. He raised his hand and directed Wladek and Stefan, two teenaged Poles who had the courage of the entire Third Reich, to enter the clearing. In the middle, glinting like precious rubies, lay two metal canisters. Edward prayed they indeed included clothes and food—maybe some canned meat or even sugar—along with weapons and ammo. He'd noticed Anna Lechon's bony knees protruding from her pants, and too many of his fighters' sweaters were held together with twine. Most of all, he hated to see the pale moons under young Anna's wide brown eyes. She reminded him painfully of his little niece back home.

And of the Polish Jews he'd seen beaten and forced into boxcars. So much like his own ancestors—accused, tortured, murdered because of their beliefs.

Anna even reminded him occasionally of Katrina. Brave in her frailty. Brave as the Nazis lined her up against a wall.

Brave unto death.

Edward blinked away the brutal images that never lurked far from the surface of his mind. He positioned the gun into his shoulder and watched with coiled breath while his two faithful partisans dashed out from cover.

The wind froze as time ticked away in their steps. More than once, a well-hidden dispatch of SS men and their dogs had ambushed a Resistance unit.

The boys reached the supply barrels and attacked them with vigor. The muscles in Edward's neck pulsed, but his breath released slowly as he watched the young men open the first drum and raise the shiny black barrel of a British "Sten." The Poles would assemble the pieces into submachine guns. *Thanks, Colonel Stone.* When Stefan opened the second barrel, Edward blessed his director for his golden heart. Stefan held up a can of coffee, and Edward could nearly taste it hit his mouth—bitter, hot, smelling of home. Stefan turned and looked directly at him, a wide grin on his youthful face.

Edward nodded, feeling relief rush through him. Maybe this spring would bring the seeds of hope. Of victory.

The crack of a rifle shattered the crisp air. Edward choked on his relief as Stefan jerked, then crumpled to his knees. Another shot sent Wladek airborne. He landed ten feet from the canister. Reeling, Edward scanned the forest, searching for the black coats of Nazi SS men. Nothing but barren trees and shadow. His partisans, however, dressed in rags of all colors, stood out like stars in the night sky.

Oh, how he hated spring.

"Let's get out of here!" Simon screamed into his ear. He fisted Edward's worn coat.

The canister pinged as another shot hit. Edward went weak at the site of Stefan crawling between the containers, his face screwed up in pain. *Oh dear Lord, please, no! The boy is still alive!*

Simon read his thoughts. "You must leave him! Now!"

Edward turned to him. "Go!" he hissed. He trained his eyes on Stefan, tasting bile at the look of terror on the youth's face. What had he gotten them into?

The spongy forest floor swallowed Simon's footsteps.

Across the meadow, Edward saw Raina had also abandoned her post, like the good soldier he'd trained her to be. Head home, fast and covertly. At all costs, don't let the enemy find you. They all knew too much about other partisan units to be taken alive. *Run, Raina!*

Marek had also fled, taking Anna. Only Edward knew the eighteen-year-old girl had escaped from the Warsaw ghetto, a secret he'd take with him to the grave. *God of Israel, watch over Your children.* He whitened his grip on his rifle and trained his eyes on Stefan. "I won't leave you, kid."

Not like he had Katrina. Never again. *At all costs.*

He crouched in the soggy earth, listening to his partisans flee, hearing gunshots, tasting despair. As the noise of barking dogs ricocheted through the forest and darkness hooded the sky, Edward felt the fingers of failure close in around him.

So much for spring.

arina dug her fingers into the soft soil, wincing as the fresh dirt wedged under her nails. The scorching early-August sun burned her neck as it slanted through the poplar tree hovering over the grave. She closed her eyes and bit the inside of her lip, but the groan emerged anyway. Her knees ground holes into the soft mound, and the cold earth radiated through her until it found her soul. She raised her gaze to the cloudless blue sky and glared at the One who had so completely abandoned her. Finally. Brutally.

She'd spent her words. Time and disbelief had reduced them to a groan, and over the past two weeks, denial had become her only comforter. God had surely been silent.

They hadn't recovered enough of him to dispatch remains. Instead, she'd received a sealed box. Initials and a number denoted the life of the boy who had laughter like the breeze off the Velikaya River and eyes that looked past her fears into her soul.

Alone. Abandoned.

Marina had buried her heart with him under the ash-brown dirt.

She rubbed the wooden marker with her palm. A splinter pierced her finger, and she yanked it back and watched as blood formed around the edges. She pried the sliver out with a dirty fingernail. The blood dripped onto the dirt, and Marina pushed out another drop, feeling a strange satisfaction as the ground absorbed it. She wished she could pour out every last drop, then climb in with Dmitri.

She sunk down onto her side and curled into a ball with her head on her hands. She tried to conjure up his face or the sound of his laughter, but all she could manage was the wail of her mother-in-law as the woman draped herself over the casket. She barely let Marina near it, glaring at her as if his demise at the hands of the German invaders were somehow Marina's doing.

The sun moved behind a cloud, and Marina shivered when the breeze skimmed over her. It carried the fragrance of a full-blooming August: honeysuckle, gooseberry, and currant bushes and the crisp scent of a nearby river. But the cheerful smells were wasted on her. Despair lodged like a lump in her throat. "Why, Dmitri? Why did you have to chase adventure to the grave?"

A song sparrow chattered at her, signaling twilight. Marina pushed herself from the ground and watched a squirrel stare at her. In a second, it scurried up a tree into a hole. Marina watched it, wishing she had a hole to hide in—somewhere to go, to escape the awful, wretched burning in her chest.

Only one thing kept her alive.

She moved a protective hand over her abdomen. Her chin trembled at the regret that boiled in her chest. Her letter was still folded in her Bible, right next to the wretched telegram. Dmitri would never know she carried his child. *Where are Your promises now, God?*

She dug into the pocket of her skirt and tugged out a

small, yellowed photograph. Her hair fell around her face, its wisps teased by the hot breeze. Marina ground her teeth into her bottom lip as she peered into the two young faces in the photo. Two women, one of them her biological mother, the other the surrogate mother who'd embraced her as her own. She focused on the woman on the left, the one who, she'd been told, bore her own sky blue eyes, although but a dull gray in the colorless photo. Marina felt the life and breath pulse in those eyes as they looked straight on at the photographer. Eyes etched with sorrow and determination. The photo never failed to raise sadness in her throat, and now a crushing feeling of despair curled around her chest.

The other woman she knew beyond the worn photo—the lean cheekbones, the high brow, the pensive gray eyes. Marina knew her by her earthy garden smell and by the touch of her weathered hands. She knew her by the sound of her voice, low and strong, humming songs of faith as she made borscht or knitted stockings. Marina owed her life to Yulia Petrov, and despite her adolescent doubts, she'd not been left lacking under Yulia's tender care.

Both her mothers leaned together against a gravestone. The gravestone of her father, who had died the same day she'd left her mother's womb. What had happened to Anton Klassen remained a mystery, and despite her pleadings, Mama Yulia refused to explain beyond a shake of her head and a murmured, "May he rest in peace." Marina had been content to settle for that. . .until now.

She traced the outline of her biological mother. About Oksana Klassen, she knew more. She knew her mother had been faced with difficult choices. She knew her mother had been beautiful and had loved the baby daughter she left behind. Still, a photograph couldn't wrap its arms about a toddler and hold it in the wee of night, nor guide a teenager through the trials of budding womanhood.

Nor could it give her strength, offer her answers to a life in tatters, or help her find her way back from the depths of grief. Her chin quivered. Abandoned. Not once, but twice.

She glanced again at the pose of her mother leaning on Anton's grave. Her mother's plight suddenly felt too raw, too close. They'd had to bury the men they loved way too early. Marina opened the ground at Dima's grave and tucked the picture into the earth, not able to face the brutal legacy.

She'd matted the pricks of grass dotting the mound and created craters where her hands and knees had begged for entrance. "I'll be back tomorrow with seeds and a rake," she promised the grave that embraced her husband.

She untied her head scarf as she trudged back to town. The wind picked at her hair, playing with the long strands. Behind her, the sparrow called again, sharper. The acrid smell of burning leaves filled the air as she passed first one house, then another. The smell thickened, and Marina watched with a frown as a black trail twisted into the sky from beyond the speckling of farmhouses. The smoke billowed, deepened.

Gunfire peppered the air. A flock of sparrows scattered in a flurry of wings. Marina's heart hiccupped, and then fear crashed over her like a wave, driving her forward in a jerky run. She sprinted toward Pskov, the scarf falling to the ground, forgotten.

Skirting Lenin Street, she headed toward her mother's two-room green shack on the south end of the city. Pskov wasn't so big that it took more than minutes to run the length of the town. Still, time slowed as her heartbeat raced. Black smoke tufted the purple-hued sky, then more gunshots, and a deafening boom shook her to her bones.

She skidded to a halt when she rounded her fenced yard and saw flames engulfing the Petrov home. Her gaze scanned to the dirt road, and she froze at the sight of a green German Panzer, its turret still smoking. Unfamiliar men in gray and green field coats, black metal helmets, and with faces like granite milled about the road, jabbing at trashcans and splicing weeds with oily black rifles. Another group leveled machine guns at a small group of women and children. Marina's mouth dried when she spied her mother standing among the other neighbors. Chin up, Yulia stared with steely eyes at three ruddy soldiers whose submachine guns fanned the group. Marina sucked her breath in horror as she heard Yulia sass them. *Mother, no!*

A spray of gunfire mowed the group to the ground.

Marina collapsed into the dirt. She leaned against the rough fence, her hand pressing her chest, hiccuping her breaths. *Dmitri, what should I do?* She heard the lock and grind of the Panzer's treads as it churned through potato patches. Wiping her eyes with her grimy fingertips, she made to rise, her eyes on the next street and, beyond, the forest.

Her hand covered her womb, held the life as she contemplated her choices.

Her blood drained from her body when the muzzle of a rifle nudged her thigh. She looked up.

"Ryki Veer!"

Marina licked her lips and raised her trembling hands in surrender. The soldier, his eyes dark and unyielding, scraped a gaze over her. She bristled, counting the seconds with her heartbeat.

"Please," she said, not sure what she was asking. The wild impulse to let him shoot, beg him to end her grief, flickered through her mind. But as the Panzer rolled by behind him, crushing potato seedlings, fences, and homes, anger coiled in her stomach. Her jaw tightened. He barked at her in his detestable language, and she frowned back. His eyes narrowed a second before he reached out for her. She stiffened, but he yanked her to her feet. The gun's aim fell away from her, but when she saw the look in his eyes, his beaklike nose, his lips licking, her knees buckled.

No. For Dmitri's baby, she'd never let the German defile her.

The Panzer boomed, and a shot exploded another home. The German jerked to look.

Marina slammed her fist into his face, whirled, and ran. Leaping a gully, she heard a shot but kept running. She cut down the alley between fences, then scooted between a crack and through a backyard.

"Perestan!"

Yeah, she'd stop when she hit Moscow. Adrenaline surged into her limbs, and she balled her fists and pumped. Slamming open the fence door, she soared over the dirt steps and landed in the street.

Her ankle screamed, but she clenched her jaw and ran. An open potato field before her beckoned, but the soft mounds would eat her speed. She headed for the packed dirt road, eyes on the cemetery and the woods beyond.

Another shot whizzed over her head. Her heart leaped out ahead of her. The roar of an engine found her ears.

Motorcycles.

Her fingernails dug into the palm of her hands. *God, please, help me!*

She refused to glance back. Her lungs burning, she dashed into the cemetery, dodging headstones, toward Dmitri's grave, then past it, up a hill, through the scrub brush and into the woods. The motorcycle whined in uneven pitches as it navigated through the burial grounds. Then a rifle cracked, and bark sprayed from the trunk of a spruce. Marina swallowed her scream.

The forest whipped her as she ran possessed, crashing through tangles of vine and sheet-sized spider webs. Branches slapped her face. Her ankle burned as she landed on roots and uneven ground. She tripped over a downed tree, scrambled to her feet, and threw herself into a knot of ash trees.

Her hands on her knees, she dragged in breaths that turned her lungs to fire. Willing her pulse silent, she strained to make out her attackers.

Only the thick, cottony silence of an overgrown forest. Sweat stung her eyes.

Another shot shredded the leaves above her head and sent a flock of birds to the heavens. Marina dove behind a wide oak and clung to it, digging her fingers into the grooves of bark. *For Dima's sake, please, God, help me!*

The sound of branches cracking nearby raised the hairs on her neck. Panic choked her in a death grip, but she turned and scanned the forest. Nothing but light, splintered by trees, dappling the foliage and spongy forest floor.

German voices to the south, moving closer. Tears burned her eyes. She clung to the tree and hung her head. She wouldn't stay here to be murdered. Putting a hand over her womb, she gulped in a deep breath and edged away from the trunk, gathering her legs under her.

A flock of birds betrayed her. Gunfire chipped bark from the trees. Marina clamped down her scream and pumped her legs.

Another shot, then another. Heat seared her, wrapping around her ribs and pitching her to her knees. The ground crumbled beneath her.

Falling.

She felt free, separated, as if she'd departed from herself. *Dmitri.*

She hit water with a numbing slap. The last thing she felt was the water's cool blanket filling her ears, her nose, covering her body as she sank below the envelope of Velikaya River.

<hr />

"Please don't ask me to do this." Edward Neumann stood with his back to Colonel Jeremiah Stone. In his mind he saw the forty-something OSS director steeple his fingers and lean back on the tree stump as if he were in a padded rolling chair.

"You know I have to, Edward. No one speaks Russian like you do. You can get past the border, hustle up your group of fighters. Think of it as the last front."

Edward closed his eyes, seeing Anna's haunted eyes, Marek's limp. "I can't leave them. Not now."

He heard a crack and jerked. Stone's gaze landed on him, and he felt the fool when he saw the broken twig in the man's grip. After three months of dodging the SS, Edward felt wrung out and raw, on the lee edge of unraveling. Like a bobcat, he paced the niche Stone had reserved for this meeting, pricking his ears for the rumble of low-flying

Messerschmitts. Or the crackle of forest floor debris. He harbored no illusions that a loyal Estonian wouldn't think twice about tracking him down and handing him over to the local Gestapo.

Estonians saw Germany as their liberators from Communist Russia.

Which made unearthing and allying with Russian partisans in Estonia particularly uneasy business.

Then again, trust across any border wasn't an easily bartered commodity in the wake of Operation Barbarrossa and Germany's blitzkrieg into Russia. Edward's ragtag partisan unit had been pushed like cattle, dodging the enemy as the Nazis overran Ukraine, then Byelorussia, Latvia, and finally Estonia as they marched toward Moscow. Thankfully, his partisans had found a niche near Tallinn and were safely tucked into an old farmhouse while he conferred with his OSS director, Colonel Stone.

"What happened, Neumann?" Stone asked quietly.

"I don't know." Edward curled a hand around the back of his neck, reliving the fateful day when ninety percent of his freedom fighters had been ambushed. Stefan, Wladek, Simon, all slaughtered. He'd found Raina's eight-year-old daughter, Irina, mauled by dogs, clinging to life, calling for her mother.

Raina never returned.

One by one, Edward had buried them. And with every shovelful, he saw Katrina's soft gray eyes, heard her sweet voice—"Don't leave me, Edick."

He blinked back the images and fought the grief rising in his chest. "I have no idea who might have betrayed us."

Colonel Stone nodded, his square face hard, his mouth set in a straight line. "You have to let it go, Neumann.

Yours isn't the only unit betrayed and wiped out by the SS. They've been unusually lucky over the past six months."

Edward crossed his arms over his chest as he stared past the knot of forest and watched the sunset paint the trees shades of orange. The piercing melody of the wood thrush raised the hairs on his neck, and he tensed. Stone caught his movement and frowned. Edward sighed and offered a rueful smile.

Stone pursed his lips and ran a scrutinizing gaze over Edward. "I should have brought you out after Katrina."

Edward looked down, studying his clenched hands.

"Her death wasn't your fault."

Edward's jaw tightened. "Send someone else." The wind hissed, and something startled the wood thrush. It scattered in a flurry of wings. "Please."

"There's no one else. Not with your contacts. This just might be the reason God sent you here."

Edward shot him a dark glance. Not fair, using his faith against him. Colonel Stone knew Edward's Mennonite roots ran deep, knew how he struggled with the traditions of a pacifist upbringing in the face of a world war. "I doubt that."

"You need to stop dodging the fact that God gave you a heritage and the ability to influence people and embrace your calling." A calling that got the people he cared about killed on a painfully regular basis.

"Listen. I may be Russian in heritage, but that doesn't make me Russian. I'm American first. Besides, who knows if this old monk she knows is friendly. . .or even alive? I'm probably walking into a death trap."

"America isn't at war with Russia—they've no reason to suspect you. Besides, you've got the training and the language skills, even if this monk won't help you to find the local partisans. I have faith in you."

Yeah. Like Raina and her daughter had. He sighed. "Anna is ill. And Marek is still recovering. I can't leave them."

Stone picked up a pebble and rolled it back and forth between his wide palms. "I brought in a new agent. They'll be fine."

"I'll take them with me."

"No, you won't." Stone tossed the rock in his grip. "I can't risk you taking your Poles with you. I know we're fighting on the same side, but there's bad blood between the Poles and the Russkies, and if you're going to succeed, you can't alienate anyone on the other side of the border."

Edward looked away. His chest tightened, and he swallowed the bitter taste of frustration.

"Edward, this war isn't up to you to win. You just have to obey orders and do your part." Stone tossed the rock away. "Don't let your failures be your Goliath."

Edward flinched. It wasn't his failures he was afraid of, thank you. It was sacrificing his heart for his successes.

"If I do this, I do it alone."

Stone gave him a hard look, then tossed the rock away and pulled out a folded map from his pocket. "Bear in mind that if you succeed, it just might cost Hitler the war. There's only one question here, soldier. What price is that worth?"

CHAPTER TWO

The sweet, heady fragrance of hay enfolded Marina as she drew to consciousness. She kept her eyes closed, letting the smells and sounds wash over her, drawing her from the depths of fever and a crushing exhaustion. The odor of earth and a hint of animal sweat filled the room, diluted slightly by the airy fragrance of summer. From far away, as if muffled, she heard the texture of low voices. Slowly, she opened her eyes and found mild comfort in the rays of sunlight slanting through a shuttered window. She recognized a barn of sorts with a gaping hole in the roof and rotting walls. A mound of lime-green field grass rose around her like a fortress. The chirp of a barn swallow mingled with the low hum of crickets buzzing in a far-off field. She took a deep breath, afraid to move, afraid that the slightest sound might summon the voices and fracture this fragile, safe moment.

A boot scraped on dirt nearby. "You're awake," said a male voice.

Marina wrestled a surge of panic. Then he moved into view—a peasant with long, tousled brown hair, dressed in brown work pants and a loosely knit grimy-green sweater. His deep, earth brown eyes radiated concern. Marina felt her coiled breath loosen. He crouched next to her. "You've been shot. Don't move."

Marina licked her lips, finding they were horribly parched, and summoned her voice. "Where am I?"

"Lydia, bring water, please." He took Marina's hand, and she discovered it smooth, even tender. No farmer, this one.

A woman appeared, a brunette with pensive hazel eyes and chapped hands, and handed him a battered canteen. He scooted toward Marina and cupped one of those hands under her neck. She met his eyes as he lifted her head. "Where am I?"

"Shh." He lifted the water to her lips, and it spilled into her mouth, across her lips, and down her chin. She drank greedily.

"Whoa, slow down."

She ignored him and let the liquid balm her raw throat, licking her lips when he took the canteen away.

"In answer to your question, you're in Pechory. Well, sort of." He smiled sheepishly. "We move around a lot, and for the past week, this little barn has been our home."

"Who are you?" she whispered.

"My name's Pavel. Dobrin. I'm a partisan."

Marina absorbed that information as the brunette crept up behind him and leaned over his shoulder. "Is she okay?"

Pavel raised his eyebrows, meeting Marina's eyes. "I don't know." He shot a quick look at her stomach. "Let's see."

She sensed probing hands move toward her blouse, and she slapped at them. Heat flashed up her side, and she moaned. "What's wrong with me?"

"You were shot." Pavel touched her hand. "I'm not going to hurt you."

Marina's lip trembled, and she clamped down on it.

"I found you in the river and took you with us when we escaped the Germans. Believe me, we mean you no harm." He cast a look at the brunette. "This is Lydia. She's the one who attended your wound. But before the war, I was a doctor. Can I look at it?"

Marina turned away, feeling heat rise through her. She nodded and pulled her arms away. Pavel lifted her blouse just above her stomach and peeked under a bandage that had somehow held in an avalanche of ache. When air hit the wound, Marina groaned and shifted in the grass.

"You're very fortunate. The good Lord was watching out for you."

"And you're pretty quick on your feet," Lydia added, smiling.

Marina smiled faintly. "You saw me running?"

Pavel replaced the bandage. "We fired a few shots back. I think I got the one who shot you."

Marina tried to read his face. Up close she saw a scar running down his cheek and parting a week-long growth of russet beard. He looked tired, with lines spidering from his eyes. Peasant or no, he bore responsibility on his wide shoulders, and she couldn't ignore the nudge to trust him. "How bad is it?"

Pavel pulled her blouse down, smoothing it over her stomach. "It grazed your ribs pretty good, but nothing's broken. You'll be fine."

Relief rushed through her.

"You sure did bleed a lot, though," Lydia said. Marina stared at her, frowning. Lydia stood up, concern knitting her brow. "You were covered in blood."

Pavel shot her a look. "She's fine now, Lydia."

Blood. Marina felt grief slap her, suck away her breath. *Please, Lord, no! Not Dmitri's baby!* She fought the rush of tears. *Please, God, no.* But as grief filled her chest, the truth burned inside her. Their child had died. One more victim of the Nazi assault. Memory seared her thoughts—her mother, defiant to her death. Her childhood home, in flames. The menace in a soldier's eyes. So much for God watching out for her. "Did you say you were partisans?" she asked.

Pavel smiled. "Do you have a name?"

Marina pushed to her elbows, ignoring the pain that spiked up her side and down her arms. "My name is Mara." *Because God has left me.*

Pavel's brow creased, and she thought she saw a flicker of pain dash through his eyes. "Mara. Do you know how to shoot a gun?"

"Teach me."

⚊⚊⚊

Deep inside unconsciousness, the musty, dank odors brought to him the nightmare.

The cellar. And as always, the dim, slanted light told him that dusk had rolled across the cobblestone road, dragging in its wake the cover of night.

"Edward." Katrina stood at the door, hands shoved into her trench coat, her blond hair piled atop her head. "Am I late?"

He felt grief knot his chest as he saw her smile, the delight in her eyes. In the back of the moment, he heard his voice speak the truth, that this was a dream. Still, he couldn't break free of the summons to surrender to the moment. He rose from the chair, his book thudding on the cement floor. Katrina laughed as she scooped it up.

"Kafka, my American philosopher? Am I so late that you surrender to fatalism?"

She went easily into his arms, and he buried his face in her hair. "Never late, Kat." Yet, despite their stolen moments, he did feel like a fatalist. Each passing day felt darker, suffocating under the grip of despair. He knew how much she risked for him, for these moments, and the knowledge ate at him. A Jewess working inside Berlin, at Gestapo headquarters, no less. A German who recognized the darkness and fought for light. He had no right to put her in danger. But he'd come into the game late and discovered that Kat had already set the rules. No commitment. No talk of forever. Just now, these moments, the passing of information, stolen tenderness to bolster hope.

Terror stalked him every minute she stepped outside his embrace. "They're watching me," he said, hearing pain in his voice. "We must be careful."

She sighed as she pressed film into his hand. "Don't leave me, Edick. Not yet."

Not yet.

He cupped his hand around her neck, leaned toward her, desperation roiling through him, emerging in a moan as he kissed her. Kat!

She dissolved even as he held her, those dove gray eyes in his.

Not yet.

Edick!

He blinked awake, the musty odor of limestone walls and packed soil filling his nose. Darkness pressed him, save for a crack of light beneath a wooden door. Edward pushed off his woolen blanket and sat up. He felt damp, rumpled, and exhausted to the bone, despite a solid four hours holed up in the fetal position, pursuing some shut-eye. Two weeks hiking into a secluded pocket of western Russia had left him worn out and hungry.

Thankfully, his grandmother's sketchy address for the monastery had been on target. Edward found the enclave nestled along the Velikaya River, the monks having moved into the safety of the caves, hoping to dodge the low-flying Messerschmitts. Evidently, in the correspondence between his grandmother and a monk over the years as they hunted for lost friends, she'd mentioned her OSS-employed grandson. Once Edward introduced himself, Brother Timofea turned out to be every inch his grandmother's predictions. Kind. Willing to help.

And a patriot.

"You'll need help," Timofea said, a spark in those mahogany brown eyes.

"No," Edward said sharply as they hovered over the map Stone had given him. "I can do this myself."

"Not if you want to do it right." Timofea pointed to the map. "There is only one train bridge over the Velikaya River, and you must believe that the Germans have it under heavy guard. You need scouts, diversions, and fire-power if you hope to destroy it. There is a band of partisans in the area. They'll help you."

"No." But Colonel Stone's words hummed in his mind. "This is a suicide mission, and I don't want anyone killed."

"Then you're not ready to do this job, American. Because until you accept the cost, you'll never be ready to embrace the task."

◆

Marina straddled the trunk of an oak and wedged her foot

hard into the fork of branches below her. Lifting the rifle, she sighted the road, a solid two hundred meters away.

It was a good perch. Back from the road, the tree towered high enough to give a clear shot of a significant stretch of the dirt highway yet hid her presence well enough to deter return fire. Using the scope, she scanned south, beyond the road, and eventually spotted Natasha. The girl waved back, one eye glued to her own scope. Marina returned a halfhearted wave. She liked Natasha, a young woman with tawny brown hair and doe eyes. She could ping a tin can with an ancient Russian Mosin-Nagant sniper rifle from a hundred meters and spent her evenings knitting wool hats from a stash of old sweaters she'd found in the barn.

Pavel had formed a motley crew of eleven, all armed with decaying Russian weapons and the fury of seeing their homeland destroyed. Marina easily fit in, working in silence next to Lydia and Natasha. Two boys, no more than twelve years old, were in charge of weapons, sleeping next to the stockpile, cleaning the rifles, and counting bullets. Skinny chaps with pale skin, they watched her and the other women with eyes that told her they missed their mothers.

Two older women, heads wrapped in dark scarves and lined faces filled with loss, cooked and gathered food from the forest and abandoned farms while the partisans trained and plotted. Pavel spent his days training Marina and two other recruits, Lev and Sasha, two feisty teenaged boys who Marina knew would send them all to their deaths if Pavel didn't teach them respect. Their cocky, irritating talk of murdering Germans made her sick—it reminded her too much of Dmitri, zealous in his foolish naïveté.

She couldn't help but be amazed at how easily a gun had fit into her embrace. She cradled the German-acquired Mauser 98-kZF sniper rifle against her chest like a child and leaned back against the hard tree trunk. She'd already made calculations for distance, wind velocity, time of day, possible escape routes for the enemy, and her own escape route. She exhaled slowly like she would right before she'd take her shot. She'd practiced from this position a dozen times over the past week in different conditions. Now, she cherished the solitude before the battle.

A cool autumn breeze rustled the gilded orange leaves around her, unlatched a handful, and tossed them hither. One landed on Marina's knitted wool scarf, which she'd wrapped around her torso and tied behind her. She picked up the leaf and twirled it between two fingers. The stem was not yet completely brittle, the leaf still pliable. But its amber color betrayed death's encroachment. Soon it would turn brown, crumble, and disintegrate into the forest floor.

She was not so different. She wondered what a dying heart looked like. Amber brown, crumbling? Marina freed the leaf to the wind and looked beyond her perch, across maple, oak, and poplar trees to the hills surrounding Pskov. Strange to be back in her hometown territory again. She felt as if it had been a lifetime instead of a month. She'd left Marina behind and returned Mara, a woman of bitterness, just like Naomi in the Bible.

The field grass was turning from lime green to a faint yellow. The setting sun leaked orange juice across the horizon, and tall birch trees pushed jagged shadows into the road. A flock of crows fought for space along a far-off fence line. A chickadee called from the weeds, warning of twilight. Marina tried to relax. She closed her eyes, breathing long and deep, fighting the tension clawing at her chest.

She lifted the rifle and scoped the road again, searching for a rising dust cloud, the faintest inkling that the supply train approached. She found Lev crouched behind a thicket, ten feet from his assigned position. Marina grimaced, foreseeing the inevitable day when a German bullet would find his chest. She heard Pavel's warnings behind her fears.

"Lev, this isn't a game. Please, remember that every shot you fire is one less bullet in our arsenal. Our job isn't to mow down the enemy; it's to keep them off balance and nervous. I want them afraid when they lie down at night, knowing that we are watching them. You have great potential to be a hero of the state, Lev. Don't let your enthusiasm destroy that."

Still, the teenager pushed the envelope, took too many risks. During the last attack, Lev had run out into the road and fired at the three right-flank guards. Sheer luck had kept a bullet from finding him—that and Pavel's aim.

Or perhaps it was Pavel's prayers. Marina bit back the taste of shame, hard and bitter in her mouth. She couldn't bring herself to close her eyes and join Pavel's prayer circle before they left for every mission. She always stood away, toeing the dirt and gritting her teeth until the prayers finished. Pavel never pressured, but his piercing eyes left wounds in her heart.

She wanted to please him. Especially when he found her while she peeled potatoes or prodded the fire to life. His gentle eyes held compassion, tugged at her grief. But she refused him entrance into her pain.

I am Mara.

A long, low whistle, the sound of a whippoorwill,

brought her scope again to her eye. She quickly studied the billow of dust tufting the fire-hued sky. Every muscle coiled as she braced her legs on the branches and wedged herself against the trunk. Her right arm and shoulder knew how to absorb the kick of the Mauser, but perched in a tree, the trunk added significant support. And balance. She propped her elbow onto a branch, steadying her shot. Already her neck muscles screamed from the weight of the weapon, but she ignored the burn and focused on the slow-moving convoy.

Eight. She counted again. Eight unsuspecting soldiers, the age of her beloved Dmitri, marching into the lions' den. She could almost taste revenge. Perhaps one of them had been the one who'd leered at her, the one who still stalked her nightmares. She longed to look him in the eyes when she pulled the trigger.

She winced at her thoughts. Pulling the rifle away, she fought a wave of disgust. What was happening to her?

Trust God, Marina.

She brushed at the moisture forming around her eyes and steeled herself against the whisper of Dmitri's voice. *Where is God now, Dima?* God had abandoned her, just like everyone else in her life. His promises were nothing but idealistic fervor.

He'd brought Dmitri home in a box.

She shoved the butt of the gun into her shoulder, relishing the pain. No, she didn't recognize herself. Marina had perished, finally.

She found their faces through the scope. One smoked a cigarette. Two others held their rifles like fishing poles over their shoulders. Two more soldiers rode atop the horse-drawn wagons. She wondered at their cargo—clothing or weapons? Their last attack, south near Ostrov, had rewarded them with a tripod-mounted machine gun with ammo and a box of hand grenades. But the partisans desperately needed clothing. Marina wore every layer she owned, and winter clawed at the morning.

Another whippoorwill call. Marina found her target. A young man, barely old enough to shave, with a lean jaw and unsuspecting eyes. His mussed uniform hung on him, betraying youth. Marina let loathing fill her mouth, her chest.

The column plodded forward. Pavel held off the partisan fire, drawing them into their fists. Marina held her breath.

Pavel's first shot dumped one of the drivers from his perch. Marina squeezed the trigger and sighted the next target before her first had fallen. The second guard moved much faster, diving for cover beneath the wagon. Marina took her time and sent a shot between the spokes of the wagon wheel. The soldier crumbled into the dirt. Swallowing the acid welling in the back of her throat, Marina searched for another Nazi.

She discovered the other partisans had dealt with the rest. Lev streaked out from behind a thicket toward the prizes. Relief swept through her in a rush. She lowered the rifle, her hands shaking.

Maybe they'd find some clothes or even food on that wagon of supplies.

She heard the grind of wheels as a shiver pierced through her spine, into her bones. A German Panzer growled down the road and behind it a cavalry of motorcycles.

Lev stood paralyzed in the middle of the road.

"Lev!"

The first shot caught him in the shoulder. Marina choked on a scream as he went down, writhing. Her hands shook as she brought the gun up, scoped her targets.

Run!

The voice thundered in the back of her brain, but she ignored it and squeezed off a round. It caught the wheel of a cycle, flipped it. Lev crawled toward the ditch.

Fury rose and battled with common sense as another shot turned him over. He lay still as the motorcade rumbled by.

Run! Already Pavel would be ordering Sasha and Lydia to take to the hills, and a smart Natasha would be sliding down her tree. Pavel's words rushed back to her. "We're not here to win the war but to keep them off balance." He'd expect her to run back to their hideout like she'd been trained.

Hiccuping back terror, she slammed the rifle into her shoulder. The Germans had taken to the fields, searching for her countrymen. She spied Lydia, her brown hair streaming behind her.

Run!

Gritting her teeth, Marina sighted a motorized soldier closing in on his victim. She sent him tumbling from his bike. Gunfire ricocheted off trees not far from her perch, but she bit down on her fear and tracked another target.

The Panzer boomed. A maple exploded into flames. Her perch rocked. She heard her scream as she pitched forward. Bark scraped her face; branches jarred her breath from her lungs. *Oh God, help me!*

The unforgiving fork of two solid branches caught her hard around the chest. Her head spun, and her lungs burned as she fought for breath. Flames from a burning maple twenty feet away reached into the sky. Smoke and the pungent odor of leaves burning rose from the forest floor like a gas. Marina blinked back tears, her eyes searing.

She heard the *rat-a-tat* of a machine gun, but it seemed muffled by the roar of the inferno. She pushed herself free, fighting the pain that made her want to double over, and balanced on a lower branch. Quickly calculating the distance to the ground, she edged out onto a limb and dropped.

Agony buckled her knees. Clutching her side, she searched for her Mauser. Clawing for it, she grabbed the barrel and tucked it under her arm. Her head spun in the rancid fumes. Hauling in a breath, she hunched over and tried to stand. Pain fisted her chest. With a groan, she sank into a fetal position on the forest floor.

Run.

Sprawled in the cool damp leaves, she heard the fire crackling, flames creeping toward her. Above, the smoke billowed, obscuring the sky. The gunfire had ceased. As she listened to her own labored breathing, a strange calm spread through her, numbing the pain. She loosed her grip on her gun. Her eyes fluttered and began to close. *Yes.*

"Miss?"

She heard the accented words, but her eyes refused response.

"Miss, are you okay?"

A touch on her cheek, cool, soft. She flinched and fought to open her eyes.

Dmitri?

She felt arms around her, and she hadn't a solid bone in her to recoil. "Let me help you."

Yes, Dmitri, I am here.

"Can you walk?" She felt an arm go under her neck.

41

Another wound under her knees.

The smoke thickened. She coughed, her body seizing against the rancid smells, the heat that seared her face.

Then he lifted her. Pain shot through her body, and she groaned. He curled her to his chest, and for a moment, her head bobbed against his shoulder. He smelled of leather and strength. It sent a jolt of longing through her. She stiffened, spiraling out of her dream.

"*Tiha,*" he said, using a Russian command for calm.

Calm?

She opened her eyes and reality slapped her.

Not. Dmitri.

Dark hair, hazel green eyes, a dark scruffy growth of beard, and the expression of worry, not love, on his hard-jawed face. Not her Dmitri.

A foreigner.

A *strange* foreigner.

"Put me down!" Panic swilled in her throat and went straight to her limbs. Marina lashed out, screaming.

CHAPTER THREE

C alm down, lady!"
        He said it in English, a fact that resonated with him seconds after she winged him in the throat. Whoops. *"Perestan!"* he rasped.

She launched out of his arms like a katoosha rocket, and it was all he could do to stay standing as he gulped fire into his lungs. Obviously, she wasn't the type to swoon into a strange man's arms. In fact, if he didn't keep up, she'd lose him in the forest and smoke, even on all fours and clutching her side. Flames leaped around them, closing in on the woman.

"Come back!"

She glanced over her shoulder, and the look she gave him, half-terror, half-hatred, should have turned his blood cold. Except, behind them, lacing the forest with gunshots, a small battalion of German soldiers hunted them like rabbits. "C'mon." He advanced on her and scooped her up by the armpits. "We have to get out of here."

She aimed a kick toward him.

"What's your problem?" He grabbed her arm as she wobbled. "I'm just trying to help you. You're going to get killed."

"Yeah. Guess what? That's war," she snarled. "Get away from me."

Edward stared at the woman. Dirt streaked her face. Twigs and bark littered her blond hair. He surveyed the dirty scratch on her cheekbone, the hard set of her jaw, and it came to him like a gasp. She was a partisan.

He wanted to groan. The rising smoke smarted his eyes, and he blinked away the burn. "No. You're coming with me."

"Leave me!" She jerked away from him, fell to her knees.

"Trust me!" He reached for her, but she shrank from his grasp.

"How do I know you're not German?"

"Because I'm on your side."

She opened her mouth just as a gunshot shredded the leaves above them. She winced, and for a second, fear streaked through her eyes, something so haunting it speared through Edward.

"I'm not leaving you out here," he said as he scooped her again into his arms. "So just stop fighting me, and maybe we'll get out of here alive."

She gaped at him, and for a moment, surprise filled her eyes.

"Hang on," he said.

She fisted her hand into his brown sweater, as if to muscle him into submission. He didn't wait for her to wing him across the chops, just tucked her skinny body tight and plowed through the forest.

The fire chewed up the drying leaves, spitting them into the air, choking and spurting as it spread like lava along the forest floor. Edward dug his boots into a wall of dirt as he climbed a small rise and put height between him and the blaze. The air thickened as he rose, filling his nose with a pungent, acrid smell. He tucked the woman's head under his chin and thanked the Lord he'd left his partisans in Estonia. Getting the lay of the land was proving to be deadly. He knew trouble was afoot when he heard gunfire, but only God's providence could have lured him to the foot of a giant oak in time to see a woman tumble from its grip.

He moved quickly, recognizing markers he'd left for himself, split twigs, a scrape of bark—the lessons he'd learned stalking whitetail deer in upstate New York. Behind him, the fire sputtered, choking on the wet soil and the still-green foliage. The black smoke splintered in the scattering of wispy clouds scraping the orange sky, creating a freakish fright-night sunset. Already, dusk muted the tree lines, deep shadows welling pockets of foliage. Edward hurried his pace.

"Who are you?" Suspicion pulled her voice taut.

"My name's Edward. I'm an American."

He glanced heavenward, feeling betrayed. Again, God had sent him into the folds of the partisans, and again, he felt swallowed whole. He glanced at the woman, and her troubled expression went right to his heart. The woman felt like a bag of bones in his arms. Edward curled her tight against his chest, wincing when she groaned, and headed toward the caves.

The monastery was right where he left it. Tucked in a clearing next to the Velikaya River, he'd found it with little trouble the first time, and returning to the enclave sent a feeling of peace through him. So it was a Russian Orthodox monastery. He could still find his God, the God of his evangelical faith, on his knees in their chapel. His spirit leapt at the glint of candlelight in one of the kitchen windows.

Reaching the main gate, he kicked it softly, hoping to nudge it open. A bearded man with a brown skullcap appeared in a tiny, face-height door and peered at him. The shimmer of a flickering light sent eerie shadows dancing across his etched face. Edward tried a smile. The man shut the door, and a moment later the gate lurched open. Edward strode in, nodded to the keeper, and made an arrow-line for Brother Timofea's cell.

Timofea was crouched on the stone floor, his whittled shoulders hunched, head hung in prayer. A long white candle, wax tearing all sides until it lumped and dripped onto a metal holder, sat on a rough-hewn table and sprayed erratic dappled light on whitewashed cave walls. Edward paused in the doorway, and when the monk didn't move, he crept in and set the woman down on a threadbare cot. He pulled his fraying wool blanket over her trembling body and made to move away.

The searching look in her eyes stopped him cold. "What are you doing here?"

"I thought you were asleep."

She shook her head. Sorrow saturated her gaze, and its depths rocked him. He knelt beside her and pulled up the blanket. She dug her hands into it and pulled it to her chin.

"What's your name?" He moved to push a chunk of hair from her face but paused when she stiffened and followed his movement. Her eyes stayed on his hand.

"Why?"

He lowered his hand. "I just want to know what a pretty lady like you is doing up in a tree with a German sniper rifle."

She bit her lip and looked away, studying the wall.

"Are you working for the resistance?"

She closed her eyes. Frustration made him wince. "I'm not going to hurt you!"

"How do you know Russian?"

Her voice held the finest edge of anger, and it raised his eyebrows.

"My family immigrated from Russia before I was born, but my grandmother insisted I learn to speak the mother tongue."

Outside, a long, low bong of the monastery bell signaled bedtime. The sound resonated through the chamber, raising the hair on Edward's neck. Timofea rose, then knelt beside Edward. His gaze moved over her, compassion and worry, and perhaps even horror, in his eyes. "She is ill?"

Edward shrugged at the monk. His brown beard, wispy and cut in a V like all Russian monks, had become thin around his cheekbones. He frowned, and somewhere from under the skullcap that descended past his ears and around his jaw began a furrow of wrinkles that pleated his brow.

"Yes, she is ill." Timofea's tone sent a chill through Edward.

When she at last spoke, it was in a murmur and confirmed Timofea's diagnosis. "My name is Mara."

Bitterness.

I must have cracked a rib, Marina surmised as she wrapped an arm around her body. Every breath seared her lungs; every movement sent agony spearing into her brain. The room spun, and she fought nausea. Still, she refused to turn away from the wall until her emotions decided to stop churning.

A foreign man had held her in his arms, and she'd surrendered to it. No, in truth, even longed for it. The betrayal in those feelings nearly made her choke. Only two months since Dmitri's death, and she was collapsing into the arms of another man. An American stranger, no less, with eyes that seemed to see into her heart. She bit her trembling lip.

Outside, she heard the low tones of the foreigner and the monk. She eyed them over her shoulder. The American towered over the shriveled monk. Wide shoulders stretched his brown leather jacket taut across his back, and lean, long legs stood soldier stance, his arms clasped behind his back in relaxed pose. His hair folded over the cuff of his jacket, as if needing a trim, and he cracked his knuckles with his thumb while the two men talked. Suddenly, as if sensing her stare, he glanced at her.

Caught. He locked her gaze, unsmiling, probing.

Marina turned away but wanted to die where she lay.

"Mara, are you feeling better?" He crouched and put his hand on her forehead. She closed her eyes, unable to face the needs his touch dredged up. Traitor! Only she wasn't sure whom she should accuse.

"You have a fever." He folded the blanket across her legs. "I want to see if you have any injuries."

"Don't touch me," Marina growled.

He gave her a hard look. "Listen, give me a little leash here. I promise I'm on your side."

Marina's face burned. She shook her head, but he gave her a look that told her he wasn't asking permission. Gently, he felt her stomach, then her ribs. She flinched, fighting the pain that threatened to skewer her.

"You might have a broken rib." He turned and gestured to the monk. "I need a sheet or a cloth for a sling and another for a swathe." ·

"Can you sit up?" The American snaked a hand under her neck. She stiffened, but he muscled her into a sitting position. Tears stung her eyes. Her breaths came easier, but when she inhaled, pain wrapped tentacles around her chest. Sweat broke out at her temples.

"You're going to be okay."

Oh, how little he knew. She might have a broken bone, but it didn't begin to compare to her fractured life, her shattered dreams. No, *okay* wasn't even in her vocabulary.

Still, maybe he wasn't Gestapo disguised as Sir Galahad. She couldn't deny the worry in his hazel green eyes as his gaze ran over her. And despite the power she felt as he'd trucked her through the forest, he looked weary. War fatigued. With his tight jaw, the dotting of russet whiskers on high cheekbones, and chocolate brown hair that fell over his eyes in a tangle, he looked about as okay as she felt.

The monk appeared with a pile of muslin cloths.

"Tear the sheet in half," the American instructed.

The monk obeyed and handed him a wad of fabric. In a moment, her "doctor" had a length of fabric tucked under her arm. His ministrations were gentle, and she was surprised to see a line of perspiration glisten his brow as he worked her left arm into a sling, tied it around her neck, secured the elbow corner, then swaddled it against her with the other length of fabric.

"I want you to take two to four deep breaths every hour. I think your rib is only cracked, but you need to stay put until it heals." His eyes met hers, and the slash of his mouth told her he was serious. "No more leaping from trees."

Oh, real funny. Still, she fought a smile.

He rubbed his hand over her forehead, drawing back the hairs that slicked to her skin. "Now, tell me the truth. Are you a partisan?"

Her smile faded.

"*Da.*" Another voice answered from the arch of the doorway.

Marina's eyes widened as Pavel stepped into the cell. She saw the American bristle as he climbed to his feet.

"Pavel," Marina said, aware of the relief in her voice. Pavel's gaze never left the foreigner.

"Are you okay?" Pavel asked.

"She has a broken rib," the monk answered, stepping between the two men.

Marina counted her heartbeats as the men stared at each other. Pavel might not have the American's size, but he had danger in those dark eyes.

Pavel finally turned his attention to her. His expression softened. "I found your gun." He held out the Mauser.

Marina flicked a look at the American and couldn't mistake the disappointment written on his face. For some reason, shame lodged in her stomach, the same unease she'd been dodging for a month.

"Thanks." She reached for the rifle as Pavel handed it to her. It felt so familiar yet cold and unforgiving in her grip. She slid it underneath the cot. The room felt hot, the cave walls giving off a stale, musty smell. Fatigue blanketed her like a woolen cloak. She leaned back and cradled her slung arm with her right hand.

Pavel stood above her. His brown eyes probed hers, searching, but without the intensity of the American's. Pavel already knew far too much to search that deep. "*Maya Doragaya.* Are you really okay?"

Marina nodded, quick and jerky. She clenched her jaw. "And Natasha? Sasha?"

One side of his mouth crooked up. "*Doma.*" Home, safe and sound.

Relief rushed out of Marina in a tired sigh. She didn't ask about Lev. "How did you find me?"

Pavel shot a glance at Marina's rescuer. "He leaves a trail like a bear."

Marina quirked a grin. The foreigner stepped close, and Marina couldn't help but enjoy the open-mouth gape. "He understands Russian, Pavel."

"Every word, comrades." The American pursed his lips and scanned a look between the two.

Pavel turned and gave him a quick examination. "Who are you, and what do you want?"

"Lieutenant Edward Neumann. OSS, US Army. I'm here to win the war."

CHAPTER FOUR

E dward sat with his back against the wall, the
stone sending cold streaks up his spine despite his
leather jacket. The candle sprayed erratic firelight
across Mara's face as she slept. He could see mere exhaustion, not comfort, had driven her to sleep's embrace. Her
eyes seemed tense, even in sleep, and tiny crow's lines
chiseled her face. He longed to rub his thumb over them
and ease the sorrow from her expression. The desire caught
him before he could shrug free, and he cringed. The last
thing he needed was to start thinking with his heart.

He'd already made that mistake before.

Brother Timofea had garnered a mat on the floor and
was curled up with a moth-eaten brown blanket. Pavel had
chosen a spot at the end of Mara's cot, sitting up with his
head drooped at her feet. Her protector. Edward read it in
his eyes, his stance.

The white walls in the dim firelight seemed to enlarge
the cell, but with four people in a room meant for one, the
sour whiff of sweaty bodies took possession of the room.
Edward longed to open the wooden door. The air outside
the chamber had cooled, and despite Mara's blanket, her
thin sweater couldn't possibly generate enough heat to
keep the chill from finding her bones.

A partisan. Edward ran two hands through his hair,

shrinking from the grime and grease that embedded in it. He dragged in a deep sigh, cursing the war. A woman shouldn't have to suffer the horrors of war. His left eye twitched, and he ran a thumb under it, working the muscle gently. It made his stomach turn to see this pretty young woman embrace her sniper rifle as if it were her best friend.

Mara. Was that her real name? Edward glanced at Pavel, who was hauling in deep breaths. The man looked exhausted. Edward slid on his knees over to Mara's bed. She'd slung her right arm over her left, protecting her wounds. He prayed she only had a cracked rib. A ragged scratch along her cheekbone had begun to turn purple. Without thinking, he ran two fingers over it. Her eyes fluttered, and he pulled away, rocked by the emotions that passed through him.

No partisans. He'd promised himself that as he'd slipped into Russian territory. Still, Brother Timofea's words chipped at him. If he wanted to take out the bridge, he needed help.

Just not from Mara.

The urge to pray for her swept through him, thumping his heart. Edward closed his eyes. *Dear Lord, she's hurting. I can feel it. I don't know why, but You do. Please, save her.*

She moaned slightly, and her lips twitched as if she was about to say something. He watched her in the fire-lit glow for a long moment. Her high cheekbones had been perfectly set in a teardrop face. Long lashes closed over her haunted blue eyes. Sorrow moved through him. "Please, Lord, use me to help her, if it be Your will."

Do you love Me, Edward?

The question, like a whisper breathing through him, made him frown. He nodded, eyes on Mara. *You know I do.*

Then feed My lambs.

Edward fingered a strand of her long blond hair and watched her sleep.

❦

Marina blinked twice, then stared at the ceiling, trying to get a fix on where she'd spent the night. She was surrounded by whitewashed rock cut at jagged angles and dimpled by shadow. The press of sunlight slinking beneath a wooden door told her dawn had long passed over. Marina shifted her weight and propped herself up on her right elbow. Pain rushed her, bringing with it the last twelve hours.

She gritted her teeth, sat up, and swung her legs to the floor. The musty, damp odor made her skin feel clammy. Holding her left arm close to her body, she reached down and felt for her rifle. The Mauser was right where she left it.

Marina slid the gun out and used it like a crutch to propel her to her feet, white-gripping it when the room decided to ripple. She frowned and fought the feeling of her stomach flopping inside her. Hunger. She pressed against her belly with her bound arm and hobbled to the door.

Voices, low and tense, made her pause. She held her breath. Pavel, the monk, and the American—what was his name? Edward. The Russian version seemed easier. . . Edick. His speech was good, but the accent singled him out as a foreigner. Still, he had a low tenor, and it rumbled through her, drawing her toward the door.

She cracked it open and spied Pavel, anger on his face. "You can't do it without us. It's our land. Our territory. You need our help."

"No. I don't." The American's tone chilled her. "I don't want any more people getting hurt than necessary."

Pavel's eyes glinted. "You want to fail."

Silence. Tiny hairs rose on Marina's neck. She pushed the door open and stepped out. Pavel looked at her with enough concern for her to smile. He reached out his hand and gripped her elbow. "Are you okay?"

Marina nodded. A low, far-off drone made her scan the sky. Bulbous, cloudlike cotton hung low and threatened rain. Through one of them, she spied a squadron of planes. Pavel stepped closer to her. "Bombers."

"Messerschmitts," the American added. "German bombers."

Marina looked at the American—his eyes were on her, and emotion flickered in them. Concern? Mistrust? She took in his tight fists, balled in his jacket pockets, and that commanding soldier stance, and it spoke to all the terrified places in her heart.

"What's their target?" she asked.

"I don't know. They bombed a village not far from here. Karamishevo." The American's jaw tightened as he said it.

Beside him, Pavel had gone white. "Karamishevo?"

Marina glanced at him, but he turned away, breathing hard. "Was it. . .destroyed?"

The foreigner gave her a sidelong glance, said nothing.

"So much death. . ." The monk shook his head, then looked at her with sadness in his eyes. She couldn't deny the feeling that somehow his words were meant for her. After a moment, he offered a grim smile to Pavel. "I'm afraid there is little left of the village. We sent some supplies, but the church there has been completely destroyed."

"Why would they bomb a church?" she asked. She glanced again at the sky, watched as the bombers headed north, toward Moscow. Fear coiled deep in her stomach.

The American sighed and ran a finger under his eyes. "They're looking for partisans."

Oh. All the same, a monastery seemed an odd place to find freedom fighters. Only. . .she glanced at Timofea, at the seasoned set of his jaw. He'd taken them in without blinking. Without question.

She had a sick feeling, one that told her to leave soon.

Marina's jaw tightened. "It's Edick, right? What were you talking about?"

The American's eyebrows rose, perhaps at her variation of his name, and the hint of a smile tweaked his lips. Then it vanished, and he cast a conspiratorial look at Pavel. "I have a little project and Pavel wants to help."

"Project?"

Edick sighed and looked beyond them to a point over Pavel's head. "I'm on assignment from the US Army."

Pavel dug the butt of his gun in the ground and stared at it. "He has to blow up the bridge over the Velikaya River."

Marina's heart lodged in her chest, and a strange ache streamed through her. "No."

"There are reasons." For the first time, Marina noticed tiny lines around Edick's eyes. "C'mon, I'll show you." He turned and reentered the cave. Marina, Pavel, and the old monk followed.

Edick unfolded a map on the monk's table. "The Germans invaded Russia through Kiev and Estonia." He pointed to both routes on the map. "They are driving northward toward Moscow. They're after this area, here"— he palmed an area beyond Kiev, in Ukraine—"because of the oil fields and fertile soil." He moved his left hand toward St. Petersburg. "We think they are hoping to meet up with the Finns here."

Marina felt numb. "Stalin said they won't reach Moscow."

Edick gave her a grim look. "Only God knows what will happen."

Marina clenched her teeth, fighting tears. If only she'd known four months ago that Hitler was going to plow over Lvov, Ukraine, with his tanks, she would have thrown herself on the floor at Dmitri's feet and begged him not to go. Her hand moved to her empty womb as she watched Edick circle the area of Pskov with his finger.

"There are three main train lines into Moscow, and right now all of them are in the possession of the Germans. One of them runs right through Pskov." He followed a black, crosshatched line. "And it ends in Moscow. That's the line we need to destroy."

"Why?" Marina leaned on the table, running her finger along the route.

Edick braced two hands on the table. "What do you know about Napoleon's attack on Russia?"

Marina shrugged. "We defeated him?"

"He defeated himself. He bit off more than he could chew and marched his troops right into a Russian winter. They froze to death. "

Pavel surveyed the map. "How far in are the Germans?"

"Far enough. The front line is within shouting distance of Moscow city limits."

"So you mean to cut off their supply line?" Marina said, tracing the railroad line with her finger.

"That's right. We'll take out their source of weapons, food, and clothing and let winter do the rest."

Marina looked at Pavel and didn't miss the gleam of mischief in his eye. "How are you going to do it?"

Edick looked at her, a steel look in his eyes. "Alone."

Pavel slammed his hand on the table. "No."

Marina flinched. She understood Pavel's frustration. "Why? We're here. We know this land. We can help!"

Edick folded his hands across his chest. Pavel's eyes narrowed. Marina glared at Edick. "Are you so proud? You don't want to work with us Russians?"

Edick's eyes widened, and she enjoyed a moment of delight at his surprise. Arrogant American. Did they think the Russians didn't know what the Western world thought of them? Mindless sheep following a wicked shepherd? Not everyone embraced communism and the ideals of Moscow. But politics didn't matter when Hitler threatened to rape, pillage, and burn as he marched across the Motherland. And this stupid American was about to discover just how freethinking and innovative the black sheep of Russia could be when their homeland burned around them.

Edick blew out a breath and shook his head. "Not even close."

"Then why?" Marina stepped up to him, so near he couldn't ignore her. "We're partisans. Messing up the Germans is what we're trained for."

Edick's lips turned into a rueful grimace. "What were you before you were a soldier, Mara? A teacher, a nanny?"

"A wife."

Silence drew out the other sounds of the monastery: chickens in the yard, the clink of pots in the kitchen.

"So you know what it means to lose someone." Edick's voice came out so low, it was nearly a whisper. Marina stared at him and saw grief flicker through his eyes.

It vanished as quickly as her breath in her chest when he fixed a hard gaze on her. "Then you know why I can't let you be a part of this mission."

"You're not letting us help because you don't want us to get killed?" Pavel's tone held disbelief. "It's not your decision."

"The last thing I need is more blood on my hands," Edick said.

"Would you prefer the blood of the entire Russian population?" Pavel asked quietly.

Marina's mouth parted in shock.

"I was a student in med school when Hitler invaded Poland and Comrade Stalin sent troops to Ukraine," Pavel said. He stared hard at Edick, unblinking. "Because of my education, they sent me to one of the collective farms in the region to tend the women who worked them." Pavel's face radiated with an emotion she'd never seen in him. "I remember when the first Nazi wave came through. I was in town, tending a child with the flu, and when I returned, not one woman was left alive." His voice dropped. "Not one."

A muscle pulled in Edick's jaw. "How many were there?"

"Two hundred and thirty-five. They were mowed down in the fields."

Marina's knees buckled, and she landed hard on the cot, unable to stand against the image of Mother Yulia crumpling into the dirt. Her eyes burned, and she fought the grief that had the ability to blindside her.

Pavel flicked her a glance. "I swore that day I would give my life for Mother Russia, fighting the Nazi fascists."

Edick nodded slowly. "Okay, Pavel. You can help me."

Marina fixed her gaze on Edick, a smile tweaking her lips.

"But not her."

CHAPTER FIVE

E ither Colonel Stone had greatly overestimated him, or his director thought he could perform miracles. Edward dug his elbows into the dirt to hold his field glasses steady as he watched movement on the Velikaya Bridge. Three men posted on the eastern end were tucked away inside a bunker with the business end of three Erma submarine guns poking from the hole like bloodhounds sniffing the breeze. Three more patrolled the bridge on foot. A German Panzer held post thirty feet from the western end with its own armada of ruddy soldiers eating from tin cans.

The Nazis seemed serious about possession of their bridge.

Edward exhaled slowly, thankful for the twilight sounds that shrouded his audible frustration. An owl awoke and hooted as if agreeing with Edward's dismal assessment of the task before him. A drone of crickets drifted upward, past the hiss of the riverbed to the cliff where Edward lay. His arms ached, and pain crept up his spine from his quickly stiffening muscles. Still, surveillance had its rewards. While the German command intended to secure their shipping route, the bone-weary soldiers spent most of the afternoon dropping stones from the bridge and watching them splash sixty feet below into the rapids. They even sent a log over.

Edward had followed it with his glasses down the river, where it disappeared into the froth of rapids and over the mouth of a fifteen-foot falls.

A low sun had turned the steel girders of the bridge copper, gilding it with majesty. Edward pictured himself standing on one abutment, looking nearly the length of his hometown football field, to the opposite end. What type of magician did Stone think he was? The drawings in his rucksack were a poor mockup of the real McCoy.

The snap of a branch behind him raised the hairs on his neck. In one move, he palmed his Colt automatic and rolled over—

"Don't shoot!" Mara raised her hands, her eyes wide on the revolver.

"Sorry." Edward lowered the gun and sat up. Mara didn't smile any acceptance of his apology as she shuffled through the leaves and crouched beside him.

"Pavel sent me to check on you." Her gaze settled on the bridge in the distance. "You've been out here all day?"

The breeze toyed with the long strands of blond hair that had escaped the brown head scarf she'd wrapped over her ears and neck. She had another woolen scarf draped over her shoulders, crossed over her chest, and tied around her waist.

"Where's your sling?"

"I don't need it."

He could argue that point. He'd seen her wince yesterday while hauling a pot of water to the cook fire. In fact, he'd been watching her all week and growing increasingly angry at her lack of concern for her injuries. She'd nearly broken another rib evading his help on their hike back to the partisan hideout, a small, dilapidated barn at the edge of a field. Her fury, sizzling like embers in her eyes, bit at his calloused resolve to keep her out of the war.

He'd learned it was better to avoid her.

"So, what do you think?" She picked up a twig and rolled it between her fingers. Although grimy, she had strong, even regal hands.

"About what?" He had his eyes on her hands and jumped when she snapped the twig in two.

"The bridge." Her condescending tone made him bristle.

"You're still angry."

"You can't do this without me."

He shook his head and rolled back over on his stomach. Picking up the field glasses, he trained his gaze on the squadron of soldiers. "I can and I will. I don't want you there, Mara."

"Why?" The leaves hissed as she turned and stretched on her stomach beside him. He handed her the field glasses. She snuggled them to her eyes and scanned the bridge.

"I don't want you hurt." Her shoulder rubbed against his arm and the smell of smoke and pine went right through him, tugging at his focus. She worried her lower lip with her teeth as she scanned the bridge.

"I won't get hurt." She handed him the binoculars. Her gaze latched onto his, and he saw the determination written in it. He forced himself to shake his head.

She slapped her hand on the ground. "I know this forest. I used to swim in this river and play on that bridge. You just won't use me because I'm a woman."

"You're absolutely right."

She sat up and hugged her knees to her chest. Jeweled leaves clung to her brown woolen pants and lodged in her shawl, illuminating all the bronze highlights in her hair. Her eyes blazed. "You might be surprised to know I'm the best shot in the unit."

"I'm not surprised in the least." He sat up and picked an amber oak leaf from her scarf. "I know you can shred a pinecone from two hundred yards."

His admission made her jaw drop. He enjoyed the startled look in her blue eyes. "I just have issues with women fighting on the front lines."

"Sometimes it's necessary."

"But not now." He picked up the field glasses.

"What if I told you I don't care if I die?"

His chest constricted. *So that's it, Mara. You're out to achieve a glorious end.* "Well, I care."

Her face twitched, and she looked away from him. He reached out and traced her face with his hand. She flinched.

"I know you're grieving, Mara, but God doesn't want you to die."

"God doesn't care about me."

Ouch. "You're so wrong."

"You don't know anything about me. You don't know what God has put me through." The tears edging her eyes softened her harsh expression. He wondered if, trapped inside the shell of bitterness, there huddled a woman who begged to be comforted.

Edward reached out, intending to hold her to his chest. She recoiled, eyes wide. Her fear stung him. "I'm sorry." He held up his hands in surrender.

"Don't get near me. I don't need your pity." Her face turned cold; her eyes narrowed. "All I want to do is repay the evil dished out to me."

"It's God's job to repay."

"Well, I'm taking over." She grabbed the field glasses from his hand. "Tell me how you're going to do it."

Edward drew up his knees and hung his arms over them. A chickadee sang from nearby, and around them, twilight hovered and spilled burned-honey rays through the forest.

"A train's coming."

Edward didn't move but heard a low rumble in reply to her announcement. Five full minutes passed while the train thundered across the bridge. He noticed Mara's grip whiten on the glasses. Her jaw tightened.

"This bridge is a truss bridge," he said as the train rolled toward Pskov in a fog of black smoke. "See how it's built like a triangle? The stress of the bridge is at the top. We take that out, the whole thing comes crashing down, like a card house."

"How?"

"Ten pounds of C-3 detonated when the train is on the middle span."

Her long fingers drummed on the glasses. "How will you detonate it?"

He turned and pointed to the bridge. "I'll run a wire up the middle pier, along the span to the abutment, and into the forest, where I'll be waiting with the trigger."

She lowered the glasses. "You mean you have to be there? You can't set up a timer?"

"I need the bridge to blow while a train passes. It will give the C-3 *oomph*. We want to make sure destruction is complete. If we only damage the bridge, they will be able to rebuild it before the first snowfall."

He reached for the glasses, holding her hand longer than he meant to. "But if we take it out completely, it will be a decisive blow, and they won't be able to rebuild until spring."

"If at all." She pulled her hand away, but he noticed her expression soften. Finally. She picked at the leaves on her pants. He fastened the leather case around the glasses. A breeze, fresh from the river and smelling of nighttime, whistled through the trees. He thought he saw her shiver.

"How did he die?" He snapped the case closed. In the silence that followed, he looked up and saw her face was pale. She met his gaze with a naked look.

"The German invasion. He was stationed at Lvov."

Edward reached out and took her hand. She didn't flinch, and he couldn't help but notice how cold and thin it felt. He traced the fine bones in it with his thumb. "I'm sorry, Mara. How long were you married?"

"Three months."

Grief felt like a fist, sucker-punching him in the chest. "And you loved him?" Her limp hand suddenly tensed, but she didn't pull away.

"More than life," she whispered. The look in her eyes made him want to cry. The longing to hold her rushed through him, but he sensed that holding her hand pushed her to the edge. Besides, holding her just might tell her more than he intended.

"How are you going to get around those guards?"

Whoa. He blinked at her, amazed at how quickly she'd gathered in all the frayed emotions in her eyes. He dropped her hand and fiddled with the binoculars. "I'm working on that."

"I have an idea." She lifted her chin, and a tiny smile tweaked her lips.

He grimaced.

"If you let me help."

"How did I know that was coming?" He shook his head. "You'll let me help?"

"You can fold the maps."

She hit him on the shoulder, but for a second, laughter danced through her eyes. "You're going to need me, and you know it."

He was beginning to wonder if, perhaps, she wasn't painfully correct.

⁓

Natasha held the candle over the map that draped the tiny square table. Light licked the grim faces of the partisans as Marina gestured, outlining her plan. Edick stood beside her, and from his hands-folded-across-his-chest stance, she knew he wasn't biting. She added another layer of determination to her voice.

"They're garrisoned here, in the city administration building, and here, at the school. I don't think it would be too hard to seal up the entrances with some of Edick's C-3." She shot him a glance and enjoyed watching him frown. "Then we keep them occupied while Edick wires the bridge."

Edick rubbed his jaw with the back of his hand. Pavel's dark eyes traced the map. "Do you think the explosion will be loud enough to draw the guards from their posts on the bridge?"

"If there were two, spaced a few minutes apart, that would bring them in." Edick braced his hands on the table. "I only have one radio transmitter. But we could rig them to set off in a series. You blow the first one, then resend the signal for the second, and so on. But you'd have to lay the cable between them."

"Across the road?" Sasha leaned forward on his stool and slid his elbows onto the table. "How would we lay the wire without alerting the guards?"

Marina pointed to the buildings on the map. "If I remember correctly, there is a drainage ditch running across Karl Marx Street, behind the administration building. We can run a line from the building to the school."

"Or you could toss a couple grenades on the first target, then blow the second after you've rattled them a bit," Pavel said. Anticipation lit his face. She smiled at her first convert. Edick, however, continued to frown and rub his whiskers with the back of his hand.

"If we positioned here," she tapped her finger on the map, "at the cultural center, we could toss some of those stick grenades right into their front yard."

"Oh, sure," scoffed Sasha. "We'll make lovely targets. Why don't we just stand up and wave? Look at the partisans, ripe for torture."

"You wouldn't have to stick around, Sasha. Just toss and run," Marina said, angling him a wry smile. Sasha's demeanor had turned from cocky to subdued after Lev's death, but the kid still had courage in his veins waiting to be stoked. "You can do it, Sasha. You're fast, and you have great aim."

He harrumphed. "You're the runner in the unit, Mara. You should do it."

She glanced at Edick. "Nope, I have other things to do."

Edick glanced at her, eyes sparking. "No."

"Yes. You need someone to watch your back. While Pavel and the team cause trouble in Pskov, you're going to wire the bridge. And I'm going to sit in the forest and pick off the dogs who nip at your heels."

The table groaned as Pavel leaned onto it. Candlelight accentuated the grim lines that etched his face. "I don't like it, but she's right. We need able bodies in the city. Natasha and Sasha can't take it alone—I need to help them."

"The whole thing is crazy, Pavel." Edick rubbed a thumb and forefinger under his eyes. "I'm going to get you all killed."

"You don't own this war, Edick." Marina stood arms akimbo. "This is our homeland. Let us fight for it. You can't possibly complete your mission on your own. You need help. Admit it."

He pushed up the sleeves of his gray wool sweater and leaned on the table. He had wide, strong forearms and muscled hands. Standing next to him, she felt the memory of being nestled in his arms, his strong, masculine smell washing through her, the rumble of his breath in his wide chest as he hauled her through the forest, and it made her head spin. She gritted her teeth, hating the fact that in his arms she felt safe.

It was just grief, perhaps loneliness stirring her heart and dredging up her wounds.

Edick sighed, long and low, and Marina recognized resignation in his voice. "You're a gritty bunch, you Russians." He cast a grim look, first at Natasha, then Sasha, Pavel, and finally Marina. "You've whittled me down to a nub." To her shock, he reached out and touched her shoulder. Warmth radiated down her arm. "As long as you don't climb any trees, I'd be honored to have you watch my back, Mara."

Oh my, the man packed a punch with simple words and low tones. She could barely nod.

Thankfully, Pavel stepped up and unleashed his ideas. The group huddled around the table, talking into the night until even Sasha and Natasha retired to their mats. Pavel finally admitted exhaustion, but Marina's nerves buzzed with anticipation. While Pavel and Edick grabbed blankets and made to curl up on the dirt floor of the shack, she slipped out the door into the night.

A cool breeze lifted the hair on her neck. She ran her fingers through it, combing out a nest of tangles. Forest sounds filled the air—the hoot of a lonely owl, the buzz of crickets. The jagged, black tree line pushed against a midnight blue sky. As a million stars winked at her, the moon reached out and pooled white light in the clearing. Marina walked into it, evening dew seeping through a hole in the German boots she had lifted from a corpse. She rubbed her arms as the wind shivered through the dying leaves.

"Are you cold?"

She whirled, frozen as Edick approached her. The wind played with his hair, begging her to run her fingers through it. She folded her arms across her chest. "No," she lied.

"Hmm." He walked past her into the pool of moonlight. "Amazing how a planet a million miles away would know to shine on the prettiest girl in the world."

Oh. Marina's mouth opened, and heat flooded her face.

"I like it when you're embarrassed. It's better than furious."

"I'm. . .a married woman," she stammered.

He frowned, his smile fading. "I see."

Marina's eyes burned, and she turned away from him.

"The Bible says God knows each of the stars by name," Edick said. "If He knows the stars that well, imagine how He knows us."

Marina rubbed her arms. "I like to think Dmitri is up there, watching me."

"Was he a Christian?"

"Yes. He loved God. He told me God would bring him home."

"He did." Edick shoved his hands in the pockets of his wool pants. "Dmitri is safe in the arms of the Lord."

"And I'm left behind." Tears stung her eyes.

"There's a reason for everything that happens, Mara. God can take the sorrow in your soul and turn it to joy."

"I don't think so."

He stared at the ground, toeing the dirt with his black boot. "I know that's hard to believe. Especially in these dark times. But if you don't hold onto hope—"

"Don't talk to me of hope. You didn't see your mother murdered before your eyes, or. . .or. . ." She fought the fury rising in her chest. *Or have your child ripped from your womb. Hope is for fools and dreamers. Like Dmitri.*

"Mara." The soft edge of his voice made her want to cry. "I'm so sorry."

Marina pressed her fingers to her eyes. "It doesn't matter anymore."

His sudden movement took her by surprise, and she didn't have the sense to complain until she was locked inside his arms, his hand smoothing her hair, her face nuzzled against his chest. The rich scent of wool and earth wrapped around her, and his heartbeat in her ear opened the wounds she'd thought had scarred over. Sorrow burned her throat. *Oh, Dima, I miss you.* She closed her eyes, relishing the pocket of comfort, painfully aware that, while another man held her, she still ached for her husband's touch.

"Don't give up, Mara. Believe that God loves you. Somewhere deep inside, you must know it."

Marina heard his words, longing to embrace them. Her entire body tingled, and the strangest sensation moved within her like a whisper.

But deep inside her soul, she felt nothing.

CHAPTER SIX

E dward crouched by the edge of the Velikaya River and watched foam gather on shore, pinkened by the hues of dawn. Behind him, a mockingbird scolded him, and the trees, at the mercy of a renegade Siberian wind, scrubbed their naked arms against the sky.

Edward turned up the collar of his jacket and sat on a large boulder. Unzipping his coat, he drew out a small New Testament. The brown leather Bible had seen him through West Point and had kept him alive after Katrina's execution. It had offered him solace after the massacre of his partisans, and now, it seemed, he needed the comfort of its guidance. How to soften Mara's heart of stone?

He'd seen it crack last night. A little tenderness, and she'd held onto him for a half hour, her thin body wracking. Then, just as abruptly as it had started, she'd pulled away and run for the barn.

He'd stayed in the chilly night, watching the wind swirl the stars, and knew only his Maker had the comfort she silently longed for.

He needed guidance and assurance that the fight he was about to start was in God's hands. He turned straight to the Gospel of John, chapter twenty-one.

Picking out a small ticket stub, he flicked it between two fingers. He'd met Katrina at the Berlin symphony house and kept the stub as a reminder of happier days, of moments when he'd thought he was the luckiest man alive.

Yeah. So lucky he got the woman he loved killed. He tucked it into the pages of his Bible and traced his finger down to verse four. "But when the morning was now come, Jesus stood on the shore: but the disciples knew not that it was Jesus. Then Jesus saith unto them, Children, have ye any meat? They answered him, No.

"And he said unto them, Cast the net on the right side of the ship, and ye shall find."

Funny how the last words he'd read still leapt out at him. Jesus asking the disciples what they'd accomplished for all their work that night. When he'd read it three years ago, the words knifed through his heart. He'd failed his mission and condemned the only woman he'd ever loved. His nets, his goals had come up empty. The memory of a blindfolded Katrina raising her chin before an execution squad rose like a taunt.

"Lord, how did I mess up so badly? I thought I was doing Your will." His eyes burned, and the Bible shook in his hands. Clenching his jaw, he read past the disciples' negative reply to the miraculous blessing. "They cast therefore, and now they were not able to draw it for the multitude of fishes."

Edward closed the book, wedging his thumb to save his place, and lifted his eyes to the rose-hued sky. "Lord, what are You saying to me? Am I fishing on the wrong side? Running fruitless missions, busying myself with tasks that aren't Your will? Is that why I can't seem to do any good, why people are betrayed, why my heart aches to hear Your voice?"

He watched the wind push around a clump of wispy

cirrus clouds. "Make me fruitful, Lord. Show me how to serve You, and give me a good catch." He furrowed his hands into his snarled hair. "Lord, please help us this day. Make my hands strong and my feet steady. Make Pavel and Natasha courageous, and let Sasha be quick and precise. Give Mara excellent aim. And please, Lord, keep her safe."

Marina eyed the branches of the hornbeam and wished she hadn't promised Edick she wouldn't climb any trees. Propped on the edge of the cliff with its roots clawing the side like fingers, it stretched two long, twisted arms over the river. Arms that she could hide in and from which she could secure a much better angle to protect Edick as he climbed the bridge.

Still, she'd made a promise. She sighed loudly and scanned the cliff's edge for a decent perch. From her position, she could clearly make out the bridge, some three hundred meters in the distance. And a few meters away, Edick, crouched behind a downed oak. He knew how to blend—in his dark leather jacket, he seemed a mass of bark in the lush forest greens. But Marina didn't just see him, she sensed him. As if his vulnerability on the bank of the river and his dependence on her to keep the fascists off his back had knit them together with an invisible, unbreakable thread.

They'd walked to the river in silence, but since waking that morning, she felt a supernatural force buoying her courage. An invisible hand had pushed her into Pavel's prayer circle, and while she couldn't bow her head or join in the words, she couldn't deny the feeling that something had changed.

Still, she refused to believe that maybe it had something to do with the moments inside Edick's arms. She had absolutely no room in her heart for anyone but Dima, and Mr. Arrogant-I'll-Save-You-American had nothing to do with the fact that today she felt stronger. Just a little healed.

So he had wide hands that felt like they could carry her burdens and a wry smile that seemed to zero in on her. She'd had her heart scooped out of her body whole. And nothing but a gaping hole of ache was left in its place. If she ever, ever let herself feel again, she needed someone who wouldn't abandon her for adventure or duty. Ten seconds after Edick blew the bridge, he would head for the border. Not a battle plan for a happy future. Still, as she stood beside him, watching the wind rake his dark hair, she'd felt a rustle in the pit of her stomach, as if her body had begun to awaken to hope.

The drum of a woodpecker tore her gaze off Edick. She stood at the edge of the cliff, casting a longing glance at the tree. Thirty meters down, the Velikaya River tumbled and frothed toward Malenki Falls, the first of two falls, the only one that a person could tumble over and survive. Bolshoi Falls, another half kilometer down the river, dropped thirty meters into a cauldron of foam and spray.

Marina shuddered, remembering herself as a fifteen-year-old tempting fate, swimming against the current above Malenki Falls. Although a strong swimmer, the current snatched her, drove her to the edge. "Marina!" Dmitri's panicked voice laced her memory, and she smiled at the memory of his arms about her, pulling her back. His wet hair plastered his face; his eyes stretched wide with fear. "Be careful!"

She backed away from the edge, his voice in her ears.

Be careful. Why, exactly, Dima?

She spied a pocket of ground ten paces ahead and bushwhacked along the edge toward it. She pressed her foot into the mossy depression. It was as if a large boulder had sprung from the edge and left its footprint in the soil. She sighted her Mauser toward the bridge. Tangled bushes and downed trees made a troublesome sight line but adequate for the defense she would wage. Hopefully, the squadron of Germans would jump at the bait and abandon their posts for crisis in Pskov.

She set down the rifle and tromped a short distance until she came to a large, decaying log. Gripping two limbs, she tugged at it, hoping to drag it over to the nest and form a wall of protection. She braced her feet and tugged.

Pain seized her abdomen. Gasping, she released the tree and fell, her arms around her body as she groaned and rocked back and forth. Hauling in shallow breaths, she closed her eyes until the pain eased its hold. Sweat dotted her forehead, and her head spun. She shook her head, furious her body wouldn't cooperate. She'd been breathing deeply and often, just as Edick had instructed; and although she'd discarded the sling sooner than he advised, the pain had subsided to a dull ache in the evenings.

Bracing her hands on a tree, she pushed to her feet. She slapped off leaves and twigs from her woolen britches and again grabbed the branches. This time, she eased into her pull, and the pain kept a distance as she shimmied the log toward her sniper's nest. Positioning it between her and the bridge, she climbed down behind it and laid her gun on top, again sighting the bridge.

Two Germans sat on the edge of the bridge, their legs dangling over the side, submachine guns across their laps.

One smoked a cigarette, dangling it between stained lips. Green helmets obscured their eyes and cast dark shadows over their faces. Marina preferred not to see their eyes anyway. She still had burned in her mind the image of the German in Pskov who'd attacked her.

The other German laughed and slapped his knees, swinging his legs over the thirty-meter drop to the river. Marina mentally squeezed the trigger and saw him drop with a splash into the river. The old, familiar hatred roiled inside her. It tasted bitter; and as she pulled the gun away from her eye, she noticed her hands shook. She drew in a deep breath and searched for Edick.

He'd vanished from his spot. Panic spurted into her throat, and she clamped down on her emotions. He was simply moving into position or checking his equipment. Her gaze traveled over the hornbeam tree, along the naked branches to the horizon, where the opposite cliff met the twilight sky. Dark, raisin-black clouds drifted overhead, and along the scrape of treetops, the sun slashed at the encroaching night in sprays of burnt sienna. The air smelled of decaying leaves and the moisture of a freezing river. Marina inhaled a calming breath and ran her mind over the mission details.

Poor Sasha. Armed with a backpack of Dyakonov stick grenades, Sasha had been dispatched to town just after dawn to garner a position across from the administration building, in the House of Culture. Marina pulled him aside before he left and revealed a few secrets from her days as a Pioneer. "You can climb up to the third-story window through the fire escape on the south end of the building."

Sasha's eyes filled with fear as Marina drew out a mental map. "Then take the attic stairs and close the door behind you. You should be able to toss out the grenades through the ventilation system. If not, go to the roof." She'd clamped a hand on his shoulder, cringing at the lack of muscle on this lanky teen. "If you throw down a rope from the third floor, you might be able to rappel down to the fire escape during the confusion."

Sasha nodded, his eyes wide.

She wondered if Dmitri had felt Sasha's fear when he stood eye-to-eye with the Germans. Had he been afraid, armed, like Sasha, with only an ancient squirrel gun that had a crack in the stock? Did his heart leap from his chest and his hands grow sweaty when the Panzers crested the horizon and the Messerschmitts droned overhead? Had he seen the brutal expressions written on the faces of the Nazi invaders? Marina's throat thickened, and she ran a hand over her empty womb. *Dmitri, did you suffer?*

Under her hand, a strange sensation brushed the inside of her stomach, a whisper, as if the wind moved inside her. She froze, her fingers spread wide. Again, the movement crossed her belly, deep inside. She pushed on her belly, slowly, deliberately and found that beneath the folds of skin, it was hard.

She wrapped two hands around herself, as if to contain the emotions that swelled within her. *No. Could Dmitri's baby be still alive, blossoming inside her?* She shook her head to dislodge the thought. The hope seemed a dangerous flame, flickering too close to her raw heart. Still, movement inside made her pause. She counted back and judged herself to be about five months' pregnant.

No. Not after falling into the river and out of a tree. Besides, God had abandoned her. Dmitri and everything about him had perished.

The thunder of two explosions shattered the silence and sent a flock of sparrows screaming into the sky.

⟡⟡⟡⟡⟡⟡

The skin on Edward's forearms rose at the sound of the grenades. He dug the field glasses into his eyes and glued his sights on the two guards dangling their legs over the bridge. They scrambled to their feet.

Edward's muscles tightened, his legs poised to jump the second the soldiers abandoned their posts for town. "C'mon, take the bait," he urged in a thin whisper.

Another explosion, this time thundering across the sky in a rolling wave, sealed the guards' seduction. The two inside the bunker emerged, yelling, gripping Erma machine guns, and gesturing toward Pskov. Edward's insides coiled, his heartbeat on overdrive as he watched them waver. Time stretched out like rubber, then snapped as the squadron jumped on three motorbikes and screamed toward town in a spray of dust and rocks.

He hoped Mara had seen their victory. Letting the field glasses drop, he crouched low, then hurtled through the brush. The weeds whipped his chest and body, but his eyes stayed on the bridge. Twenty feet short of the first abutment, he slowed and scanned the road. A billow of dusty smoke signaled the all-clear. He prayed Mara had her sights on him as he edged out onto the bridge.

For the briefest of moments as he ran down the span, he wished Russia had joined the twentieth century and built a cantilever or even a suspension bridge. One ten-pound charge of C-3 on the end of an abutment on those bridges would send the entire main span crashing into the rocks below. But this truss bridge required him to climb to the very top of the triangle struts and plant his C-3 where it would destroy the tension and collapse the bridge from the center out. He was glad he wasn't afraid of heights as he peered over the edge to the churning river below. He threw a leg over the outer rail and began to climb the supports.

The *rat-a-tat* of machine gun fire and smaller explosions that sounded of German pull-grenades sent his stomach to his feet. A crow screeched at him from the cliff line, and the wind cooled the sweat from his brow. Rivets tore into his hands, steel bit his knees and shins. He wedged himself into the top V and reached up inside the ridges of the uppermost girders to place the C-3.

Another explosion from town. The partisans were attacking with his American Mk2 fragment grenades, a gift from his own arsenal.

He'd already worked the C-3 blocks into putty and now quickly attached the fuse wires into the pack. Reaching high, he set the explosive onto the top of the triangle steel casing, wedging it hard into the underlying girder section. Ten pounds of C-3 should shatter the joint, but he'd feel better if he could place a similar charge on the opposite truss.

Unwinding the fuse wire as he shimmied down, he tacked it with nonexplosive putty along the girder down to the span. Sweat dripped in rivulets down his cheek and saturated his shirt. He shot a look downriver, where he hoped Mara had him in his sights. He saw nothing of her, which only pumped up his respect. He smiled in her direction, hoping she caught the expression of success.

In the distance, the rattle of machine guns and explosions died to a smattering. Nakedness crept over him. Leaning over the side, he ran the wire along the end, tacking it every ten feet toward the abutment. The air had become strangely still except for the lone, piercing cry of a hawk soaring through the riverbed. He worked quickly, precisely, feeling victory in the palms of his hands. Once the wire was laid, he'd simply camp out until the first train passed. Then, methodically, he'd dump the train, along with the bridge, into the rapids below.

Score one for the Allies.

He wiped his sweaty palm on his pants. His heartbeat thundered in his chest as he fed out enough wire to allow him to leap over to the cliff.

A blow between his shoulder blades sent him to his knees. His head fogged, but he tucked, and rolled, and felt another blow skim his ear.

"Haltestelle!"

Edward turned, and beyond the blur of green, he made out the definite outline of the business end of an Erma submachine gun swiveling toward his face.

Mara, where are you?

CHAPTER SEVEN

Marina drew a still breath, held it, and squeezed the trigger.

A scream echoed off the steel girders. She reloaded as the German crumbled at Edick's feet. As Edick scrambled backward, a second soldier flashed across her peripheral vision. She ignored a sick feeling and fired.

He dropped. Searching for Edick, she found him feeding out a line of wire and running toward the cliff. She left him and scoped the road, her heart stopping at the sight of four motorcycles churning up a plume of dirt behind them. "Hurry, hurry, Edick."

Hoping to buy him time, she picked off the front tire of the first motorcycle. The machine toppled in a wild zigzag and careened into its neighbor. Four soldiers went airborne. Marina didn't watch to see where they landed. She turned her sight on Edick and watched him secure the fuse line on the abutment and leap to the cliff. Slamming another bullet into the chamber, she returned her gaze to the road.

The soldiers had reached the bridge and were running along the cliff line toward Edick. She sighted them in her crosshairs, but her angle would only chip off twigs and dirt. She tried anyway and dug out a swath of bark from a large oak. Frustration welled in her chest. Her second try pinged on the bridge. She lowered the rifle, panic driving adrenaline through her. She had to find a better angle.

Tucking her Mauser under her arm, she ran to the hornbeam overhanging the river. "Sorry, Edick," she muttered as she climbed up the trunk and shimmied out on a long branch. She didn't look down but turned and propped her right foot in the joint of two skinny branches. She curled her left leg around her perch. Slamming the butt of her rifle into her shoulder, she forced her breath still and ran her sights along the shore until she found her prey—two Germans in green field coats plowing through the forest after her American.

She tracked the lead pursuer, a lanky fellow whose blond hair made a shimmering target in the fuzzy green foliage. With steel in her heart, she pulled the trigger.

The recoil slammed into her hard and dislodged her foot, sending her backwards. She dropped the gun, her arms spinning, grabbing at the air, catching nothing. Then she heard a crack as her perch split under her weight.

She spilled down its smooth trunk and out into openness. Marina screamed as she pedaled backward, legs kicking the misty river air.

Edick dove into a thicket, rolled, and came up with his Colt. Smacking himself up against a tree, he looked behind him, scanning his back trail for pursuers. They crashed like bulls through the brush.

A woman's scream raised every hair on his neck, and he whirled, searching for Mara. *Please, O Lord, let her be safe!* What he saw turned him cold. Mara, fanning the air as she tumbled through the sky toward the river below.

"Mara!" Forgetting his attackers, he stumbled to the edge of the cliff and searched the water. He made out her blond head bobbing down the river at the mercy of the frothy current.

Gulping in a deep breath, he calculated the distance between her and the falls. Two hundred yards at the most.

The sound of cursing behind him sealed his decision. Taking a deep breath, he flung himself over the cliff and toward the water below.

He spliced the water like a needle, feet first. The numbing cold sent a thousand spikes into his skin. He burst to the surface gasping, pain pulsing in his head, pinching his lungs. Treading water, he searched for Mara. He spied her thirty feet ahead, a speck in the raging swirls of rapid. Water crested over his head and tugged at him, gathering him into the current. He swam with it, yelling her name. "Mara!" Swells of white water and spray drowned his voice.

Fear and cold had paled her face. He lunged for her. Missed.

Mara went over like a slice of raw bacon, limp and long, feet first. Edward fought to bring his feet around in the water, backstroking to keep his balance. The falls sucked him in and threw him over the lip like a slingshot. He landed and went deep as a thousand gallons of water emptied into his wake. Kicking violently, he fought for the surface. He broke through, gulping air. "Mara!"

The river had swallowed her. The current slowed in the fall's pool, and he swam through it, resisting the flow that continued to tug him downstream. "Mara, where are you?"

"Help!"

He spied her grabbing at low-hanging reeds along the shore, each one sliding through her grip like wet noodles.

The river clawed at her, hungry to suck her back into the downward spiral toward a lower falls.

"Hang on!" His voice was wasted in the roar of the river. He kicked hard toward her and in a moment had sped past her, towed by the river's grasp. Turning, he clawed for branches and rocks. Panic began a death march as his numb grip slid uselessly over decent holds. *O God, please help!*

He thudded against a submerged boulder. The river tried to spin him around the obstruction, but he wedged his fingers into a crack and held on. Shaking the water from his eyes, he searched upstream for Mara. She still fought for purchase along the shore with more grit than he'd pegged her for.

"Mara!" He pulled his legs around and straddled the rock, letting the pressure of the river hold him fast. Digging his ankles into the rock, he felt a couple layers of skin peel off. He opened his arms. "I'll catch you! Let the river have you!"

She met his eyes, and he saw right into her terrorized soul. *I won't let you go, I promise!*

She landed with a thud in his arms. He locked them tight around her. The river wrestled him for her, but he refused surrender. She coughed as she clutched his shirt. Around them, the river roared in fury.

"Let's get out of here." Edward helped her turn and grab a branch hanging out of the water. Her hair was matted to her cheeks, and she had the coloring of a bloated fish. Still he couldn't help admire the way she dug her knees into the mossy bank and worked her way to safety.

He followed her ashore, crouched on all fours, his chest heaving, his breath burning his lungs. Beside him, Mara had curled into a ball, shivering, hiccuping back sobs.

"I'm sorry," she said, shaking. "I'm so sorry."

"Me, too," he said, not sure what she might be apologizing for. She'd saved his life.

Feeling weak, he leaned over her, shushing her sobs, his words meant for himself as much as for her. "You're okay now, Mara. Please, don't cry."

She covered her head with her arms, her knees drawn up to her chest.

O Lord, help me. What was it about this woman that ignited all his protective urges? He wasn't about to let another woman climb into his heart only to see her murdered. And Mara had set her sights on martyrdom. Still, the way she held onto him last night despite her defenses churned up deep-buried longings. In his wildest dreams, he was a hero, an answer to prayer, a man who saved lives.

A man Mara could trust.

So far, he'd been the source of betrayal. Of death.

Not anymore. Gently, he scooped her up and held her on his cross-legged lap. She continued to hide her face and sob.

"Mara, you're safe now. It's okay."

She shook her head. "It's not okay. What. . .if. . ." Her sobs annihilated her sentence.

He pulled her arms down gently and met her red-streaked eyes. "There's no 'what if.' We're okay. You're okay. We'll just have to have another go at the bridge."

She shook her head, her eyes shimmering with tears, her lips purple and quivering. Edward ran his hand over her face, cupping it with his palm, rubbing her tears away with his thumb. All words left him at the bravery of this wounded woman.

How was he supposed to heed the warnings in his

heart as well as common sense screaming like an air-raid siren in the back of his head when she looked at him with those blue eyes, ripe with need, reeling him in? Almost without thinking, he cupped her cheek and kissed her.

She tasted salty and cold and for a moment froze in his arms. He leaned back, his breath caught in his chest. What had he done?

Except she'd stopped crying, and fear had vanished from her eyes. Then sadness broke out over the face, and she closed her eyes. "Please, kiss me again, Edick."

Oh, no, he wasn't ready for this woman, wasn't prepared for her to invade the long empty places inside. Still, he wrapped his arms around her, pulled her to himself, and kissed her. She moved into his kiss, and he felt her pour her emotions, her fears into her response. She touched his face; her tears wet his lips as she kissed him with an abandonment that suddenly scared him. She was quickly peeling back the walls that kept him moving forward, dodging his past, his wounds, and it all threatened to crash over him and pull him into a vortex beyond his control. Groaning from his vulnerability, he pulled back, dragged in a ragged breath, and searched her eyes.

They widened, and the horror seeping into them chilled him to the bone.

"What have I done?" She covered her mouth with her hands, then disentangled herself from his lap and stood. "No, no!" She backed away, shaking her head.

He felt raw. "What? Mara, I'm sorry. I didn't mean to offend you. I just. . .you are. . ." His words lodged in his chest.

She entwined her hands in her wet hair and stared at him. "I can't love you, Edick."

"I know you're grieving, Mara. But maybe there is time for us, in the future—"

"No!"

Her answer stung. So maybe their kiss had more to do with the moment, with relief. But certainly some part of truth lived in her response. "Why?"

She suddenly dropped to her knees, her hands on her stomach. Her face twisted. "Oh no."

Edward scrambled toward her. "Are you hurt? It's your ribs, right?"

She shook her head as she moaned. "No, Edick. No." She curled into a ball. "No, Edick. I think. . .oh no. . .I think it's the baby."

CHAPTER EIGHT

How could she still be pregnant?

Marina wrapped her arms around her stomach. The contraction washed over her in a wave, numbing all other thought. She couldn't bear to look at Edward, to see the look in his eyes, nor could she face the guilt that burrowed into her heart.

She'd kissed him. And for a terrible moment, lost herself in his embrace.

She felt like a harlot.

Swallowing deep breaths, she willingly lost herself in the pain. It crested, then subsided slowly, like a yawn. Soon all that remained was the fear that she had somehow killed Dmitri's child when she'd fallen into the river. She leaned forward and clutched the mossy ground, shivering violently and waiting for the next pain to overtake her body.

To her shock, Edward knelt in the dirt beside her. She mustered her courage and looked into his eyes. The confusion on his face made tears spring to her eyes. She'd never once since she met him seen him afraid, but as he stared at her, his face waxed white, his hands out, hovering above her, as if she were made of spun glass. She recognized a man's fear.

"The baby?" he repeated weakly. "Why didn't you tell me before?"

She sat and pulled her legs up to her chest. With the river wind snaking through the trees and the moist air creeping under her sopping wool shawl, she fought a teeth-chattering chill. "I didn't know. I thought I'd lost the baby, and I guess I couldn't believe. . ."

"That God might be watching over you?" Edward still didn't touch her, instead running his gaze up and down her body. "I can't believe I let you help me attack the bridge. What if you'd been killed?" He raked a hand through his hair. "I'm such a heel."

He shook his head, looking unraveled.

"It wasn't your choice, as I recall." She fought to steady her voice. "You needed my help."

"Not at the price of your child." He hung his head. "What was I thinking?"

She tasted the bitter steel of regret. "Sometimes there is no choice."

He met her eyes, his lips a drawn line. "I failed. We lost the bridge."

Marina blinked at him. "No, you didn't, how could it be your fault?"

"I should have worked faster."

She grabbed his jacket, felt him tense under her grip. "We'll try again. We'll think of something. Pavel knows what he is doing."

She didn't want to consider the idea that Pavel and Natasha and mostly likely Sasha could be wounded. . .or dead.

Edward didn't respond, but he stared at her with such a horrified expression, she felt like weeping.

Another cramp started in her abdomen, reaching out like fingers across her stomach. Marina opened her mouth and felt the blood drain from her face. She held perfectly still, but Edward met her eyes. She tried to tuck her emotions away, but he must have seen them, for his face twisted with worry.

"Another pain?"

She could barely nod.

"Are you in labor?" He tucked her wet hair behind her ear.

The possibility stretched her voice whisper thin. "I don't know."

"I need to get you somewhere safe." He slid his arms around her and lifted her. She groaned and clutched his sweater.

"Wait, I can walk."

"Not if you're in labor. Try and kill that stubborn streak and let me take care of you, please."

His words wrapped around her heart like an embrace. She settled her head onto his soggy shoulder and closed her eyes. Around them, the river roared and the wind whistled through the trees, but the strongest sound was his quiet voice, praying for her and her child.

━━━━━━

Wrapped in a monk's cloak, Edward leaned against the cell door and fought a chill. Inside, Mara lay on the cot against the wall, curled in a fetal ball, finally sleeping. Thankfully, the contractions had been few and had subsided as Mara relaxed in his arms. Still, Edward's emotions felt raw, realizing the enormity of what she'd nearly lost. Edward raised his eyes to the milky black sky, sighted the North Star, and prayed.

"God, who made the universe and knows even the stars

by name, protect Your Mara and the child within. Please, don't let her lose this baby after all she has suffered. Heal her body and her heart with this child." His voice broke on the last sentence, and he closed his eyes, remembering the feel of her lips on his, her head nestled into his chest, the hard-won surrender of her trust. His hands tightened into fists. "Please, Lord, don't let my mistakes steal this child from her arms."

Guilt raged unchecked through him. If he'd known she was pregnant, he'd never have let her leave the hideout, let alone take on the German army. He'd wanted to shake her when she'd collapsed in the dirt and surrendered her secret. How could a woman not know she was pregnant? Her foolishness and hatred had driven her to this precarious situation, and from this moment onward, he'd do the thinking for her. Revenge pushed her beyond the envelope of rational thinking, and she couldn't be trusted with her own body.

Frustration burned like a coal in his heart. He raised his hands, palms up, to the sky. "Why, oh why, do You put me with stubborn women?"

He was in big trouble, and he knew it. If her kiss didn't tug out his desires, the look in her eyes as he carried her to the monastery had completely unraveled him.

What was he thinking? She carried another man's child. Still, God had taken that father and, for whatever reason, plunked Mara into Edward's life.

Edick's life. It wasn't lost on him that she called him by the same name Kat had. Was she also destined to Kat's fate?

For both their sakes, he had to rid his heart of her. She didn't belong with an American. Her child needed a Russian father, and she, a Russian husband. Perhaps Pavel, if the partisan had lived through the attack.

The thought sent a wave of ache through him. The partisans. He wondered who had survived.

And who hadn't.

He turned and entered the cell, watching Mara in the soft bath of candlelight. Dressed in a monk's cloak, which swallowed her frail body, she looked fragile and nothing like the gritty fighter he knew her to be. Her hair fanned out around her on the cot in a gilded halo of light. He wanted to reach down and run the back of his fingers along that stubborn mouth that felt like velvet and had made his heart tumble through his chest. He forced the urge into the category of never and stepped away from her. Today was just more evidence that he brought only pain to the people he tried to help.

Brother Timofea entered the cell, a reed mat under his arm. "Peace to you, Edward." His craggy face broke into a smile. "She is asleep?"

Edward took the mat. "For now."

Brother Timofea wove his hands into the cuffs of his monk's robe. "Come with me," he said quietly.

The crisp night air froze the sweat dotting Edward's face as he followed the monk outside. The compound was quiet, the monks shut away in their cells for the night. Two large bulldogs lay at the front gate with heads on their paws. Shiny black eyes blinked at him, sending a shiver up his spine. Edward turned his attention skyward and for an awestruck moment lost himself in the brilliance of winking lights.

"Sometimes, on nights like these, I feel but a mustard seed," Timofea said, putting words to Edward's thoughts.

Edward shrugged. "We are."

"That depends on your perspective. When we look up,

yes. But when we look inward, our lives seem to consume us. We see only ourselves. It's the vanity of man, telling ourselves that we matter, that we can change the world."

Edward sighed. "Is there an escape from that?"

Timofea nodded. "Again, perspective. We *can* change the world. But only as tools of the Master Designer. The sure cure for vanity is humility—a proper view of who we are in God's eyes and a determination to walk in His will."

Edward smiled and scuffed his boot into the dirt. "I sure wish I knew what that will was."

"I thought you were here to blow up a bridge and save Mother Russia."

Edward caught the tease in Timofea's raspy voice. He shrugged, embarrassed, failure mocking him in Timofea's words.

"Or could you be here for different reasons?" Timofea cast a glance toward his cell.

Edward shifted and curled a hand around the back of his neck. "I don't think so, Timofea. After today, I wonder if I'm supposed to be in Russia at all."

Brother Timofea nodded. "The scripture says He sets the stars in the sky. Imagine, if God arranged Cassiopeia and the Orion, He certainly knows why you are running around here in Russia. God put those stars in the cosmos. Just as He put you here, Edward."

From far away, the low hoot of a great horned owl lifted and carried across the compound. A breeze kicked up dirt and raised the hair on the back of Edward's neck.

"So, how are the other partisan groups doing?" Edward's voice was so low, he barely heard himself speak.

Brother Timofea shuffled closer. "We had a shipment today. More MN-Carbine rifles with ammo and three crates of Dyakonov stick grenades. From Moscow."

"I don't like it, Timofea. It's a dangerous game you're playing. Sooner or later the Jerries are gonna find you and uncover your entire operation."

Brother Timofea raised his hands. "I put it in His hands. Twice already the Germans have sent their Schmitts over, and twice God protected us."

"They're hunting the partisan supply line."

"And it's right under their noses."

Edward wondered if it was a sin for a monk to laugh so hard at deceit. He couldn't help but add his own wry chuckle.

"Just don't take any chances, Brother. I'd hate to see you swinging the next time I stop by."

Timofea clamped him on the shoulder, his bony hand clenching him in a spidery grip. "You know, when I first saw you, I immediately recognized the Russian man in you. You remind me so much of someone I once knew— another young man like yourself. Young, full of energy and vigor, and oh, he loved a cause. He believed in his Mennonite way almost as much as he loved his wife. Once he made up his mind to love her, he was committed until death. I think her love made him stronger, and she became a tower of strength for him on the outside, just as God was his internal strength."

Edward stared into Timofea's blue eyes, seeing history. He guessed the monk must be about forty years old. "What happened to them?"

"I don't know." The gleam in Timofea's eye dimmed. "I do know that wherever God took them, my young friend lived what he believed with passion and purpose, just as he loved with the same vigor. You cannot shy away from your purpose because of fear of loss." Timofea flung his arms out wide. "Life and love are gifts. Some of us have them longer than others. We shouldn't waste them out of a fear to act."

Edward eyed him with a smirk. "Are you sure you've been a monk all your life?"

Timofea tucked his hands back into his sleeves. "Not all my life." He smiled. "I am not afraid of the Nazis, Edward. I am afraid of not obeying the will of my God. Of not loving those He sends me to love, of not participating in the fight to save lives. This is what I fear."

Edward nodded, eyes pricking. "I just don't want to lose you, friend."

Timofea looked him in the eyes, his gaze piercing his soul. "This is your weakness, my son. This is what keeps you from finding peace."

Edward stood under the stars, hands in his pockets, pondering Brother Timofea's words long after the monk shuffled toward his cell. The night seemed cold without the man of God beside him, but the words sizzled in Edward's soul. He longed to be used by God—and blowing up the Velikaya Bridge could have been His purpose. Stop the Nazis. Defeat Hitler. Save humanity. It had seemed like a God-ordained path.

As for love, he'd left that long behind in Berlin and had no business hunting its path here in Russia, no matter how tempting. He shivered, suddenly chilled to the bone.

He eased open the cell door, making every effort to be quiet, and quickly unrolled the mat, stretching out on the hard ground, then pulling a blanket over himself. But sleep couldn't dent the images of failure that rattled through his mind like machine gun fire. An Erma machine gun staring him in the face, the fuse wire dangling from the bridge, tangled in the weeds. The sound of Mara's scream as she tumbled toward a frigid river.

Failure. The bridge stood, his partisans may have been slaughtered, and now the Third Reich would double their security. Edward clamped an arm over his eyes, regret sluicing through him.

He prayed for sleep and the precious oblivion into which he could escape.

❧

A feather touch whispered across his cheek and startled him awake. His eyes blinked open, and he shielded his eyes with his arm, protecting himself from the light that crept through the door and across his pallet. Laughter filled the small stone cell and drove away the lingering gloom from the night before. Stunned, he lowered his arm and peered past hooded eyes to the source.

The shock of seeing Mara leaning over him, blond hair shimmering like a halo, smiling, brought him to his elbows. He gulped and wondered if, perhaps, he was still dreaming, still lost in that place between awake and asleep where he met her, just like this, on more than one occasion.

"We need to go." Mara's blue eyes sparkled, and in the plain monk's robe, her simple beauty made him swallow hard. Yes, this was a dream. And a good one.

The door opened, and Brother Timofea walked in on the tail of a crisp autumn wind. His craggy face looked that much more stern when he peered at Edward. "Breakfast was served hours ago, and the sun is climbing. Germans will be tromping through the forest. You must leave now or stay until nightfall."

Edward nodded and sat up. His blanket fell to his waist,

and he shivered when the nippy air slid over his bare skin. He noticed Mara's gaze flicker across him and the accompanying blush as she turned away. Pulling the monk's robe around him, he stood. "Are our clothes dry?"

Brother Timofea tucked his hands together in his wide sleeves and shook his head. "They will need the sunlight." He nodded to a folded bundle on the table. "But they are freshly washed."

Edward fingered the robe. "I'll return it next time I come."

"That would be wise. But use it as long as you have need. Our things belong to God." He bowed slightly.

Brother Timofea turned to Mara, and a smile creased his face. "Pregnancy agrees with you, child."

Mara ducked her head.

"How are you feeling? Any more cramps?"

"No." She placed a hand across her body and looked up at him. Indeed, pregnancy refined her, drew out the gentle, soft curves of her face, the sparkle in her eyes, the lilt of her lips. It infected Edward, and he smiled despite the worry festering in the back of his mind.

He was such a fool. A fool in way over his head.

"I feel great," Mara said.

"You look it," he heard himself say. *Oh, and her blush adds just the right amount of innocence.* He reached out to tuck a strand of hair behind her ear.

Her face darkened, and she stepped away. The soft moment fractured as he weighed her expression. Fear. No, *loyalty*. Dmitri rose up like a ghost and hovered between them.

Ouch. He hadn't expected it to hurt that much. He dropped his hand and felt something inside him twist.

He turned toward the rough-hewn table and scooped up the pile of clothes. "Thank you again, Timofea."

Timofea nodded, then handed Edward a slip of paper. Frowning, Edward opened it.

"Who are they?" The two names written on the paper, *Tikhonov* and *Voloshin*, meant nothing to him.

Timofea glanced at Mara, who was combing out her hair with her fingers. "Two Russian generals. Caught behind the lines when the Third Reich swept Estonia and Byelorussia. A partisan brought us this message this morning—a Russian resistance group in Estonia has found them and is sending them to us." His eyes twinkled. Edward couldn't ignore that the monk made a perfect spy.

"What can I do?" Edward asked.

"If they come your way, don't accidentally shoot them."

Edward rolled his eyes and tucked the paper into his pocket.

The monk walked them through the sunlit yard toward the gate in silence. They scattered a pecking cluster of chickens, and Edward's stomach knotted at the smell of baking bread that trickled from the kitchen. He longed to ask Brother Timofea for a snatch of breakfast, but he feared he'd already pushed the monastery toward the jaws of the enemy. He stalked past the kitchen window without a glance inside.

Timofea opened the gate. "Our prayers are with you."

<hr />

The last time this feeling set Marina's feet dancing was the morning Dmitri laid a collection of lupine, hollyhocks, and delphinium on her open windowsill and asked if she'd be his wife.

If she'd only known that within the same year she'd bury him along with all her dreams. . .except one. She smiled, the feeling of hope lifting her from this patch of forest, beyond the copper maples and golden oak trees to a place where happiness lived, a place where she would never feel sorrow, only the weight of a baby in her arms. The heady feeling pinched something deep inside her heart and made her gasp.

Edick turned, a frown creasing his brow. "Are you okay? Maybe we're going too fast. We can rest anytime. Just tell me. I can carry—"

She held up her hand, strangely delighted at his over-flowing concern. "I'm fine." He squinted at her, his expression twitching confusion. She walked past him, tucking both hands into the long folds of her sleeves.

The sound of him walking beside her—the crunch of twigs, the swish of grass and brush, his soft breaths—turned her thoughts toward the moment, yesterday, when he'd gathered her into his arms. Guilt stabbed at her, but she dodged it. She'd drawn the line between them today and had seen understanding written in his eyes. Under-standing and the faintest spark of hurt. It pierced her heart to see it, but last night as she'd wept a thousand apologies to Dmitri, she had realized she couldn't allow herself to fall into the charismatic, embracing personality of this broad-shouldered American. Aside from the obvious fact that Edick wouldn't live through the war, she could never belong to anyone but Dmitri. Not now that she knew his son grew in her womb.

Still, Edick's gentle protection as he carried her through the forest to the monastery rooted in her a grati-tude she would never know how to repay. Edick Neumann, maverick American, had a heart of honor, even if it did edge on the reckless and often bossy side.

They walked in silence. The sun winked from high overhead, but jealous towering aspen, elm, and oaks gulped its rays, leaving only tidbits for the forest floor. A nuthatch twittered, and the rush of the wind shivered the treetops, scattering leafy jewels southward.

Marina pulled her hood up over her face, her thoughts on her fellow partisans. "Do you think they're dead?" Her voice came out in a low hush, as if the trees were eavesdropping.

"Maybe."

She glanced at Edick. A muscle jerked in his jaw, and his eyes didn't meet hers but stared straight ahead.

For the first time since Dmitri's death, she had the sudden urge to pray. She turned the hard edge of anger against the impulse and sliced it from her mind. She would have no more communion with a God who allowed evil to rampage the world.

"Have you been in the war long, Edick?"

"Too long."

"You've seen men die."

"And women and children." He turned his gaze on her, and the raw pain in it made her shrink back. He quickly hooded it. "Too many victims. Hitler has to be stopped."

"Did you lose someone you loved?"

He flinched. She swallowed, regretting the question but for some reason desperately needing to know.

"Yes. I lost my fiancée. She was a spy in Germany before the war, working for the Gestapo. She knew their agenda long before the rest of us. She saw into Hitler's heart and tried to warn the world."

"Did they catch her?"

He looked away from her as he spoke. "I was young and foolish. I knew they were watching me, but I thought I could outsmart them." He lifted his eyes to hers, and they were red-rimmed. "I was undercover as an English professor at Berlin University. Katrina warned me, but I didn't take her fears seriously enough." He paused, and his voice turned ragged. "I led them right to her."

"What?"

He flinched at her word, and she felt sick. He closed his eyes, covering them with his hand. A strong urge rose and shook her—the urge to run her hand along his whiskered face, to touch his forehead to hers, to wrap her arms around him. She took a step away.

"Oh, Edick, I'm sorry."

He sighed and turned his face from her view. "I knew they were watching me, and still, I went to Katrina, hoping to convince her to leave Berlin. I was supposed to be meeting a courier, transferring information, but I was near her house, and I couldn't stop myself. I missed her." His voice fell to a tortured whisper. "Instead of completing my mission, I led the SS right to Katrina. They were searching for her, and when they saw me, they knew." His eyes met Marina's, and she ached at the grief in them. "They executed her."

She closed her eyes, feeling too well his loss. Perhaps he understood her better than she thought. Maybe they could comfort each other—

She shook away the thought and forced open her eyes. He'd tucked his hands into his robe, looking somehow lost, as if the admission had emptied him.

"I'm sorry. You can't help difficult choices, nor can you

be blamed for loving her. This is war, Edick, and all you can do is keep fighting."

He nodded, mouth grim. "Why do you call me that?"

"Edick? It's Russian for Edward."

"Hmm. That's odd. I thought *lapichka* was short for Edward. It's what my grandmother always called me."

She chuckled. "It means 'little, sweet one.'"

"Oh." And he looked, suddenly, just like the little boy she imagined on his grandmother's lap. She nearly reached up and brushed his hair from his forehead.

"Perhaps they are still alive," Mara said quietly, fighting to get a grip on her rebellious impulses.

Edick's face again turned solemn. "Perhaps."

The sunlight moved lower in the sky as they hiked on. Hunger pinched Mara's stomach, but her pace quickened as they came to familiar landmarks—a broken fishing boat, a pile of rusty, metal traps, a decaying outhouse. The smell of soot and smoke thickened in the air as they worked their way to the partisan hideout.

"Oh, no," Marina said as they edged in on the clearing.

Flames shot from the barn's windows, billowed black smoke into the sky.

Beside her, Edick was silent, his face pale and stern.

"Now what?" Marina whispered as she backed away.

Edick looked bereft, and he shook his head. "I don't know."

The sound of a magazine locking into a submachine gun stopped her cold.

"Perestan!"

Marina froze at the order, scanning the forest for movement. Two men appeared from behind a thicket, their faces shrouded by shadow under green helmets. But Marina clearly recognized the muddy field dress of the German infantry.

The soldiers raised their weapons and pointed them at Marina and Edward. *"Ryki Veer."*

orry, but Edward wasn't going to let the Germans murder another woman under his watch. He grabbed Mara and shoved her behind him. His brain backtracked, aware that he'd only had half of it engaged in the game.

The other half had been trapped inside the look Mara had given him, the one that spoke compassion, not indictment.

The one that wheedled past his defenses and seeded the soft places in his heart. He should not, should not start letting his heart do the thinking.

Because as reality reminded him, when he let his emotions off their leash, he only led the people he cared about straight into the lions' den.

"Haltestelle!" he yelled in his best German. "We are monks! Men of peace!" His adrenaline wound his chest tight while his mind scrambled over his options. Their disguises wouldn't buy them more than precious seconds if the traitorous wind kept snatching at Mara's hood. He advanced a step, praying his German wasn't as wretched as it sounded to his own ears. "Don't shoot."

The soldiers advanced, their heavy black boots crushing the field grass.

"Mara, run!" Edward hissed, coiled to spring on the first

one. Maybe he could divert—

"Pavel?" Mara said, peeking out from behind him, her voice tweaked high.

The German lowered his gun. "Mara?"

Fury spiked through Edward as the soldier pushed back his helmet and smiled at him. With a roar, Edward ran at Pavel.

"Edick!"

He heard the shouts as background noise as he took Pavel down and sent his fist into his face.

Pavel butted him upside the head with his rifle. "Get off me!"

Edward shook off the flash of pain and grabbed the partisan about the throat. "You could have killed us," he hissed.

Pavel grabbed his wrist, wrestled with the grip at his neck. His face was white. Edward felt hands on him, pulling at him, but all he could see was his fear of Mara lying in a bloody heap.

"Sorry, Edward. We didn't know," Pavel rasped.

"Edick! Let him up!" Mara yelled at his ear, pulling at his grip.

Edward bit back a word and let the man go. He stalked away to the edge of the clearing. The smell of smoke burned his nose and watered his eyes as adrenaline shot through him.

Get it together, pal. Edward closed his eyes, fighting the impulse to whirl and unload his frustration, or maybe fear, into something solid like Pavel's jaw. So much for wanting to inspire confidence and earn Mara's trust.

"Edick, are you okay?" Mara touched his arm.

He glanced at her and felt gut-kicked by the worry—not

anger—in her incredible blue eyes.

"No," he groaned, and to prove it, he reached out and crushed her to his chest. Relief shuddered out of him as he held her, painfully aware that he might have well declared to the world, or at least to the partisans who worked with him, not only that he was just slightly half-cocked but also just how much he cared about their stubborn sniper.

To his surprise, her arms went around him. "Thank you."

He closed his eyes, letting her words balm the ragged edges of his anger. Taking a deep breath, he released her. Whirling, he poked his finger into Pavel's chest. "Don't ever do that to me again."

Pavel's face darkened. "And how was I supposed to guess you'd show up in an abbot's robe?"

Edward rubbed a thumb under his twitching eye. "Where'd you get the uniform?" He looked at the other guard and shook his head. "You look fairly intimidating, Natasha." The partisan smiled at him, but sadness edged her red-rimmed eyes. He swallowed hard and didn't ask about Sasha.

"We stole them off two guards right before Sasha lobbed the first grenades. It was the only reason we made it out alive." Pavel pulled at the collar. "I think this one gave me jiggers."

"Who fired the barn?" Mara flipped back her hood. Her hair shone golden in the sun.

"We don't know," Natasha said. She dropped the helmet on the ground and kicked it, hard. "Nina and Milla are gone."

Edward winced at the thought of the two babushkas who fed the partisan crew crumpling under the vise of Nazi torture.

"We saw boot prints." Pavel motioned them to a thicket of forest. "I think they followed us."

"Then how did you escape?" The sick feeling in his stomach began to spread to the muscles in his neck. First the city, then the hideout? Perhaps these German uniforms weren't a farce. It wouldn't be the first time a spy filtered into the ranks, role-playing partisan while feeding information to the enemy. His fists tightened under the cover of the long robe's sleeves.

"Natasha and I went to look for you." Pavel walked ahead, his back to Edward. His voice didn't waver with any hint of deceit. Then again, a good spy knew how to deliver his lines. "What happened? The bridge is crawling with Germans."

Edward measured his words. "I'm not sure. Some of the guards must have doubled back from Pskov. They caught me just as I was laying the fuse line." He replayed the moment in his head, still baffled at how they had snuck up on him.

Perhaps they had been warned. By Pavel? A sick acid filled his throat. He was having a hard time not tackling the man in front of him. Training told him to wait, but suspicion drummed blood into his fists. A solid right and maybe Pavel would spill it all.

"I fell into the river." Mara's statement made Pavel stop.

He looked appropriately worried when he whirled. "What? Are you okay?"

"Edward jumped in after me and pulled me out."

Pavel looked again at Edward. His dark eyes registered something Edward didn't want to acknowledge. He didn't need Pavel's respect when he was trying to convict him of treason.

"How did you fall in?" Pavel took a step toward Mara, and Edward couldn't ignore the flare of something hot and dark in his chest.

Down, boy. If anyone should be edging in on Mara and her heart, it was Pavel. If only that didn't make Edward want to hang him from the nearest tree.

"I fell out of a tree," Mara said.

Pavel raised one eyebrow, glanced at Edward. "I thought Edward said no climbing trees."

Edward suddenly wished he could be like Pavel. He enjoyed the man's dry humor, even if he was a spy or. . .his competition. Maybe he should be the one falling out of trees—a good bang to the head might knock him back to sanity.

"I couldn't help it." Mara smirked at Edward. "Edick was losing a footrace to two Germans."

Pavel's eyes twinkled, and a slight smile edged up his face. "So she saved your hide, huh, American?"

Edward didn't return the smile. He brushed past the partisan. "Let's get going."

⚜

"I don't like it, Edward. It's too risky." Pavel sat at the edge of a tiny fire, stirring the coals with a charred stick.

"You'd prefer they were tortured?" Edick paced in a tight circle just outside the ring of light. Marina tensed at the expression on his face, the way his eye twitched, the set of his jaw. She reached over and took Natasha's hand. It was cold, evidence that she was also listening to the two leaders' exchange.

"Of course not!" Pavel stabbed at the fire, sending sparks into the night. "But we're already down to four. Four!" He

111

threw the stick into the fire and pounced to his feet. "I started with eleven. Do you have any idea what it's like to lose people who depend on you?"

"I do." Edick's voice dropped but contained an edge. Marina winced for him.

Pavel stared at Edick. In the firelight of the damp cave, his Slavic features with the high, angular cheekbones and dark eyes seemed dangerous. Even threatening. "Then you know how hard this decision is. I can't afford to sacrifice Natasha or Mara. We have a bridge to blow, if I recall."

Edick shook his head. "It's over. There's no way I can blow the bridge with the amount of C-3 I have left." He turned and walked out to the edge of the cave, his hands shoved into his leather coat pockets. His wide shoulders made a dark outline against the charcoal blue of the night sky. Marina drew up her knees and wrapped her arms around them. Why was Edick abandoning the mission? She rested her chin on the well of her knees. Was he afraid? For her?

A drip of water somewhere far in the recess of blackness that extended beyond the mouth of the cave accentuated its musty dampness. Edick had led them right to the hideout, as if he'd scouted it out earlier. And when he showed up not long after with a pack of supplies—tins of food, two Colt automatics, and a map, she knew he'd been at this cat-and-mouse game with the Germans far too long. Unfortunately, the Russians' weapons, their cache of food, clothing, and everything they owned in the world had been destroyed in the fire.

Pavel walked over and crouched beside her. "How are you feeling?" She met his gaze, and the tenderness in it moved a soft smile up her lips.

"I'm fine, thank you." Had Edick told him about the baby? Pavel took her hands in his and rubbed them. "I'm glad you didn't get swept over the falls."

"Me, too." Marina couldn't help but be touched by his kindness. All her emotions felt raw and battered, yet Pavel always seemed to have the right words to soothe her ragged edges. "Pavel, how did Sasha die?"

Pavel's face twisted, and he looked down at her hands. Slowly, he turned them over, rubbing her palms. "He never made it off the roof. I don't even think he tried." When he looked up again, his eyes glistened. "He just kept lobbing grenades, even after we blew the school. They fired the cultural center, but we heard shots long after the flames engulfed the roof."

Marina shuddered and shut her eyes. She saw Sasha's cocky grin, his lanky face, his laughing brown eyes. Her throat thickened. "What about the babushkas? Shouldn't we go back for them?"

Pavel's lips drew into a tight line. "It won't do any good."

Edick turned from his stance at the door. "Why not?"

Marina stiffened, seeing Edick cross his arms and Pavel's dark expression. Tension strummed the air.

"Why not?" Edick repeated, and his voice held danger.

Marina held her breath. Pavel sighed and stood up. "Because they're already dead."

Cold fear streaked through Marina at the expression on Edick's face.

***

"And how, exactly, do you know that?"

The echo of Simon's smile and Irina's laughter hit Edward like a slap, and the memory of their deaths put motion to his anger before Pavel could answer.

"Edick!" Mara's voice cut through his charge, and had it not been for Pavel's shock and Mara's fear, he would have collided with the man with a force that would have broken heads. He stopped just short of Pavel, dragged in a breath, and grabbed him by his wool sweater. Pavel didn't flinch.

"How do you know they're dead?"

"Take your hands off me." Pavel stepped back. The sweater stretched as Edward dug his fingers through the knit. Edward had a healthy five inches on him, and the meager supplies and slim pickings from the ransacked potato fields had left the man wiry. Still, defense sparked in Pavel's partisan eyes.

"Answer my question."

Edward turned his fist into the sweater's weave and tugged. Mara grabbed Edward's upper arm and dug in her nails, but he barely felt it through his jacket. Natasha stood behind Pavel and scoured Edward with a look that revealed her loyalties. Well, he wasn't out to make friends. Not when there could be a snake in their midst. He ignored the women and glared at Pavel.

Pavel's eyes narrowed. "I saw their bodies."

"Where?" Natasha gasped.

Pavel fixed his gaze on Edward, his eyes cold. "In the forest, not far from the house. They'd been shot." He glanced at Natasha, who'd turned white. "I thought it might be better for you to believe they'd escaped."

She slapped him. Mara drew in a breath that bared her horror. Edward released him with a shove. "Show me."

Pavel smoothed his sweater. "No. I want you to be-lieve me."

Edward clenched his fist, fighting his Mennonite

roots. He might be a soldier fighting a war, but he'd never solved his problems with his fists. Until he met Pavel. No, until he'd seen the woman he'd loved being murdered by Nazis.

He'd pretty much forgotten everything he believed in at that moment. Including the faith that had kept his eyes on an eternal purpose.

Now, he could barely muscle through from dawn to dusk. He felt like Peter after Christ's crucifixion, throwing down his net, coming up empty, trying to sort out the rest of his life.

"Why should I believe you?" Edward demanded of Pavel.

"Why? Because I lost one of my best men to you. Because I don't know you. Because I'm not the one who waltzed into my unit and dangled an unrealistic, fruitless mission in our faces like caviar."

"I didn't ask you for help."

"But you knew we would offer. As soon as you discovered we were partisans, you knew we'd jump at the bait." Pavel grabbed Mara's arm and pulled her to his side. "You're the stranger here, American. Not me."

Edward looked at Pavel's hand on Mara's arm, then traveled his gaze to her ashen face. She lifted her chin, as if in defiance. But her eyes begged him to trust Pavel.

Okay, so maybe he had gotten them in over their heads. Especially Mara. Still, he couldn't deny the suspicions that ate at him. The German uniform, the fact that they'd escaped from a virtual suicide mission, the sudden appearance of German troopers on the bridge, and now the dead partisans, at Pavel's word, stacked the evidence against him.

Edward released his hold, and backed away. "I'll just sleep outside tonight."

He whirled, not sure that he wouldn't just keep going, right to Estonia, and maybe just to London, when he felt a jerk on his arm. He turned, fists clenched, and startled at Mara. Her eyes blazed. "No you won't. You'll trust us, or you'll leave."

"Since when did this include you?" Edward wanted to shake her, to force her to look at the evidence. A false romanticism had blinded her to Pavel's betrayal. "I don't suspect you, Mara."

"Pavel dragged me from a river. I was shot, and he nursed me back to health." Before he could react to that, she jerked up her sweater.

Ouch. A hideous red scar traced her left side. "He taught me how to shoot so I could fight for Russia."

He was staring at the scar, and he barely heard his words. "No. So you could get even."

Mara flinched and stepped away. Edward focused on her, pretty sure that he'd spoken for himself, understanding with clarity the need to find a place to put his despair, his fury. "Don't kid yourself," he said quietly. "Revenge and hatred, not loyalty, drove you to learn how to pick off the enemy at three hundred meters." He glanced at Pavel. "He used that. He used *you.*"

"How would you know? You're not even in this war. America wrings her hands while the rest of the world stumbles under the foot of Hitler." She took a step away from him, hurt twisting her face. "You have no idea what it means to suffer."

He felt punched. "Oh, really?"

Her eyes filled, but she managed to keep that glare

that darkened her pretty face.

"I. . .Edick, okay, I'm sorry. But you can't accuse Pavel of treason. Not after everything we've been through."

He couldn't look at her. Didn't want to give in to the urge to forgive her, to forgive them all. Obviously, the nightmares of Ldosk still haunted him when he saw traitors in his own freedom fighters.

He closed his eyes, feeling tired.

"I am sorry, Edick," Mara said again, softer. "But it's your anger indicting Pavel, not reality. Can you really believe he'd send a teenager not old enough to shave to his death? How about two lovely old ladies who did nothing but tend our wounds and make borscht? Why is Natasha still alive if Pavel's a Nazi—and don't say she's a spy, too."

He felt her hand on his arm. "I've seen too many soldiers fall under Natasha's aim. And Pavel's. Edick, won't you believe us? Because, like it or not, we're on your side." She touched his chest, right over his heart, and the warmth made him wince. Wounded Mara saw his bitter, betrayed heart and offered him healing. His throat closed, painfully aware that he didn't deserve her trust.

Painfully aware of how much it meant to him.

He opened his eyes and stared into hers, so devastatingly beautiful, especially with unshed tears.

"I'll prove to you we're not Nazis." Pavel stepped up beside Mara. "Give us another shot at your bridge, and we'll make sure this time it lands in the Velikaya River."

CHAPTER TEN

Marina crouched on a ridge overlooking the road to Pechory, her nerves strumming as she sighted the road some one hundred meters to the south. Yes, this was a good perch. She'd scouted two others, but only this view, cleared by the overzealous reports of a German Panzer and protected by a fall of boulders, gave her the shots she hoped to take.

"I'm not letting you do this."

She put the rifle down but didn't have to look to see who had crept up on her. She felt the low rumble of his voice just below her skin. Breathed his scent of leather and forest. Knew him by the way heat filled her veins. She could peg American Edward Neumann blindfolded and in a Bolshevik riot. "Yes, I am doing this."

Edick sat down next to her. She peeked over her shoulder, bracing herself. He looked devastatingly handsome in his fraying leather jacket and tousled dark hair. And he'd shaved in the last twenty-four hours, something that always surprised her. As if he couldn't let himself get too rumpled? *Drzastvotya*, they were fighting a war. Life was rumpled.

Still, he smelled clean, and the scent drifted off of him and did traitorous things to her heart rate. She shouldn't be relishing this moment away from camp, the sun warming overhead, the sky as blue as *zhimilist*, caught in a moment of peace with a man who had turned her heart into a war zone.

She spent way too much time analyzing his movements, his smile, watching his hands as he loaded weapons or outlined ideas. And the fact that he'd cracked open that brave heart and told her his secrets, his heartaches. . .well, a smart girl would pack up her Mauser and run for the hills before he took a permanent foothold in her heart.

"What are you doing here?"

He cracked a half-smile. "Trying to get on your good side."

"Yeah, well, you'll have to try and keep a lid on your chauvinistic comments. Sorry, *paran*, but you're in Russia, and here, the women do the fighting."

"We have women in the armed forces in America, too. Just not on the front line."

She shrugged. "Then maybe you should loosen up about my fighting."

"Not as long as you're under my watch," he said. His hazel green eyes seemed like they could peel layers off her defenses and find all her vulnerabilities. She looked away before he saw the effect of his words.

"Here, I brought you this." He handed her a can. Inside were chunks of fried fish and mushrooms. "I did some fishing this morning."

She couldn't deny the delight that swept through her. She was famished. But more than that, the idea that he'd thought of her. . . Okay, maybe she shouldn't read so much into his kindness. But again, it furrowed places in her heart she thought had hardened over.

"Thank you."

"You're welcome."

Was that a blush? Something about seeing Edward Neumann, bold American, with a slight blush made her stomach get up and jig.

"Mara, I don't want you to attack the supply troop with us."

Oh, what a shock. She gave him a look while she scooped the fish into her mouth. Trout. She'd never tasted anything so good. "Sorry. I'm a sniper. I promise I'll stay out of the way."

"I can't protect you way out here. I have to be down there with Pavel."

"So?"

He wore his frustration on his face and blew it out on a hot breath. "C'mon. I don't want you or your baby hurt."

"Neither do I. But you'll have to trust me. Let me do my job."

He grimaced before he turned away. Marina finished off the fish. "This was delicious. Did Natasha cook it?"

He didn't look at her. "I did."

"No."

"Yeah." His half-quirked smile spoke mischief. "I used to fish in the Schoharie River, right near my house. Mom would make me clean and fry my own fish."

"Maladyets. Dima couldn't cook to save his lif—"

Oops. It amazed her how grief could rush at her and consume her whole in one unguarded moment.

Edick glanced at her. His smile faded. "Still, he sounds like a great husband."

Yeah. Young. Rash. But my first love.

First?

Only.

121

Marina handed back the tin. "Your mother sounds like mine—stern but with my best interest at heart."

Edick smiled at her, and for a moment, she saw him young with a boyish grin and a stringer of fish over his shoulder, the sun kissing his nose and cheeks, wearing a shirt cut off at the arms. She would have probably fallen for him just as quickly as she had Dima. "You would have liked my mother," she said, fighting the tug of guilt. "She could take a couple of old potatoes, a beet, and some field grass and make a meal that would have impressed even Lenin."

"What happened to her, Mara?"

My, he had a way of slicing through her buffered emotions and drawing blood. Tears pricked her eyes. "Where did you grow up?"

He hesitated, his eyes searching hers. She looked away. *No, Edick.*

"Upstate New York," he finally answered. "A little farm outside the town of Schenectady. We had family and farmland for miles."

"How did you get into the war?" Her chest loosened as he picked up a leaf and began to shred it. She had no desire to free the memories when they'd successfully scarred over.

"I blame it on my parents, I guess. They were originally from Russia. Came over in 1914. We lived in a good-sized Russian community, and there were immigrants from all walks of life—serfs, Mennonites, the bourgeoisie. I even knew this one girl who everyone called the czarina. She spoke several languages fluently and carried herself with an almost regal bearing, as if she just might have some sort of royal Russian blood or something."

Oh. The sharp prick in her chest surprised her. "Do

you still keep in touch?"

"No. She moved to Virginia before the war. Married a rich guy."

Marina offered a sad smile. "We haven't had a czarina for about twenty years. We're not even allowed to talk about the royal family."

He nodded. "I heard stories about them, though. From my grandmother, who left Russia in 1918. She met a woman on the boat coming over who actually worked for Czar Nikolai. Baba told me that something horrible had happened to this woman, something she could never quite speak of. It was a dark time—the Bolshevik Revolution. Because of it, my grandfather never made it over, but his story always intrigued me. Despite his pacifist beliefs, he was a man of great courage, and according to my grandmother, he faced death without flinching."

"How did he die?" Marina asked.

Edward shook his head. "It's a horrible story. Suffice to say, the revolution caught up to him. And because of it and my Mennonite upbringing, I believed that I would never be involved in war. In fact, I was a history professor in Berlin before the war, trying to teach the ways of peace, hoping the mistakes of our past wouldn't repeat themselves. But when I saw what the Nazis were about, I couldn't stand by and watch them herd human beings into a cattle car. I guess I came to believe that sometimes fighting is the only way to peace."

He wore a far-off look, and she suppressed the urge to trace her fingers across his angular face, to draw forth the memories that laced his eyes. "You're a brave man, Edick. I'm thankful for what you're doing here. We'll blow that bridge. I promise."

He turned to her, and the look in his eyes rocked her. "I don't want you anywhere near that bridge, Mara. It hurts me to even see a gun in your hands. You're going to be a mother—"

"A mother who has to fight for the country her child will live in. Imagine what Russia will be if Hitler takes over—"

"Not to be harsh, but Stalin hardly seems better."

Her mouth parted, and reflex made her glance over her shoulder. "Don't say that. Not aloud, please."

Edick frowned at her, but she couldn't bear to dredge up the horrors she'd seen over the past twenty years, the Cheka patrols who stole men and boys from their families, who executed dissidents without trial. No, Stalin wasn't any better than Hitler.

But she wasn't fighting for Stalin. She was fighting for her future. For Dima's baby's future. For a land that had been Russia for centuries.

"I'm sorry, Mara, I didn't. . .well, you don't strike me as a communist."

"I'm. . .not." She barely spoke the words and leaned close to him. "But we can't choose our leaders, only our beliefs. And I believe in fighting against fascism. Then maybe someday, we'll tackle the sins of our own country."

He sighed, closed his eyes, and shook his head. The breeze sifted his hair and raised the collar on his jacket. She turned up the collar on her own military coat.

"Do you ever wonder what would have happened if we'd met before the war, Mara?"

His question swept the air from her. *I would have still been married. To Dima.* Still, the image of meeting Edick at a different time without the cloak of war to darken their perspective sent a whirl of pleasure through her. She said nothing and let herself be caught in his thoughts.

"I would have taken you to the Bolshoi and walked along the Volga at night, watching the moonlight caress your face."

She stared at him, unsure whether he knew he was speaking aloud. His expression seemed far off, seeing past her to some distant place.

"I always wondered what it would be like to visit Russia. The sounds and smells of a country that takes up a healthy chunk of the world. The grandeur of the czars written in the architecture—"

"Now, it would be the glory of Stalin, I think," Marina said softly. She giggled "I didn't know you were such a romantic, Edick." She smiled at his blush. "But I would have enjoyed meeting you in safer times."

She felt the melancholy in her words resonate between them. He reached out, touched her hair. "Maybe someday we can start over. With fresh and clear tomorrows."

"*Da,*" she said softly. "Maybe."

Edick's gaze ran over her slowly, running past her mouth, stopping at her eyes. Gently, he touched her hand. "You be careful tomorrow, Mara. Russia needs you."

She turned her hand in his, grasped it. "No, Edick. You need me. You just don't know it yet."

He stared at her, his mouth a grim slash. "Just don't get killed." He turned away, the wind raking his hair, suddenly looking much older than his, what, thirty-plus? years.

"Edick, how old are you?"

"I'm twenty-six."

What? Okay, he looked about forty, and suddenly she knew why.

It was more than watching the people he loved die. It was feeling responsible for their deaths. And the burden of keeping them alive.

Without thinking, she touched his cheek, wanting suddenly to pull him into her arms. She wondered what it might be like to be the object of Edward Neumann's die-hard affection.

She swallowed the swell in her throat. "You can't protect everyone, you know."

He glanced at her as if startled by her touch or maybe her words. "Well, maybe I'm just supposed to protect you."

Oh. Her mouth dried, and sadness welled in her throat as she withdrew her hand. "I don't think anyone can do that, Edick. Not even you."

⁂

Edward watched the road, hearing Mara's words, feeling the band around his chest tighten. *Not even you.*

Then who, Lord?

He didn't gaze heavenward or let an answer resound in his heart. Yes, God could protect her a billion times better than Edward ever could, except she wasn't letting God within shouting distance.

Oh, Mara.

He huddled beneath the grasp of an oak and watched for the plume of dust. Behind him, hidden in the shade of boulders, Mara scoped the road with her German rifle.

It made him nearly retch to think about it.

But they needed supplies. C-3, bullets, and grenades. He felt like he was selling their lives for a packet of ammo.

Across the street, Pavel's whippoorwill call signaled his all-ready. Natasha, the other sniper, hid down the road, at another angle of attack.

Please, God, make the Germans. . .cowards. He'd like more than anything to see the soldiers drop their weapons and make for the trees.

Most of them weren't any older than his younger brother.

He heard the sound of a mechanized vehicle and groaned. He'd hoped for horses. Then again, with the right demolition, they could detour the truck, lift its cargo, and vanish without a trail of blood.

He pulled out a pineapple and grasped the pin. *C'mon, closer.*

Two trucks. He coiled his breath, hoping that Pavel was thinking on his trail.

The first truck barreled closer. Edward counted the guards. Two in the front, probably two in the back. And two hanging on the sides.

He pulled the pin, tossed the grenade, and ducked.

The explosion caught the truck under the front axle. The truck flipped onto its side, dirt and flames shooting from the ignited fuel tank.

Another grenade, aimed for the truck behind. The soldiers scattered before it exploded, and Edward picked off one running across the field, tracking his attention to the next before the first fell.

Screams and distant gunfire popping told him that Mara and Natasha had sighted their targets. He leaped from his niche and ran for the second truck. A soldier rolled out from underneath and aimed for him. He kicked him across the chops and kept running.

He rounded the back of the truck and nearly plowed over Pavel. "What's the cargo?"

Edward climbed in while Pavel dove under the chassis. Shots pinged off the frame and through the canvas. Edward ducked behind wooden crates, reading the German labeling. "C'mon, please have demolitions."

German—*Sturmkanones*—assault cannons. And ammo. Enough to supply the entire eastern front. He slammed his foot into a box, cracked the casing just to confirm.

"What are they carrying?"

"Stuks."

Machine gun fire shredded the canvas. Edward ducked, feeling the urge to dive. "Don't these guys know these things are explosive?"

"That's probably the point!" Pavel fired off three shots. "We gotta get out of here."

"You run. I'll cover you."

"Nyet. You run. We need you."

The image of Stefan mowed down by the SS sliced through Edward's brain. "No. We go together. On three."

"Bad, bad idea, American."

Still, Pavel counted, and Edward leaped off the end of the truck. He saw Pavel in his peripheral vision shooting, yelling, and aimed for the other ditch.

He dove, landing hard, and came up on his feet.

Right into the sites of an MP-38 submachine gun.

The soldier shook, his aim iffy at best. This one looked barely old enough to shave.

Certainly not old enough to rip a man apart.

Still, Edward wouldn't have pegged Mara for a sniper, but look what war and fear had done to her.

Edward dropped his weapon, raised his arms. Oh, this wasn't going to be pretty. And most of all, he was sorry Mara had to watch—

A gunshot. Blood appeared at the man's throat. He pitched forward, nearly into Edward's lap. Edward gulped his heart back into his chest and scooped up his weapon.

A blow caught him at the shoulder. He pitched forward, scrubbed his chin on the ground. Rolling, he caught the movement of gun butt just as it found its target.

His head.

He blinked twice, and black dots appeared before his eyes. He felt hands on him, dragging him, and he thrashed at his captor.

The hands dragged him behind the truck. Threw him to the ground. He looked into the dark face of a helmeted soldier who pressed his boot into Edward's neck and screwed his Erma into Edward's temple. "Quiet."

The shooting had stopped. The eerie sound of birds calling, the rush of the breeze through the stripped-for-winter trees. The smell of burning fuel.

The groan of the man Edward had kicked.

Then, "I found her!"

What? Edward's gut churned. *Oh, this can't be good.*

Above him, the soldier smiled—something even Edward could make out between the splashes of darkness. "We got your sniper," he sneered.

Why, oh why, didn't Natasha listen to her? Marina watched as they wrestled the partisan to her knees. The wind had kicked up, and Marina mentally did a readjustment for wind velocity. Her shot pinged off the truck's undercarriage.

One guard looked up, toward her perch.

Marina ducked, hoping they hadn't spotted her. She'd seen Pavel make a run for the woods, but for all she knew, he was face first on the forest floor.

She tasted bile in her throat when she watched the soldiers pat Natasha down, then slap her, hard.

No. Natasha wasn't going to die raped and tortured, hung from the gallows in Pskov Square, or worse, turned over to some labor camp. Marina knew what Hitler thought of Russians. . .the *Untermenschen*. Subhuman. He'd made a point of maiming his way across Russia, sparing no distinction between peasants and soldiers.

Marina counted her opposition. Three still standing, one moving under the truck, and possibly two more in the woods after Pavel. Edick lay on the ground, but she saw him writhe, which meant he still lived.

She wasn't sure just how she'd make it past this moment if they killed him. She blew out a hot breath and forced herself calm.

She sighted the first guard, again readjusted for wind, and squeezed the trigger.

He spun twice and fell.

The other two turned, shock on their pasty faces. *Yes, boys, you're in trouble.* Marina fought to still her heartbeat and again uncoiled her breath. Natasha was inching toward Edick while the two guards dove behind the downed truck.

Another shot, from another direction—*Maladyets, Pavel!*—and the final guard ran out from behind the truck and dove under the chassis, nearly next to Edick. Not bad for a doctor.

Edick, to his credit, had climbed onto all fours and inched toward Natasha.

Marina sent a shot between the wheels, just to remind the guard to keep his nose down, away from Edick, who now hooked his arm around Natasha's waist.

They rose, staggered toward the ditch.

Marina pinged the German's Erma as he rose against them. She watched, relief whooshing through her as Edick and Natasha ran for the woods. *Run.*

It wasn't until they were safely inside the grip of forest that she realized she was crying.

<hr/>

Edward plowed through the forest, Natasha slightly ahead of him. Thankfully, she had sure footing, and aside from a red imprint on her cheek, she seemed fine.

Rattled. Terrified. Traumatized. But fine.

He felt the hot trickle of blood down his cheek but didn't bother to wipe it. His head throbbed; with each step, it felt like it might explode.

Still, he couldn't deny the euphoria that filled his lungs.

For a long, agonized moment, he thought they'd caught Mara. And while it hurt to see them backhand Natasha, seeing them hurt Mara just might have gotten them all killed. Because it was quite possible he would have lost all measure of sanity. Right there.

Which would have been an ugly way to end this operation.

Then again, he had a sick feeling that the longer he stayed, the more he tried to complete his mission, the closer he brought this entire partisan unit to the devil's lair. If he were wise, he'd leave them or at least hook them up with another partisan unit. Timofea had informed him that Moscow was organizing a partisan movement committee, which, along with useless bureaucracy, would lead to coordinated guerilla efforts, weapons, and ammunition—and maybe even food and clothing drops.

He had no doubt it was soldiers like Mara who would win the war against Germany. Pit-bull tenacious. Brave unto death. Creative and sacrificial.

Heroines like Katrina. Like Raina, the partisan mother he'd lost in Poland. Women who had died under his watch. That fact should be sending him a message. Perhaps he should just keep running, right to the border.

He caught a branch across the mouth and tasted blood. Natasha crashed through the wall of brush ahead of her, and he followed into the tangle. Grabbing at her, he pulled her down.

"Shh," he said and listened. He couldn't hear gunfire or even the strident voices of followers. His pulse thundered in his head, and his breath came in razor gasps against his lungs.

"Did we lose them?" Natasha asked.

He held a finger to his lips.

A branch cracked. He stiffened. Then he heard a voice by his ear, something sweet and light and painfully welcome.

"Good shooting, *da*?"

Edward turned to eye a grinning Mara. She looked every inch a misplaced partisan in her cock-eyed *shopka*, her oversized army jacket, and the Mauser dangling from her grip. "Just. . .let's get out of here," he growled.

She eyed him, then glanced behind him. "I told you that you needed me." Then she smirked and angled off through the forest.

He stifled a protest, feeling his chest clench. Oh yeah, he needed her. Only that scared him more than an entire battalion of Third Reich soldiers.

CHAPTER ELEVEN

It was when she was quiet, nestled in the forest, listening to the wind scrape the trees, the river rush toward the sea, that Dima's baby moved. Marina stopped weaving branches and twigs into the military jacket she'd lifted off a dead soldier and placed her hand over her belly. She stilled her breathing.

A tickle. No, a whisper. Of hope. Of life.

She felt it clear to her soul, and even there, it nudged.

She closed her eyes, conjuring up Dima's smile, and felt a pang of panic when it seemed grainy. How could she so easily forget—

"Mara?"

She jerked, opened her eyes, and slicked the tears from her eyes.

"I thought I'd find you out here." Pavel edged up to her. He wore his own confiscated German army coat, and his brown hair, long and scraping the collar, spiked out of a worn woolen cap. His eyes warmed as he smiled and sat next to her. "What are you doing?"

She lifted the jacket. "Making camouflage." She'd taken a knife, separated the fabric in tiny slits, and had woven into the upper back and shoulders foliage from the nearby trees. "I figure that I'll be less noticeable if I look like an oak tree." Besides, it wasn't lost on her that she couldn't run near as fast as she used to. . .and Natasha's near capture had rattled her to her bones.

She wasn't going to stop fighting. But she wasn't going to be an easy target, either, thank you.

Pavel smiled his approval at her handiwork. "I brought you something." He reached into his pocket and pulled out a wad of wool. He handed them to her. "They don't even have any holes."

Marina took the gift, opened it, and a wave of delight rushed over her. "Gloves! Where did you find them?"

Was that a blush? She felt something inside curl in delight at his boyish chagrin.

"One of our German benefactors."

She wrinkled her nose at him, resisting the urge to plant a kiss on his cheek. "Thank you."

He reached out, took them, holding them open for her. "I don't want those pretty hands of yours to freeze."

Pretty hands. Right. There might have been a time, perhaps when she was a child, that she had had pretty hands—musician's hands, her mother had said. But now, welts and scars puckered her skin, her nails chipped and sawed down to a nub. She slid them into the proffered gloves.

"Edward told me how you saved his life, by the way," Pavel said, but a sadness tweaked his face. "I always knew you'd be an excellent sniper."

She gave him a rueful smile. "I guess the war dredges up unexpected talents." She stripped the end of an oak twig down and began working it into the jacket, weaving it through the holes she'd created. "Certainly you didn't expect to ever be a partisan."

Pavel laughed. "Oh, I don't know. I spent my childhood fighting the white army with birch sticks."

Marina laughed. "I can see you in your stocking cap and *valenki* boots, stalking the Cossacks with your deadly birch pistol."

"Oh, I was fearsome." He grinned at her, white teeth, mischief in his brown eyes. "Sadly, birch-branch warriors weren't widely esteemed in my village."

Marina quirked an eyebrow.

"My family was Baptist, and in Karamishevo, we weren't popular. Probably because my father was one of the church leaders."

"You grew up in Karamishevo? I was there once when I was young. We visited some graves, and an old woman, who I remember, fed me *krugla*. It's sort of a—"

"German cake. I grew up on it." He leaned back on his hands. "My mother served it with strawberry preserves, and I can still remember fighting my brother for the jar."

Marina laughed. "You have a brother?"

Pavel's smile dimmed. "Had. He was at the front when Hitler invaded."

Oh. *Da,* the war. For a moment there, Pavel's laughter, his story had swept her back, right into her mother's kitchen and the smells of *tikva* kasha, and cabbage *perog*.

She looked at her stolen German gloves, at the coat, spiked with twigs, and grief knotted her chest.

"I'm sorry." She looked away from him toward the bridge, past it to the horizon, which bled out the day in splotches of cinnamon and marmalade. "I never had a sibling. My father died before I was born." Her mother, too, for that matter, but then again, she'd had an adopted mother who more than made up for the one she'd lost.

"Yeah, my papa died when I was a child, too. Probably where I got my birch-branch tendencies."

Marina eyed him.

Pavel picked up a stick, drew in the loam at his boots. "The NKVD came through not long after Stalin came to power and closed the church. We moved underground, but slowly the church brothers got arrested and disappeared. I woke up one morning and discovered that my father had been taken in the night. They told us he was shipped off to gulag and died of a heart attack. But just a few years ago, I found out that he'd been shot that very night after a mock trial."

Marina's breath left her, and her heart simply refused to work. What?

"It's okay. He knew what he believed in, and God watched over us. But it did shake my faith, and I struggled with the goodness of God—until I realized that God never promised us an easy time of it. Just His faithfulness during the dark times."

Marina had no words to respond. But when Pavel lifted his head and met her gaze, the look tugged at her heart. What was it about Pavel that made her feel not only calm but. . .hopeful? It made no sense. Not now. Not in the face of his story.

"No wonder you wanted to fight the communists."

He shrugged. "Naw. They were just the scapegoats. Actually, my beliefs run more along the lines of, 'Precious in the sight of Him are the death of his saints.' My father and the rest of the brothers were Christians. I'll see Papa again."

Marina felt her eyes burn. How long had it been since she'd let that thought grip her heart, thread through it, strengthen it?

She'd see Dima again.

"Besides, I had a great mother who taught me to praise the Lord even in the dark times. She loved Psalm 147. It goes something like this: 'How good it is to sing praises to our God. How pleasant and fitting to praise him.'"

Marina looked away from him and stiffened. For some reason, she resented the fact that Pavel's mother had chosen faith in the face of her loss.

"'He heals the brokenhearted and binds up their wounds. He determines the number of the stars and calls them each by name. Great is our Lord and mighty in power; his understanding has no limit. The LORD sustains the humble—'"

Marina wanted to cup her hands over her ears, to force the words away. But she couldn't deny that they found the nooks of her heart and lodged there. Tears pricked her eyes, and she stared at her hands, feeling the baby shift inside her as Pavel spoke.

"'His pleasure is not in the strength of the horse, nor his delight in the legs of a man; the LORD delights in those who fear him, who put their hope in his unfailing love.'"

Yeah. His unfailing love. She felt so beyond hoping in God's love, she nearly laughed aloud.

"You should have been a priest," Marina said, deflecting the impact of his words.

Pavel smiled. "Maybe someday. Or maybe I'll have a son who devotes his life to serving God. If I live to have a family, that is."

"Don't talk that way, Pasha. You're going to survive the war and live to be eighty."

He gave her a sweet, lopsided smile, and something flickered in his eyes. It rustled the melancholy in her heart and lifted it from its moorings. What was it about being around the partisan doctor that made her feel safe? Encouraged? No, he didn't have Edick's charisma, nor did he stir her heart like Edick, but Pavel possessed a sweet gentleness, and he could certainly push a blush into her face with a sideways glance or unexpected smile.

Pavel picked up a rock and tossed it off the edge of the embankment where she sat. She heard it skip down the side, into the river below.

"You'd be a good father, Pavel," she said softly. Patient. Strong. Kind. The kind of father she'd hope for her son.

Except, she'd already picked out the father for her child.

"I hope so. I'd like to get married. Have a son. Be a doctor again. We'll see what happens. Like the verse says, God's pleasure isn't in our abilities but in hoping in His love for us. And despite this dark place, I believe God loves me." He angled a smile at her. "And you, Mara. God loves you very much."

Her mouth cracked open at the look in his eyes. Sweet, yet sad, and not a little longing. *Oh. My.* She swallowed, looked away.

For a physician, he sure had a way of making her feel like he could see right into her soul.

Sadly, if he looked hard enough, he'd find it barren.

Edward wasn't sure which he hated more: the dampness that came with the erratic fall weather or one more cup of birch bark tea. He downed the last of the bitter liquid, then put the cup into his pack. Against the glow of the firelight, Mara had begun to lay out her blanket, and he watched as she moved. Protective, yet still lithe despite her enlarging bulk. He still couldn't believe no one had noticed the change in her. Couldn't they see her face had rounded, that her countenance had become softer?

It made for a harsh and shocking picture when she put the Mauser to her eye and squeezed the trigger. Still, her pregnancy must be affecting her, because a slight bruise ringed her eye, and she favored her shoulder, evidence that she hadn't hugged it against her when she pulled the trigger. The recoil had to have left marks.

How he hated this secret.

He saw Pavel rise, stride out past the camp and into the ring of darkness. From his tree nook, Edward watched him go, aware of the tension in his chest whenever a partisan left the camp.

Obviously, he still hadn't recovered from losing Raina, or Simon, or. . .his Katrina. Sometimes, especially in the wee morning of his watch when his thoughts roamed loose, he saw her, her blond hair unfurled, her eyes searching his as she strode toward him, her mink smile on her face. "Edick," she said, "don't leave me."

And then with a roar, memories chopped him off at the knees, and he saw her brave and defiant, lifting her chin to the firing squad.

Sometimes, he could still hear the reports echoing against the pane of his soul.

He closed his eyes, hoping to wipe her face from his memory, and against the darkness, he saw Mara. Defiant. Brave. Smiling, as the wind took her hair. "See, you need me."

Oh, did he need her. She'd somehow twined through his chest until he couldn't escape her. Her smell, her blue eyes, her smile.

The images of her walking Red Square or leaning

against him as the moon kissed the Volga. Inside those dreams, she wrapped her arms around him, let him weave his hands through her hair, lower his mouth to hers.

In those dreams, she kissed him with the passion he saw behind those beautiful eyes.

And sometimes his dreams betrayed him. Memory merged with fears, and he heard gunshots, felt her crumple in his arms.

Bile filled his throat as he stuffed the image into the dark, uncharted places inside. No. She wasn't Katrina. This wasn't Berlin. And he was going to keep her safe, as long as he had a beating heart in his chest.

He heard cracking, the forest shifting under footsteps, and he stiffened.

Pavel appeared, his dark form lit only by the dent of dying firelight as he reentered the camp. Edward watched while Pavel hovered over Mara, perhaps checking her blanket, then moved over to the fire and warmed his hands.

Edward still hadn't convinced himself that Pavel wasn't a traitor, and the man's unexcused excursions into the dark didn't help allay his suspicions.

Although, Edward could admit that he did feel a nudging to trust the partisan physician. It wasn't lost on him that Pavel had risked his life attacking the German convoy or that the partisan had taken out a guard to free him and Natasha. And true to the doctor he claimed to be, Pavel seemed genuinely concerned for Natasha and Mara. More than once, Edward had stalked Pavel as he followed Mara into the forest and watched as Pavel sat guard over her as she took target practice or scouted the bridge. It wouldn't be reaching to surmise that Pavel had feelings for Mara. Still, Edward had been ambushed too many times to turn his defenses down to a simmer, and he wasn't going to let Pavel off his tether, despite the man's apparent dedication to the cause.

The sooner he blew the bridge and delivered Mara to a hospital in. . .where? He shook his head, afraid of where his mental excursions had taken him. Yes, okay, he could admit that he saw her on the farm in New York, her son fishing in the Schoharie River, running barefoot through the fields. His chest actually ached at the thought.

Yes, if he didn't blow the bridge and get out of Russia soon, he'd find himself in over his head.

Oh, who was he kidding? He settled his gaze on Mara and let himself watch her sleep.

CHAPTER TWELVE

Snow peeled from the steel gray clouds. Edward handed his field glasses to Pavel and leaned back on his knees. He zipped his leather coat up to his neck and blew into his reddened hands. "They've beefed up the watch to two squads."

Pavel pasted the glasses to his eyes, scanning the Velikaya Bridge, some three hundred meters in the distance. "I see that."

Their perch on a high bluff to the north of the bridge had become a second home. Not as clear or as close as his previous bunker, still, the position afforded him a spectacular view of the gorge through which cut the great river and the route he'd tumbled trying to save Mara. The afternoon sun turned the bridge a dark bronze and rimmed the low-hanging snow clouds amber.

"They're afraid." Edward turned up his collar. "They know that if they lose this bridge, there are only two other routes to Moscow. And they need supplies."

"Praise God for *Rasputitza*. I've never been so thankful for the season of mud." Pavel lowered the glasses. His eyes were cracked with red streaks, and the skin sagged under his eyes. "Supply columns are locked in goop on the road through Pskov and tanks are trying to free guns and trucks all over Russia." He gave a wry chuckle. "The ghosts of Napoleon's Grand Army are rising up to haunt them."

"And the Siberian winter is closing in like a vise." Edward returned Pavel's smile, but wariness kept him from surrendering to camaraderie. Pavel, for all his appearances, seemed driven to the task. Still, memory cautioned Edward to rein in trust. He reached for the field glasses. "We're running out of time. Every day that train brings in more food, more weapons, more clothing." He watched a clump of dour-faced Jerries smoke cigarettes on the east end of the bridge. He saw one turn up the collar on his threadbare wool coat. "And Timofea told me that Stalin can see the troops from the spires of the Kremlin."

Pavel leaned against a smooth ash tree and closed his eyes. Edward couldn't help noticing the fatigue lines etched around Pavel's eyes. His gaunt face betrayed hours of surveillance without a care to food or warmth. "So, have you come up with a plan?"

Edward pursed his lips and shook his head. Digging into his rucksack, he pulled out a tin can of C-rations. "I'm not sure how we're going to get near that bridge." He sliced open the can with his knife and picked through the hardened contents. Stew, with fragments of meat clustered at the bottom. He stirred it. "I'm running out of supplies. I don't have enough C-3 to blow the bridge."

"Maybe we need a little raiding party, pick over the German supplies."

Edward handed the can of food to Pavel. "Eat up."

Pavel frowned. "No, I'm okay."

"I hate stew. You'd be doing me a favor." Edward watched Pavel eye the tin. Their last meal had been roasted squirrel the night before. He agreed the stew wasn't much better, but he hated to see the hunger in Pavel's eyes.

Pavel took the tin. "Thanks, Edward." He used the knife to ladle the stew into his mouth. Edward leaned against the tree and wished for coffee. The cold seeped through his jacket and made his bones stiff.

"I thought of something," Pavel said between bites. "What if the bomb were on the train?"

Edward arched his brows. "Go on."

Pavel scraped the edge of the can, peeling off every layer of juice. Edward wondered if Mara was this hungry. To his knowledge, no one besides himself knew she was pregnant. The bulky layers of sweaters hid any hint of the life inside her.

"There is a refueling station for the train just outside of Pechory. What if someone planted the bomb during its stop?"

"Then blew the bomb while it was over the bridge? With a remote detonator?"

Pavel closed the lid on the can. "You could be here, watching. I'd send word through your two-way radio when I planted it."

"You'd plant the bomb?" Edward narrowed his eyes.

Pavel nodded, a "no arguments, please" look on his face.

The snow fell heavier, sifting into Pavel's hair and frosting his green German field coat. Edward's chest tightened.

"You gotta trust somebody, Edward." Pavel handed him the empty can. "Why not a comrade in arms?"

Edward packed the can into his pack. "I've done that."

"Well, how about a Christian brother, then?"

Edward frowned. "How did you know I was a believer?"

Pavel worked his hands into the cuffs of his coat. "I've seen you praying out by the river. And I saw your Bible."

Edward smiled wryly. "This isn't a trick, is it?"

Pavel's expression betrayed his disappointment. "I'd hoped you'd guessed. I'd hoped my actions would have communicated my love for Christ."

Shame seeped through Edward. "Of course, Pavel. I saw you pray, I just. . .didn't know what to believe."

"Russians can't be Christians?"

"War is not a good incubator for trust."

Pavel raised an eyebrow. "Do you trust Mara?"

Edward's jaw tightened. He shook his head.

"Why not?"

"I trust her loyalty, her anger and hatred of the Germans. I don't trust her common sense. In fact, I don't want her to be involved with any part of blowing up this bridge."

Pavel's face darkened. "She's a good soldier. I'd trust her with my life."

"What if it was a choice between your life and her baby's life?"

Pavel stared at him. "What are you telling me?"

Edward rubbed his hands together. "Mara's pregnant. I found out when she fell into the river. She says she didn't know, but I'm not sure."

Pavel gave him a strange look. "Two questions, and pardon the first one, but. . .ah. . .well, you didn't have anything to do—"

"No!" Edward heard his tone and realized he might have betrayed too much of his emotions in that response. So he wasn't the natural father; he couldn't deny a growing part of him wanted to fill her dead husband's shoes. Probably too big a part of him. But the thought of twining her golden hair through his fingers and the memory of her in his arms, kissing him like. . .like she *cared*—well, it kept him awake more nights than it should.

"So the baby is Dmitri's."

"Of course."

"She thought the baby had died," Pavel said quietly.

"How do you know?"

Pavel blew on his hands. "We found Mara when she was escaping the Germans. She'd fallen into the river near Pskov after being shot. The river was full of blood, and Mara must have thought it was from the baby."

Edward's heart twisted, sick that he'd mistrusted her. Her shock had been genuine. Shame burrowed into his soul.

"I can't believe she didn't tell me." Pavel lifted his head. His eyes edged frustration. "She could have been killed."

"I think that was her plan."

"Mara."

"What?"

Pavel shook his head. "I think she adopted her name when she became a partisan. A new identity."

Edward cringed, feeling the despair in Pavel's words. "The baby has changed her, made her softer. I've seen her wrap her arms around herself as if protecting the life inside."

"It's all she has left of her husband."

Edward mentally traced Mara's face, his heart breaking at the grief that still lined it.

"Sometimes we reject hope and comfort for the familiar. In Mara's case, grief." Pavel drew a line through the glistening clusters of snow with his finger. "In your case, mistrust. You rely on no one but yourself, Edick. I wonder, do you trust in God, or is even the Almighty untrustworthy in your eyes?"

Marina could feel the heat of the summer sun on her face

as she lay in the grass, head resting on Dmitri's arm. "When we're married, will we still sneak off to the meadow and watch the clouds, Dima?"

"Perhaps." The faraway tone in his voice, as if a whisper, made her turn her head. She traced the outline of his face, his high brows, his strong, angular jaw, the hint of molasses-colored stubble along his chin.

He twirled a long-stemmed daisy between his thumb and forefinger. "I think I'll be busy in the fields and you with our home, with our babies."

His words twisted her heart, and for some reason, she sat up. "Will you be happy, Dima?"

His brown eyes settled on hers and embraced her. "With you, I will be."

"You won't leave me?"

He laughed, his eyes twinkling, his face creasing in delight. "Never!"

She gasped as she saw his face slack and loose color. His lips turned blue, and the fire in his eyes died. "Dmitri?" She reached out for him, but he began to dissolve, his form fading like the mist of a rainbow in the glare of the sun. "No!" Panic welled inside her. Her breaths came in hiccups. She began to moan, "No, oh please, Dmitri, don't leave me."

"Mara." The voice threaded through her dream. The meadow turned dark and hazy. A warm breath filled her ear. "Mara, wake up. You're having a nightmare."

She blinked as she shook herself out of the subconscious world and into the land of the living. Around her, eerie shadows flickered against the cave wall. A soft touch brushed the hair from her cheek. "Mara. You're safe now. Wake up."

Marina wiped the gritty salt from her swollen eyes and recognized Edick, *and* his worried expression, in the dim firelight. "Are you okay?"

She would never be okay. Not even if she had Dmitri's baby. She had nothing, no one, and she never felt so alone, so overwhelmed.

Her lip trembled, and she worked out a smile. "*Da*," she lied.

Edick scanned her face with his too-perceptive hazel green eyes. "Can I get you anything?"

She shook her head, wanting to climb back inside unconsciousness and grieve Dmitri. The jagged cave walls pressed in around her, dampness and chill threading through her layers of wool to find her bones. She shivered.

"You're cold." Edick pulled the threadbare blanket up to her chin. "Come and sit by the fire for a bit. I'll heat you some soup."

The longing to give in to his ministrations swept over her. Her pregnancy had crept up on her, tightened the grip of exhaustion. She found herself nodding.

He helped her to her feet. They walked to the mouth of the cave where the fire smoldered. He arranged his blanket on the ground next to the fire, then draped hers around her shoulders. Stars peeked from between cloud cover in a black sky. The firelight pushed the folds of darkness to ragged edges of the forest. Over the fire pit, she and Natasha had constructed a makeshift rack, and on it Edick placed the leftover *shee*, full of fish heads, potatoes, and carrots they'd managed to pilfer from the cellar of a burnt house not far from Pskov. They'd also buried the family, a mother and two sons who'd fallen with pitchforks in their grips.

Edick found a tin soup bowl and filled it. The smell sent

her stomach into convulsions. Funny how her appetite had swelled along with her belly. Although she'd been able to keep the secret hidden under her clothing, she knew discovery wasn't far off. Pavel had started to look at her with curiosity, and she'd noticed Natasha's eyes linger on her more than once. She had to tell them. Then she had to leave.

A week ago during an argument after the supply column ambush, she'd made her decision to depart the group and head east in one of the many convoys of women and children going into Siberia. Despite the fact she'd saved his life, Edick had rounded on her.

He'd practically accused her of trying to get herself killed.

And for the first time, she wondered if his words didn't ring with truth.

She'd joined the band to avenge her motherland, and the partisans were counting on her. Still, she couldn't move as quickly as she had, and if she were caught. . .well, maybe it would be better if she left before she cost lives.

Edick glanced at her, a bare smile on his face, worry in his beautiful eyes. Oh, she would miss him. Locked in the most private places of her heart was the memory of his embrace, his lips on hers, needing her as much as she had him. When she shook free of the guilt, she could admit he'd found fertile soil in her heart in a way Dima never had. Dima had youth, passion, and a sweetness that had sent her heart soaring.

Edick made her feel safe. And she had the uncanny feeling that he'd battle the entire Third Reich for her.

The thought left her breathless. And afraid. She'd dodged him over the past week for her benefit as much as his.

He'd leave another gaping hole in her chest when she left. Just when she thought all her wounds had closed over.

She watched Edick in the firelight, the way the orange glow played on his strong hands and rippled across his whiskered face. He shaved now and again and nicked himself with the straightedge so it left gaps in his whiskers. Again. She decided it was because he never let himself relax long enough to get a clean swipe. He had an energy that rippled under his muscled exterior, one that told her he never truly slept.

Or maybe his restlessness had to do with the war, the losses in his life. The worry hiding in his eyes.

The burden to protect his partisans. To protect her.

He looked in her direction, and his expression softened. "Something to keep the baby kicking." He handed her the bowl of soup.

She thanked him and lifted the bowl to her lips. The tin burned, but the soup warmed from the inside out. Edick settled behind her, wiped the hair from her neck, and settled his wide hands on her shoulders. Gently, he began to work her weary muscles, tense from countless nights on a rocky floor.

"Mmm. That's. . ." *Great.* She closed her eyes, aware that Dima had never stirred her emotions the way this American could. Dima had been her breath, her heartbeat. This man found empty places in her soul.

He'd probably be relieved to know she was heading east with all the other wives and mothers whose homes had burned, their children slaughtered. She'd have to make her way to Moscow, but from there, she'd catch the Trans-Siberian rail. And Dmitri's baby would be born safely inside the great white expanse of Siberia, out of Hitler's reach.

And out of the reach of Edick's tender care. The decision turned her throat raw. Somehow she couldn't form the words to tell him she was leaving. She set her soup bowl on the ground. She would simply slip away one night and be out of his life forever.

"I'm leaving soon, Mara."

Edick's words froze her heart in her chest. She turned and gaped at him. "What?"

"I need supplies. I'm going to Estonia, where my own partisan band is working. I have contacts there who can get me what I need to destroy the bridge."

Relief made her breathe out and restarted her heart. "So, you're coming back."

He looked at her, a sly smile lifting the side of his mouth. "Of course. Someone needs to keep an eye on you."

Her eyes burned, and she looked away at the fire. "I don't need your help, Edick."

"You need it, but you don't want it." He scooted closer, reached beyond her, and picked up a charred poker. He pushed it through the coals. The fire hissed.

Silence permeated the forest around them. Winter's grasp had sent the birds south and the animals into hibernation. Only a slight river wind shivered the trees.

No, she didn't want his help. She'd learned too well the pain that came from depending, needing, loving. But as she watched him work the fire, need overwhelmed the stubbornness that wanted to wall him out. Fear and a misplaced fidelity kept her from enjoying Edick's friendship, from allowing him full entrance into her life. She pressed her fingers against her eyelids. Betraying tears fell over them and down her hands. Lately, it seemed that all her emotions had a life of their own, acting without permission. And tonight, it seemed her mouth was following suit. "Edick, what will happen to me?" she whispered. "To my baby?"

She felt his hands on hers, drawing them down from her face. "Mara, God knows you're afraid. He'll watch over you." He cupped a hand on her cheek and thumbed away her tears.

She shook her head. "I don't trust God." She touched Edick's whiskered face, her emotions swelling. "I trust you. I want you to take care of me."

His jaw slacked. "Oh, Mara." His eyes roamed her face for a long moment, moving from her eyes, to her nose, and finally her mouth. "You have no idea what you do to me." He closed his eyes. "I will take care of you as best I can. But it's God whom you must trust." He raised his eyes, and they glistened.

Oy, did he pack a punch when he allowed his emotions into his gaze. She smiled weakly, so utterly aware that, again, she longed to bury herself in his arms, to lose herself in his touch. *Please.*

He swallowed hard, as if gathering composure, and one side of his mouth tweaked up. "I can't call you Mara any longer."

She opened her mouth to protest, but her words died when he sat next to her and pulled her to his chest. Tucked close, with his long, powerful legs wrapped around her, his leather, Edick-meets-the-woods smell swept through her. She nestled close, let her fears swirl out of her, leaned her head against his chest.

She felt nearly whole.

"Why not?" she managed.

"Because it's the wrong name. God has not left you. God loves you, and He is watching over you."

She stiffened at his words, but he tightened his arm around her and brushed her hair back lightly with his fingers. "I will call you Magda."

"Magda," she repeated. "What does it mean?"

"It means tower of strength. After Mary Magdalene, the prostitute Jesus forgave. She became a powerful witness to His love after her sad, bitter life." He traced a finger along her face. "You are Magda, my tower of strength. The woman who falls from trees into great rivers and survives. The woman who testifies to God's great love."

She wanted to bristle at his words. She wasn't the testimony of love, but of grief. Still, never since Dmitri's death had she felt so protected, so loved. Suddenly, everything within her longed to be held by Edick, to touch him and forget the war and the grief that ravaged her heart. She brushed her lips at the well of his neck.

He trembled, and with a sudden intake of breath, he entwined his hand in her hair. "Magda," he whispered, his mouth a breath away. "How can a man not love you?"

She closed her eyes, her heart in her throat. Dima was gone. But Edick had charged into her life and maybe, just maybe, God was giving her a second chance.

So, maybe the Almighty hadn't abandoned her, after all.

She lifted her face, felt Edick's hand on her chin. Yes—

A gunshot echoed through the forest. And in its eerie wake, a scream lifted the tiny hairs on Marina's arms.

And in her embrace, Edick bristled, as if memory had devoured him whole.

CHAPTER THIRTEEN

E dward paced the ring of firelight that pushed against the forest. His gaze darted toward the darkness as if waiting for a ghost—or a demon—to pounce from its murky interior.

"Maybe it was a cat. We have lynx in this area." Pavel stood beside him, rubbing his arms, blowing in his hands.

"I've heard that scream before; I know it." Edward rubbed his twitching left eye.

Pavel grabbed a stick and handed it to Edward. "You first, American. But I can't help think it would be better to wait until morning."

Edward shook his head. "In any case, there's a woman out there, and she's in trouble. Can you leave her to the bobcats, or worse, the Nazis?"

Pavel pushed a torch into the fire and lit it. "You'd better hope it's not a trap."

Edward smiled, finding it easier with each day to release his grip on mistrust. He turned to Magda, who was huddled under her blanket. The firelight added color to her gaunt face. Her eyes met his, spoke her pleas without words.

"I'll be back," he said softly.

She nodded.

The snowfall from days ago had melted, but the sodden leaves barely crunched in the darkness. Edward held his torch out before him, moving slowly, saying nothing. Ten paces behind him, Pavel did the same. Something familiar about that scream had spiked every hair on the back of his neck. Deep in the well of memory, he knew he'd heard it before. Probably it was his nightmares replaying in the dead of night. It seemed fair, somehow, to have them spill out into reality. A warning that yanked him from making another mistake. Namely, Magda.

He would have kissed her. He felt the desires still piled against his chest.

What was he supposed to do when she looked at him like he was some sort of answer to her prayers? He was just a man, one who wanted to be everything he saw in Magda's eyes.

A real hero might remember that they had a negative-chance future. He'd be smart to push her into Pavel's arms and race for the border. Because, as he so easily forgot, he only caused the death of the people he loved. If he wasn't careful, he'd repeat history in yet another country.

He must be setting some sort of world record for stupidity.

He'd have to keep her at arms' length if he hoped to keep her alive—and his heart intact.

Birch and oak trees lurched to great heights, blotting out the winking stars. A crisp wind threaded through the forest and ran up his spine.

"Edward," Pavel hissed, "this is foolishness. Let's go back to camp."

Edward kept walking.

"We'll never find her."

"You could try earning some of that trust you're so eager to get." Edward clenched his jaw and whirled. "I have a gut instinct on this."

"My gut says it's cold out."

Another scream pierced the air. Pavel's eyes widened in the dim torchlight. Edward listened. "That's not a bobcat. We had those in upstate New York, where I grew up, and that scream is definitely human."

"I think it's west of us, near the river. The wind is carrying it." Pavel turned and began working through a crisp clump of bushes. Edward followed, turning in all directions.

Ten paces later, they stopped and listened. The wind hissed but carried no human voice. Edward listened to the thundering of his own heart.

Another crack. Gunfire. Edward's pulse raced. Pavel froze, stock-still. Then another shot and the sound rolled right over the top of them. "It's not a gun," Pavel said. "I think it's branches echoing."

"Stay still." Edward held out a hand and crouched low. He dropped his torch onto the ground and stomped on it, snuffing it out. Bringing his finger to his lips, he crept away from Pavel, who stood frozen in his tiny glow of light. Edward drew his Colt from his belt and shrank behind the trunk of an elm.

The cracking stopped, replaced only by the hiccup of his heartbeat. An eerie silence swelled through the dark forest. A familiar and horrible panic birthed the night he'd lost his Polish partisans vise-gripped his chest. This was all wrong. Something wasn't right—

Pavel raised his hands slowly, his face drained of all blood.

Edward lifted the gun and scanned the circle of light around Pavel. Shadow melded into a form—slight, but menacing enough with a gun pointed at Pavel's head.

Edward swallowed hard as recognition nearly buckled his knees. "Raina, don't shoot! It's Edward!"

⚜

Marina crouched with her back to the cave, fanning a handgun across the darkness.

Natasha stood beside her in similar posture with her sniper rifle. "What is it?"

Marina shook her head. "A wild animal, maybe."

Natasha shuddered.

A flicker of light dented the darkness. Marina tightened her grip on the gun. Adrenaline ran through her body in hot currents. She trained her eyes on the light and moaned relief when Edick's outline sharpened. But three paces later, she read his expression, and it shook her to the bone. "Are you okay?"

He didn't answer, and when a young woman emerged from the clearing, she aimed her weapon. "Stop."

Edick held up his hand. "No, Magda, this is a friend. Her name is Raina."

Raina's dark eyes ran over Marina, and she couldn't help but shiver at the coldness glinting in them. Fierceness was etched into the tiny lines around her mouth, and her sunken eyes spoke of exhaustion. With her hair tucked into a brown woolen cap, her high cheekbones and thin jaw cut a lean, hardened image, accentuated by the bulk of weaponry shrouded under her padded wool jacket. Marina narrowed her eyes, refusing to lower the gun. "Who is she?"

"A freedom fighter. From Poland." He turned to the woman and spoke to her in Polish.

Raina nodded at Marina, then shuffled over to the fire. She pulled off two knitted gloves and held her bare hands against the flames. Marina's gaze roamed from her to Edick, who had curled a hand around his neck, to Pavel, who still held the torch at face height. Natasha stepped forward, her rifle at her hip. "Can we trust her?" Her face darkened. "How did she find you?"

Edick pursed his lips. "Go to bed. I'll talk to her." He crouched next to the woman. Marina watched his curiosity soften to concern and then shock as the woman spoke.

Pavel dropped his torch into the fire. "Mara, go to bed. You need your sleep." Pavel turned her toward the cave. The soft voices dispelled into the crisp air as she moved to her bed. She wrapped the blanket around her but sat with her back to the wall and laid her gun in her lap.

Raina settled onto the ground, and Edick moved the soup pan of borscht to the flames. Firelight illuminated the concern on his face, and a fist clawed at Marina's heart. When he moved an arm around the woman and drew her to his chest, Marina's eyes burned. She looked away.

Pavel was staring at her from across the room. The pressure of his gaze drew heat into her face. "Go to sleep, Mara."

She ducked her head.

"Who is she, Pavel?"

"I don't know. But she needs our help."

Marina didn't answer.

Near the fire, Edick sat with his strong arms around Raina, his chin buried in her stocking cap. Marina couldn't take her eyes off him. Her hand moved to her growing stomach. She prodded gently and felt the outline of a limb. Pushing, a strange delight rose inside her when the little limb pushed back. Her throat thickened, and her view of Edick blurred.

A hollow, fragile sensation took possession of her extremities. Trembling, she crumbled onto the mat. Salty tears spilled into her lips. Siberia loomed before her like bait, luring her to safety. Tomorrow. She would leave in the morning before Edick shattered her heart. She should have known better. She'd stood at the brink of giving him her heart and nearly toppled off. Her decision steeled her trembling and chilled her tears. Tightening her jaw, she curled on the mat and pulled the blanket to her chin. She settled her head on one hand and curled her other around the barrel of her rifle. The moment before she closed her eyes, she looked out at Edick, at the scene of tenderness before the fire.

But while Edick held a sobbing Raina in his arms, his gaze looked past the Pole, and his beautiful eyes locked on Marina. The intensity of that look dried Marina's mouth, and she closed her eyes, lest her resolve shatter.

───────

Raina's thin body shook with silent sobs, but as Edward held her, he saw only the pain on Magda's face. The firelight barely illuminated her thin outline, but he felt her question. *Who is she?*

When she closed her eyes, he groaned.

Raina wound a hand through his leather coat. "Edward. I can't believe I found you." Exhaustion stretched her voice thin. He smoothed her hair, soothing her in low tones.

"I thought you were dead," she sobbed. "When I finally made it back to the cave, everyone was gone."

Including Irina. His heart wrenched, and he tightened his hold around her. How to tell Raina her precious daughter, the one she hovered over to the point of obsession, had been mauled by SS dogs and had died in his arms? How to tell her that she alone remained? He'd never met her husband or three sons, but during their year together, she'd slowly unlocked her heart, spilling out her grief to him. He'd come to feel their loss written as his own. It fueled his fury and his passion to cripple the Third Reich. Now, the memory of Irina's cherub smile and blue eyes made him want to scream. He leaned away from Raina, searching for a way to tell her.

She lifted her head, and her blue eyes were haunted as if she already knew. "I'm so glad I found you. I couldn't wait until you came back to Estonia. I had to find you."

He put her away from him, wrapping his hands around her upper arms. It seemed she'd gained weight since he last saw her. "Why? If we hadn't found you. . .what if another partisan unit had discovered you? Or worse, the Germans? You could have been killed."

She gaped at him, and her eyes filled. "Irina. My daughter. Edward. . .I have to know. What happened?"

He closed his eyes, seeing Irina's torn body, feeling her limp form as he buried her. He said nothing but pulled her again into his arms, held her tight. "I'm so sorry, Raina."

He clenched his eyes shut at her awful gasp. "I buried her under that wide oak near the caves."

Raina hiccuped sobs, and he didn't know how to help her. *God, You sent me here to wound Hitler, but so many pay that price. Katrina, Irina.* Despair stalked his soul. He'd joined the war to make a difference, thinking it was God's will, hoping that while he parried Hitler's efforts, he'd also save lives, perhaps even souls. The emptiness of that hope, that prayer, echoed in the moan of the wind.

A snake of cold air shifted through his hair and down

the collar of his coat. He glanced toward the cave. Magda had drawn her legs up and lay in a huddled mass of darkness. The urge to creep into the cave and hold her and perhaps the life and hope growing inside her swept through him like a wave. It sent him trembling, this need to be near her, to look into her eyes and see that fire, the determination that inspired him, infuriated him, and drew him like a warm blaze. Magda.

As Raina's sobs subsided, he moved away from her and rested his hands on his knees. Rubbing the worn wool with his thumbs, he stared into the fire. It danced and sent orange sparks into the sky, only to be swallowed by the inky darkness.

He felt painfully aware of the fact that he was letting his emotions run him into destruction. War made no exceptions for love. Cruel, even calculating, love could serve only the enemy. He closed his eyes and buried them into his clenched fists. Frustration chewed at him.

Magda wasn't his. The baby wasn't his. And he had no right to love her. For both their sakes, he'd have to keep her at arms' length. She'd been the wiser of the two to dodge him. . .until he made the mistake of pulling her into his arms.

He wanted to hit something. Hard.

Raina leaned into his shoulder. He sighed and curled an arm around her. "How did you find me?"

"Through the partisan network. I followed you north to Estonia and found your unit in Tallinn. They told me what you were up to."

He frowned. He didn't recall telling anyone in the group of his plans, not willing to sacrifice more lives. But perhaps Colonel Stone. . .

Raina looked up at him. "I'm going to stay and help you."

"No." He looked away, out toward the pitch darkness. "I've buried enough women and children."

Her jaw tightened. "This isn't your war, Edward. It's mine and Irina's and Marek's."

He shook his head. "You've lost enough, Raina. I don't want your help."

She smiled, but her eyes seemed hollow. "Too bad. I'm here, and I'm not leaving. Not until my mission is finished. I have nothing left to lose."

She stood and moved toward the cave, pulling on her gloves. "Where do I sleep?"

He cast a glance at Magda, huddled against the wall, and couldn't ignore the dread stealing through his heart.

CHAPTER FOURTEEN

Marina lugged the bag of potatoes to the cave entrance and plopped down on a boulder. Digging into the bag, her thumb punctured a soft potato. She yanked it out, grimacing. Potatoes. She was cleaning *potatoes* while Raina, the Polish partisan, scouted the bridge with Edick. Gritting her teeth, Marina drove her hand back into the bag and extracted a potato. Wrinkled and dangling with long roots, it looked like something she and Dmitri would have fed to the pigs. She chopped at it with vigor. It bent beneath her hand, and she missed, gouging out a piece of flesh from her palm. Crying out, she dropped the cursed potatoes and pushed her grimy thumb into the cut.

Laughter filtered through the trees on a crisp wind. Marina pursed her lips and searched the forest. Raina's green camouflage jacket melded into the foliage, but her golden hair drew Marina's gaze like a beacon. Behind her, head down, Edick swung a sniper rifle, listening to Raina's words.

Marina slammed her knife into the potatoes and rose to her feet. A sharp pain clawed at her abdomen, but she fought it and stalked away in the opposite direction. She heard Edick calling, but she hunched her shoulders and ignored him. She should have left weeks ago. If it weren't for Raina, she'd be on a train to Siberia right now.

Nearly two weeks she'd watched the two flirt, watched Raina sidle next to Edick at night near the campfire, had seen the tender way Edick looked at the woman. She didn't care that the Pole had lost her sons or her daughter. Pavel's quiet explanation did nothing to soothe her irritation. Perhaps if Edick had stopped to explain instead of avoiding her like she was second-hand merchandise.

Her jaw clenched, and she stalked through the forest, not caring where she was going or that the frost crackled and bit at her legs.

"Magda!" The sound of branches shredding behind her made her quicken her pace.

"Magda, please stop. What's wrong?" The worry in Edick's voice tugged at her heart, but she drove her feet forward. Only his grip on her arm made her stop. Even then, she refused to look at him.

"Are you trying to get yourself killed?" The anger in his voice brought her head up. His hazel green eyes flecked with frustration. "You can't go tromping about in the woods. Not in your condition." He looked pointedly at her belly, which had decided to pop out like yeasty bread, filling her sweater. She hitched two hands on her hips and met his fiery gaze. "I don't need you to take care of me."

"We've been through that," he said, his eyes dark. "And you may be right. But you're still not going anywhere."

His words cut through her. She wanted him to refute her rejection like he had before—to acknowledge that surely if she didn't want his help, she needed it. . .and needed him. Emptiness roared through her, and she shrank back from him. "Let me be."

"Please, come back to camp." She noticed the deliberate

softening in his tone. "If not for yourself, for us."

She closed her eyes.

"If they find you, they'll find us."

She flinched. So, this wasn't about her. She barely had the strength to shake her head. "I'd never betray you, Edick," she managed through her constricting chest.

"Of course not. Not willingly, at least. But war forces a person to do the unthinkable." He stretched his arm out before her and leaned it on a smooth elm. His spicy masculine scent surrounded her, and she knew she could happily drown in his arms, if only he would curl them around her.

No, no, no! She shouldn't let him back in her heart. Hadn't she learned how easily he replaced her? Please. She'd practically begged him to be a father to her child, and he hadn't so much as mentioned it. Some impact she'd made on his life. Tower of Strength, indeed. More like Tower of Stupidity.

"Please come back," Edick said, his voice soft.

No.

He brushed her hair away from her face, tucked it into her hat. "I'm worried about you."

She shuddered at the emotions coursing through her. Not fair that he could unravel her resolve with one lazy smile, one glance from his devastatingly beautiful eyes. "Don't. You have your hands full. Obviously."

He recoiled, backed away. "What do you mean by that?"

"You know what I mean." She turned, furious that she teared so easily. She couldn't seem to get a grip on her emotions these days. "You have a job to do."

She heard his breath release, even heard him swallow. "Yes, I do."

A tear ran down her cheek. What an idiot she'd been

to read more into his kindness than what it was—responsibility for his partisans.

Spreading her hands over her stomach, she looked at the bulge. She couldn't afford to lose another man. She still had a piece of Dmitri, but Edick was only a shadow crossing her path. She'd understood that on the day after Raina arrived, as she watched Edick talk with her, share memories, and show her their supply of weapons. She'd thought of herself as Magda, someone special in Edick's life. But she was simply another partisan. After the Velikaya Bridge was dumped in the river, he would leave and all her hopes, these feelings, with him.

She closed her eyes, indictment screaming in her soul. She'd traded her loyalty to Dmitri and their love for an impossible dream. Edick offered her no future, and she'd been a fool to think it. She refused to love another man whom she would lose to war. She could depend on no one but herself to take care of her. And her child.

"Let me alone, Edick," she said. Or at least tried to say. But he'd closed the distance between them. He put his hand on her shoulder. "Magda, please. I'm just trying to do what's best—"

"For whom?" Okay, her feelings were completely out of the corral now. Almost as if she were watching, she saw herself round on him, saw her anger as she pounded her fist into his chest. "Just stay away from me, Edick. I can't believe I trusted you."

Fisting her hands at her side, she whirled and stalked back to camp. She would leave after the partisans had bedded down for the night.

Raina sat by the bag of potatoes, sifting through them, dropping them, one by one, back into the sack. Her face registered disgust. Defense rose in Marina. If only the Pole knew the hours she and Natasha spent digging them out of barren fields.

Marina grabbed her knife and squatted beside the bag. She fished out a potato and began to peel off thin curls.

"Have you known Edick a long time?" Raina's question, spoken in accented Russian, sounded twisted and spoiled.

Marina squinted at the woman, not sure what to say. Raina didn't fit. With her white blond hair down and swishing about her face, she seemed as bedraggled as the next partisan, but her high cheekbones and eyes as deep blue as the murky depths of the Velikaya River betrayed a rich Polish heritage. Perfect Aryan. A different country, and Raina would be a princess instead of a peasant. Marina pushed up a sleeve of her tattered, mud brown sweater and swiped at the potato.

"He saved my life," she answered.

"Mine, too." Raina came close and squatted near the pot. "Soup?"

"Borscht." Marina stared at the pot but felt Raina's gaze run over her.

Marina had spent a good part of the first night watching the woman, wanting to claw her eyes out when Raina curled up on the floor, gladly accepting Edick's only blanket. Edick had tucked her in with few words and taken a position near the cave door, staring at the stars.

When Marina awoke that next morning, he was gone. A strange draft filtered through her heart until he returned hours later, laden with firewood and a sack of lumpy potatoes.

"Did you have a husband?" Raina picked up a potato

and proceeded to peel it with a grimy hunting knife she'd drawn from her black boot.

Marina nodded. "He died when the Nazis took Ukraine."

A low sun sent murky orange streams through the forest. The smell of snow layered the air. Marina eyed Raina's thick wool jacket and clenched her jaw. Raina worked the potato clumsily, slicing fat chunks of meat off with the chip of her knife, whittling her potatoes down to a nub. Marina bit her tongue as she watched the layer of thick skins pile in the dirt.

Edick crouched near the fire, sending curious looks at her as he built the blaze up, working it to perfection. He grabbed a dented pot, scorched black, and brought it over to Marina. She began to slice potatoes into it. His gaze burned a hole into her neck, but she refused to look at him. She already had him imprinted in her mind: his tousled, unruly brown hair with those shimmering copper highlights, hazel eyes lined with the power to see right through her, those high Slavic cheekbones betraying his Russian patronage. When he handed her a potato, his long fingers touched hers briefly. She bit her lower lip and focused on the blurry pot.

Dinner barely soothed the hungry claw in her stomach. She didn't miss the fact that Raina took a place beside Edick, but a secret pleasure rushed through her when Edick rose to refill his bowl, then moved to sit next to Pavel. The two men huddled as if schoolboys. Natasha leaned over to her.

"They're planning something. I can feel it."

Marina nodded. "Pavel has that look." She set down her bowl. "It's the bridge. I think they have a plan." Despite the few ambushes they'd made over the past weeks, her focus had been survival. Eating. Staying warm.

Dodging Edick.

Edick set down his bowl and cleared his throat. Marina watched him rub his hands on the knees of his pants. The memory of those hands dragging her from a river rushed up at her. She ripped her gaze away from them and stared at the fire.

"Pavel and I are leaving." Edick didn't look at her. Instead his gaze fell on Raina. He translated into Polish. Marina snatched a look at Raina. The woman's jaw had slacked.

"I don't have enough supplies to wire the bridge, so I'm returning to Estonia." He glanced at Marina, and she saw worry written on his face. She clenched her jaw but felt raw. She would be long gone by the time he returned. She picked up a long stick and poked it into the fire, preferring the show of sparks to the tender concern in his eyes.

"Pavel and I have a plan, and I'll explain it when I get back."

Natasha started to protest, but Edick held up a hand. "Trust me, please. You'll be safe here, especially now that Raina is with you." He pointedly looked at the Pole, dragging Marina's gaze along with him. Raina jutted her chin, but the smug look in her eyes turned Marina's stomach. Poor Natasha. She'd be here alone. Guilt nipped at her.

"I'll leave all the grenades and my ammo. I should be back in two weeks. A month at the most."

Marina couldn't look at him. A month. Her baby was due soon after that. Hopefully, she'd be safely in Siberia, perhaps even to Vladivostok by then. Natasha grabbed Marina's bowl and stood. "How will you get there?"

His slight smile drew Marina's gaze like sweet honey. "I'll ride like a rabbit."

His words stung, and for a moment, Dmitri shimmered before her eyes. Riding like a rabbit—a colloquial term for jumping the train, something Dmitri had always threatened, long before their courtship. The reminder shook her to the bone.

"And the bridge?" Raina asked, her Polish accent distorting the words.

Edick nodded. "When I come back." He scanned a serious look around the group. "This time, we won't fail."

Marina rose and followed Natasha to a dented metal bucket, where the girl dumped the bowls in. Natasha bent and began to wash them, shooing Marina away when she offered help. "You rest," she said, eyeing the bulge in Marina's sweater.

Natasha smiled. "Perhaps you two should be. . .alone before he leaves?" She panned a look at Edick, her expression pity.

Uh oh, Natasha didn't think. . . Marina's heart plummeted to her knees. "It's not his," she mumbled. Except, somehow, over the past three months, it felt like it. Her throat raw, she turned away. The hollow feeling again roared through her as she shuffled to her mat. Sitting with her back to the wall, she wound her hands into her woolen sweater sleeve and calmed herself, hoping she'd feel the baby move. Often, the child moved at night when she was still. She loved to lace her hands over her belly and trace the outline of his legs and arms or feel the push of his head. The hope that seeped into those moments frightened her.

Edick and Pavel sat near the fire, talking. Edick held

his bowl in his hands, rubbing the edge. Now and again he glanced at her—she felt his eyes on her like a hot breath. Still, she refused to meet his gaze. Deep inside she was cracking, and should she look straight into those eyes, she knew she would shatter.

⚜

Edward pulled the string on his rucksack, tied it, then leaned back on his heels against the wall of the cave. Pavel stood outside by the dying fire, staring into the black forest, his own pack dangling in his hand. The man was fast becoming an ally, something Edward wasn't sure he wanted. He had to trust Pavel. . .but his gut and experience told him to watch his back. He pulled his Colt from his belt and checked the ammunition load. Two more clips lay in his pack. He had to travel fast and light—he'd leave his rifle and the extra ammo with Raina.

As he slipped the handgun back into his belt, his gaze fell on Raina, long since huddled in a ball near the entrance of the cave. Her wispy blond hair fell over her sculptured face like a silk scarf, but even the softness of it couldn't erase the lines of sorrow etched there. Raina was a tomcat, and she'd protect Magda from harm. If the woman could track him from the forests of Poland, surely she could keep Magda and Natasha safe. For the first time, gratefulness surged though him at her arrival. Despite the brutal memories she brought with her, she also offered him solace. Magda would be safe under Raina's watch.

Clutching the pack, he rose and tiptoed through the cave toward Pavel. The breath of winter and the taste of imminent snow filled the air. Edward stood beside Pavel and stared at the stars, diamonds on black velvet.

"Ready?" Pavel asked.

As Edward opened his mouth, foreboding gripped his chest as if something, someone pulled at him. "Just a moment." He turned back to the cave.

Magda's eyes bore into him like knives and speared his heart. His throat thickened, and without thinking, he strode back into the cave and knelt on her mat. Tears cut furrows down her face; her eyes were swollen. He felt sick. Laying a hand on her wet cheek, he kissed her forehead. The smell of her skin, earth and spice and the faintest scent of pine, nearly broadsided him.

What was he doing? Since yesterday, when he'd found her in the forest, it was all he could do not to scoop her up and run for the border. She'd gotten under his skin with her stubborn patriotism, but even more so, he longed for her to believe that he might be. . .what? A father to her child? Her husband?

I can't believe I trusted you. Her words of yesterday stung even now as he stared into her beautiful eyes. "I. . .wish I could take you with me."

She swallowed, and he saw pain flash through her eyes. "Was I wrong?"

What? "I don't understand."

"You. . .said that you. . ." She made a wry face and turned away from him. He wanted to groan. He'd said he loved her. Sorta. Then he did an end-run around her every time she got close to him.

Because he'd been afraid of just how true his words were. And it scared him more than he could voice every time she picked up her weapon. His words stopped as he searched her face, her eyes. "Magda. . ." Her hand dug into his sweater as he spoke. "You weren't wrong."

He wanted to kiss her. He could nearly taste her, feel her soft lips on his.

"Magda, please." He leaned away, his breath thick. "I–it won't work. You're. . .pregnant."

"Yes. And my baby needs a father."

"And I'm not the man for you."

He could see the question in her eyes. He felt like a heel, a number one palooka. She deserved so much more than this.

"You have no idea how much I want to scoop you up and run for the border. But you're Russian, and you need someone like Pavel. Someone who can give you a future."

"Someone who isn't going to sacrifice his life to the war? Obviously, you don't know Pavel that well."

She pushed him away, betrayal in her expression.

Magda, please don't do this.

"It's okay, Edick. I'm not your responsibility. I never was."

Oh, how much that was not true. The moment she practically dropped out of the sky at his feet, she'd been his. His heart. His breath. His Magda.

He saw himself react, felt his intentions take possession a moment before he moved, and still, it shocked him. Reaching out, he cupped her neck, leaned close, and kissed her. It wasn't a kiss that he'd hoped for, the kind that spoke of the way he wanted to love her, with sweet tenderness. No, he kissed her with the desperation that he'd tried to ignore, the fears that he'd dodged every time he saw her pick up a weapon. He cupped her face in both of his hands and kissed her like he just might be leaving her forever.

And to his sweet surprise, she kissed him back.

As if she knew exactly how he felt about leaving—and felt the same.

"Edick," she murmured, and he felt as if his chest might explode.

"Oh, Magda, please, please be okay until I get back." He tipped his forehead against hers, his breath thick.

"Take care of yourself," Magda whispered, her eyes glistening. A tear tipped the edge and rolled down her cheek.

Edward dodged the desperate look in her eyes and instead traveled his gaze to her belly. "May I?" He reached out, his hand hovering over the tiny life.

Magda took his hand and placed it on her belly. Instead of giving, like he thought it might, it was firm and warm. Suddenly, something moved between his fingers, an arm or a leg perhaps, something long and slender and alive.

"Whoa. That's. . .alive."

She gave a slight giggle. "Yeah."

Unable to stop himself, he put his other hand over her womb. The baby squirmed under the warmth of his touch, as if trying to reach back. Her stomach moved like a great mountain of water. "Oh boy."

Magda put her hands over his, lacing her fingers between his. "I know. He loves to move at night when I am quiet."

Edward sat down facing her, all his protective instincts flooding over him. "I shouldn't go." He raised his eyes and found hers. They were sweet and beautiful and trusting, and he suddenly wanted to cry. He so didn't deserve that trust. But he wanted to try, at least. His chest tightened. "Oh, Magda, I have to go."

"I know. We have a mission to complete."

He cringed, her words piercing his soul. A mission that

suddenly paled in comparison to hers. She had life *inside* her, growing. The future of Russia in her womb. He was here to take lives, to destroy the future. The comparison made him raw. Hollow. Some servant of God he was—destroying lives, putting women in danger, sending children to their deaths. "I'm sorry," he mumbled, more to God than Magda.

She touched his cheek. "Be safe, Edick."

If he didn't leave now, he never would. "Magda, listen to me. I'm coming back. I'll do everything I can to come back to you."

"So you can destroy the bridge and leave again." Her chin quivered, and she caught her lower lip between her teeth.

He flinched. Okay, so maybe she'd thought this thing through more than he had. "I'll take you with me."

Where did that come from? Her eyes widened along with his. But a plan began to form, to crystallize. Didn't Stone say he needed him? Perhaps he could do a little bargaining. A smile creased his face. He cupped her face in his hands and drew her gaze to his. "Magda, you take care of yourself and your baby. I'll come back. And then—"

She reached out and clutched his jacket, drawing him closer, leaning into him. Her lips found his, and they were soft and pliable, hungry as they kissed him.

He gathered her into his arms and kissed her again, knowing he'd unlatched his common sense. Salty tears wet his lips, and with a jolt he realized they were his own. Drawing back, he felt as if he'd left his heart behind and given her a piece of his soul. The agony of leaving her left him gasping. "I'll come back," he rasped.

She nodded, a faraway look in her eyes. It frightened

him. Trembling, he placed his hand again on her stomach and reveled at the feeling of the baby.

Indictment slammed into him. He couldn't promise her that he would return. It wasn't in his hands. *Oh Lord, how to make her trust You instead of me? Have I blown it?* His lips tingled where she'd kissed him. Already, his arms felt empty. Despite his hopes and the plan forming in a shrouded place in his mind, the war loomed above them like a guillotine. His throat thickened. He couldn't leave her with human promises. He had to leave her with trust in the Almighty.

"No matter what happens, you remember this. God loves you." He fought to steady his wrecked voice. Her jaw hardened at his words, but she nodded. Her beautiful eyes glistened. He drew a strand of her tangled blond hair behind her ear as an odd peace swept through him. "I'm going to pray for us."

Her brow knitted and she recoiled, but he took her hand, laid it over her womb, and cupped it with his. "Lord, please, I beg You, watch over Magda and her baby. Keep her safe from harm. Help her to see You in her life, watching her, protecting her, loving her. Give her and her baby hope— and a future." His voice echoed through the cavern. He prayed that his words plowed through the cobwebs of her heart. "And if it be Your will, please bring me back to her."

She inhaled a soft breath.

"Amen." He lifted his eyes and traced her face one last time in a desperate attempt to imprint it as an eternal memory. Round blue eyes the color of a stormy sky, full lips soft and so kissable, a determined lift to her chin, blond hair that haloed her face, and a firm, strong body that bulged with life. Magda, his tower of strength.

"Good-bye." He kissed her again on the forehead.

He left quickly, scooping up his backpack and striding into the forest lest his courage shatter and the look in her eyes draw him back and convince him to abandon his mission completely.

Marina watched him go without a sound. His long, powerful legs took him away. His wide back rigid, his strong hands gripped the rucksack in a white fist. In his wake, the wind whistled into the cave and right through her heart. The hollow, empty feeling returned with a roar. For a moment, while he prayed, she'd felt warm and full, as if God truly was looking down at her, holding her in His hands. As soon as Edward left, however, she knew it had only been the man's encompassing presence. Ache curled her into a ball and made her lie on the mat, shivering from the inside out.

At the mouth of the cave, the dying embers of the campfire made an eerie glow against the pitch black of the forest wall. Inside the cave, Natasha's deep breaths mingled with Raina's as they lay sleeping, wrapped in balls underneath their threadbare blankets. Winter's grasp had nearly found them, and without supplies, they would all die.

She had to leave. The decision felt like a hot ball in her chest, but she knew it was the only thing that would keep her and Dmitri's baby alive. She touched her lips with her fingers, feeling Edward's touch, his taste, the passion he'd momentarily unleashed, enough to leave her breathless and awaken hope. Until she realized he was saying good-bye. In their final moments, he'd surrendered to the longing that had saturated his eyes and hued his expression for weeks. Perhaps it was love. More likely, it was loneliness. Like her, he'd lost a loved one, fought to survive, and needed comfort. His kiss had nothing to do with love and everything to do with need, fear, and desperation.

She, however, had kissed him with every ounce of love she possessed.

But did Edick love her in return? No. Hardly.

She was afraid. And she'd just lost her husband—of course she was needy. Lonely. Edward Neumann was probably the last man she should let herself love. Especially since, at the moment, he was hiking out of her life.

They had as much chance at everlasting happiness as Hitler did of surviving the Russian winter.

She let herself smile.

She had to admit, however, that Edward's friendship had crept into her cold heart like sunshine over the frost. His belief that God watched out for her nurtured her feeble spirit. She'd begun to buy into his words, to want to hope that he was right. She'd found herself at odd moments lifting her eyes upward into the heavens and searching the clouds, wondering if God's eyes were upon her.

Edward ignited hope, and if she wasn't careful, her feelings for him would build to an inferno—one that could destroy her.

Now wasn't too late to pick up her rucksack and make a run for Siberia while her heart was still whole in her chest. Because if she stuck around, she'd watch him die. He was a partisan, and his life was the war. And until a month ago, she'd thought she could live that life, also. But now. . .

As if in response to her thoughts, the baby thumped her under her ribs. She gasped and put a hand over her stomach, reveling in the feeling of life. Edward's wide-eyed look flooded into her memory, and she smiled despite the loss. He'd have made a good father. Every bit as good as Dmitri. She bit her trembling lip.

Movement in the shadows against the far wall where Raina lay riveted her gaze. Every muscle tensed, and adrenaline burned her veins as she saw Raina rise. She hooded her eyes, feigning sleep, and peeked through her lashes. Raina moved like a cat as she reached for Edward's US Carbine rifle and the ammunition packs he'd left behind. The Pole tucked the packs into her jacket and crept out of the cave with no more sound than the wind.

CHAPTER FIFTEEN

A hawk screamed from the slate gray sky. Although the haunting shriek frayed Marina's nerves, it concealed the echo of her footsteps. A quarter kilometer in front of her, by using her rifle scope, she could make out Raina's dark form in the shards of daylight piercing the eastern treetops. The first warmth she'd felt in hours permeated her sweater. She rubbed her arms with numb hands, wishing she'd taken the blanket. But all she'd had time or sense to grab was her rifle. She was tempted to pull the trigger when she raised the sight to her eye and spotted Raina edging out into a foggy meadow.

She congratulated herself on not losing Raina's trail. Edick—no, Pavel, would be proud of her. Edick would give her one of those "you'll just get hurt" looks.

She wondered how far they'd gotten. She fought the urge to shoot a prayer heavenward. Over the past month, however, she'd found her gaze drifting above the landscape of despair, lifted by hope.

Wondering if God might indeed be knitting together the shredded places in her heart. If He'd send to her a new tomorrow.

She followed Raina's sounds, Marina's history in this woods allowing her to filter the natural from the man-made. Breaking branches echoed like a shot against barren maple, stripped elm, and frigid oak trees. Marina moved like a panther, despite her bulk, unwilling to betray herself. Where was Raina headed? And why?

She'd let out Raina's tether as the sun rose, afraid the woman would turn and spy her behind a spray of brush or hear her sometimes labored breathing. With the scope of her rifle, she could see three hundred meters and if need be wipe the smile off Raina's face. The woman moved with purpose, her wispy blond hair tucked up neatly in her dull brown cap, carrying her gun at arm's length.

Marina felt an old, familiar anticipation course through her and heat her weary muscles. The sensation wasn't an entirely welcome one. Somehow, she'd felt cleaner during these past weeks of inactivity, distanced from the bloodshed and guilt. Following Raina rushed all those mottled feelings back to her in stinging reality. The unease that had been building since Raina entered the camp turned Marina's grip white on her gun.

She pushed forward, careful to brush silently past low-hanging branches. Her stomach moaned now and again, and at times, the baby in her womb stretched, tensing the muscles down to her knees. She gritted her teeth against the pain and made sure Raina never became less than a vivid speck in her scope.

The landscape changed, and the forest began to thin. She stepped into a pocket of glowing sunshine and drank in the fresh, cool air. It smelled somehow familiar, laced with wood smoke and earth—

Pskov. She should have recognized the terrain. Even occupied by Germans, women cooked bread, washed laundry, survived invasion by performing the simple, everyday tasks of life.

Why is Raina headed toward my hometown?

Fury hustled her pace. She paused behind a gnarled oak, digging her fingers between the bark, and watched Raina stride through the graveyard and up the road. She waited until Raina had paced into a dip, then Marina scampered out, crouching between the wooden and stone headstones. Her heart in her throat, she dropped to all fours and crawled up to Dmitri's resting place. Decaying leaves—red maples, orange and yellow oaks, and brown elms—littered the site. She clawed them away, then palmed the marker. As if Dmitri himself was reaching out to her, she felt strength surge through her arm.

"Will God bring you home?" Her own question echoed through her memory. He'd knelt next to her, taken her hand in his. "You can count on it," he'd answered. Marina bowed her head. God *had* taken him home. Away from this agony, this grief, this fear. Truly he was in a better place, and for the first time since his awful death, a trickle of joy filled her. *Dmitri in heaven.* That was a thought. Probably riding rabbit on some cloud or regaling the angel choir with one of his wild boyhood stories. She thought of his tousled black hair, his dark eyes, and crooked smile, and it made her smile.

She set the rifle beside his grave and placed a hand over her stomach. "Dmitri, this is your son." Biting her lower lip, she grinned sheepishly. "Or maybe your daughter, with your dancing eyes and your sweet laughter. Do you see her?" She traced his name, carved out of the wooden marker. "I forgive you, Dima. I forgive you for leaving me." The metallic taste of grief filled her mouth, but she swallowed it, knowing Raina would soon be out of sight. "I miss you so much. But I can't hang onto you. It's too hard." She hung her head.

"I'm going away, east, to have our baby. But someday I will return and show her to you." Her eyes filled. "Someday." She pressed her hand to the mound as if touching the breast of her husband and felt the crunch of paper. The photograph. She clawed the ground open and tugged it free. Although the photograph had been overlaid by leaves and dirt, she could still discern the faces of her mothers, resolute to the life before them despite their grief. They were women of strength. Just like the daughter one bore and the other raised. She tucked the picture inside her shirt, then curled her hand around the cold stock of her rifle and worked herself to her feet.

She lifted her gaze to the sunrise, to the indent of sparkling color creeping into the pale sky. How strange that Raina's covert strolls should lead Marina to this moment, as if she were standing on the threshold of tomorrow. She had a sudden urge to turn back. To not discover what Raina was doing. To dash back into the woods and head north, straight to Moscow and to the Siberian train.

Or maybe west, after Edick.

I'll take you with me. His voice pulsed in her mind, rippled under her skin. She hated how much she wanted to burrow into that idea. To wrap herself inside his attention and imagine a life with Edick on his farm in America. He seemed to be everything Dima hadn't been. Safe. Dependable. Not given to rush after his ambitions.

But how much of that desire was just her imagination filling in the gaps in her barren heart? Edick didn't love her. He felt pity for her. Her child.

And if she stuck around, he'd die trying to keep them both alive.

She glanced again at the grave, at Dmitri's marker.

Someone had carved an inscription in the wood. She squinted at it, making out the rough scratching. Psalm 100:5. Who would etch that into her husband's epitaph? She had a vague impression that she knew this verse, but she couldn't recall the text. What pulsed clearly in her soul was the command to follow Raina.

She skirted the potato field, knowing exactly where it ended and how to work her way into the village of Pskov. As she drew near, disgust pitched her stomach at the wake of destruction plowed by the Germans. Cattle lay bloated and decaying in the fields. Trampled and churned-up potato plants littered the dirt. The smell of wet, blackened wood dampened the crisp air. She passed a farmhouse, its coal chimney stark around charred timbers. A flock of crows watched her with interest from an upturned cart, the wheel creaking in the nudge of the wind. She steeled her courage and jogged toward the village.

Marina entered on the eastern side of the city, opposite the burned culture center, the bombed administration building. The Germans had obviously considered the poor peasants on the outskirts of the town not worth destroy-ing—the ancient squatty houses with flapping tar paper and thick, decaying logs seemed untouched. A trickle of smoke from the stone or metal chimneys evidenced life and tinged the air with the promise of warmth. Uneven fences con-structed with remnants of wire, scraps of wood, and the odd metal bracing made a windbreak for garbage and paper. An occasional cow looked up from tall piles of hay as Marina shuffled past. Laundry snapped on clotheslines: dull white underwear, brown and red knitted sweaters, black socks. Marina glanced at her threadbare clothes.

Loose gravel spilled behind her, and she dashed toward

the remnants of a blue-painted wooden fence. When a pack of hungry dogs trotted past her, one mangy chow chow baring his teeth, she glared back and shooed it away along with the idea that the canine would make a good meal. She cringed. When had she begun to entertain such thoughts?

Where was Raina? The woman had walked into the city on the main road—the brazenness of that behavior stumped Marina. She was either itching for a fight, or the Pole had nothing to fear.

A chicken squawked, startled, and skittered toward its yard. Marina lowered the gun to her side and wished she looked like a peasant woman. Her woolen trousers, raggedy sweaters, and oversized military jacket pegged her as a freedom fighter at one glimpse. The sniper rifle certainly didn't help.

She ducked into the yard after the chicken and made a beeline for the house. Whoever was inside, she hoped they were friendly. Or at least stocked with food.

The smell of weathered logs and cement greeted her with memories of her mother's home. She opened the outside door without knocking and paused in the foyer. A pair of muddy boots sat on a threadbare red throw rug, and a ragged leather coat lined with grimy sheep's wool dangled like bait from a metal hook. She reached out for it, then stopped. She wasn't a thief, and war would not turn her into one. A killer perhaps. . .but didn't war allow for special circumstances? Opting not to battle the morality of her choices, she began to back out of the foyer.

The thin plank board under her foot groaned.

In an instant, the inner door swung open. Marina froze, face-to-face with a chipped kitchen knife and a babushka who looked like she could take her head off with a swipe. Marina raised her hand as if in surrender. *"Zdrastvootya.* I'm not going to hurt you."

The elderly woman, dressed in a fraying gray sweater over a thin housedress, wool leggings, and black *valenki* boots, edged forward. Marina eyed her, standing her ground. The babushka took in Marina's gun. Then her stomach. Her brow knit. "Come in," she mumbled and lowered the knife.

Relief *whooshed* out of Marina as she closed the door behind her and stepped into the tiny room. A blast of heat from the brick cookstove hit her with a smack. From the doorway to a smaller room, a small girl watched with wide eyes. Memory rushed back to Marina, swallowing her whole, and suddenly she lay in Mother Yulia's bed, snuggled under layers of wool blankets. She felt Yulia trace her hand, listened to her quiet words.

"Your mother said to me, 'Yulia, God promised my Anton that He was good and His love would endure forever, that His faithfulness would continue through all generations. She told me, 'The Almighty alone knows what plans He has, and He will carry us.'" Yulia's head bowed low, her voice soft. "And so your mother left, and you became mine, my own precious *lapichka*."

Marina shook free of the memory before grief could crumple her. "I need help."

"You need to sit and eat." The woman's stern tone felt somehow comforting. "Your baby needs nourishment, and you look on the edge of death." The woman grabbed Marina's wrist and pulled her to a rough-hewn table. "You'll eat. Then you'll tell me why God brought you to my door."

"Have you ever done this before?" Pavel crouched under the cover of tall, pale reeds. His voice lifted over the roar of a locomotive engine barreling down the tracks.

"A couple times!" Edward shouted back. He positioned his legs under him, ready to spring as soon as the engine and its German guards had safely passed. The dawn pushed the gray sky hither and decimated their cover. He prayed, no *begged*, God to help him board the freight train without getting himself or Pavel killed.

The engine roared past them, the great machine bellowing even as it hissed and gathered speed from its stop in Pechory just minutes before. Edward waited until the engine passed, then shot out of his hiding place like a grouse. "Now!"

Pavel sprung behind him. Edward raced along the track, balling his hands, his feet churning up loose gravel. Straining, he reached out for the stairs that ran down the side of a wooden boxcar. His ankle screamed, and, for a panicked moment, he saw himself wrapped around the unforgiving steel wheels. Righting himself, he lunged at the ladder. His left hand curled around the bottom rung.

"*Arrgh!*" The train jerked his arm nearly out of its socket as he stumbled to catch up to his white grip. He gritted his teeth and hauled his other hand up to the rung. He tripped, and the train dragged him like a sack of potatoes. His shoulders screamed, and the wheels sucked at his legs.

"Edward!" He heard Pavel's cry but couldn't look back. With a groan, he pulled himself toward the bar. Working his hands up, he slowly cleared the wheel's jaws. The cold wind whipped his face and tore at his clothes. He looked behind him, hoping to spot Pavel.

The train bed was empty. "Pavel!" His breath seized in his chest. Had Pavel gone under? He doubled over, feeling raw and exhausted. If he hadn't taken the partisan along, the Russian would still be alive. He should have known Pavel was too thin, too weak to survive this trip. Frustration drove him up the ladder to the top of the boxcar.

"You've done this before, huh?" Pavel sat, legs straddling the middle seam, the wind parting his hair from behind. The crazy grin on his face made Edward want to topple him off and make him start again.

"Glad to see you." He sat down opposite Pavel, breathing hard. His left arm screamed where he'd pulled a muscle, and sweat trickled down his chest. The wind was chilling it fast. "We need to get inside."

Pavel nodded. "I think I saw an open door a few cars up."

Edward followed him, balancing like a drunk down the boxcar. They climbed down the end ladder, leaped the coupling, and climbed up the next boxcar. Pavel peered around the side and nodded at him. "This is it!"

Leaning over the side, Edward groaned. No side ladder. "We'll have to go over the top." They inched along the roof seam. The wind flattened Edward's wool pants to his legs and ran cold fingers through his grimy hair. His hands broke out in a sweat as he scooted down on his stomach and slid over the edge. Dangling by his numb fingertips, he swung into the cavern of the boxcar like a trapeze artist. Pavel followed and landed with a thump beside him.

"I've never had so much fun," the Russian said, grinning.

Edward's muscles knotted in relief as he leaned his head against the cold wood of the boxcar. Exhaustion strummed his nerves, and he was cold to the bone. Eight hours of walking had netted them fifteen kilometers and a safe jumping-on place, but they still had a country to cross and Jerries to dodge while doing it. He pulled out a compass.

"What's that for?" Pavel watched the needle quiver, then settle on north. The train arrowed west.

"I need to know when to get off. When we start heading south for a long chunk of time, we'll ditch this ride and find another." Edward snapped the compass shut and slipped it into his coat pocket. "Hungry?"

"Famished. I could eat a wooly mammoth."

Edward harrumphed and dug into his rucksack. He'd packed enough potatoes to last them a week and hoped they would find a squirrel or rabbit, but the season seemed late. For now, he opened a C-ration. "Kasha." He made a face.

"Give it to me." Pavel reached out and eagerly took the tin. Edward dug back in the bag and found a rag-wrapped potato that he'd roasted in the fire last night. Even cold, it filled his empty belly and calmed the beast roaring within.

Estonia, with its lush pine forests cut by farmland and meadow, rolled by in a sea of brown and green. Unlike Poland, Estonia and the other Baltic states were fairly free of Hitler's scourge. First taken by the Russians and then conquered by the Germans, the Estonians, a fiercely independent bunch, looked at their new invader as liberators. Edward's only allies came from the now-trapped Russians who supplied him with a solid force of freedom fighters. He prayed they were still alive in the forests outside Tallinn.

The man he really hoped to contact was Stone. His director would need some serious convincing, but the man owed him a few favors, and Edward had more than earned his leave time. To clear the road for this plan, Edward was counting on the fact that Stone had a wife of his own and a grandchild on the way. The thought of Magda and her baby meeting his parents, swallowed in his mother's ample hug, learning how to tend the family farm in Schenectady slid a smile on his face. He'd always wanted to return, and, perhaps with a wife, the homecoming would be easier. Maybe then, his peace-loving Mennonite parents would forgive him for choosing to face Hitler with a gun as well as a prayer.

"This is good." Pavel ran his grimy finger around the inside of the can, cleaning the last bit of porridge. "My babushka's was better, but this will do, especially coming from the good ole '*Sa-Shaw-Ah.*'"

At Pavel's use of slang for USA, Edward angled him a look. "My babushka's kasha would bring a grown man to his knees, begging."

"You had a *babushka*?"

"How do you think I learned Russian?" Edward blew on his hands. "She never spoke anything but her native language. If I wanted to talk to her, I had to do it in the right tongue."

"What was your Russian *baba* doing in America?" Pavel stretched out and crossed his legs.

"She came over shortly after my parents with a group of Mennonites from Hierschau. She didn't want to leave, even though my mother and father begged her to come. Baba Tonya just couldn't leave her beloved Russia—until the Bolsheviks starting killing the Mennonites who wouldn't fight."

"Isn't Hierschau in Ukraine? I think I remember hearing about it when I worked on the collective farm."

"Yes." Edward watched his hands. "It's by the Black Sea. Someday I'd like to visit—to see my grandfather's grave."

"How'd he die?"

"Some sort of raid. The Red Army stormed their village, looking for a group of young men who had refused to fight. They were Mennonites and, of course, didn't believe in violence. Still, Lenin and his crew thought they could force them to go against their beliefs."

"I remember hearing such stories." Pavel drew his legs up and hooked his elbows around his knees. "Instead of defending themselves, they would barricade themselves in a house and refuse to come out. As I recall, the Reds fired many such houses."

"My grandmother and the other women were across the street, hiding in a cellar, when the Reds stormed through their village. They watched their fathers and husbands die for their faith."

"Some got away. Even snuck out of the country and headed for America. Your babushka must have been one of those."

"*Da*. She stayed with family for a while; then when my mother settled, she came to New York and moved in with us."

"And you came back to Russia." Pavel chuckled wryly.

Edward rubbed his eyes. "I didn't plan to."

"Well, God prepared you all those years ago for a reason. He certainly equipped you for the job."

"I don't know. I have to wonder if I'm doing any good. I signed up with the OSS to keep tabs on Hitler. I heard about what he was doing to the Jews and it made me sick—especially after hearing my grandmother's stories of religious persecution in Russia. But I never dreamed He'd send me to Russia."

"Or to Magda."

Edward stared at him.

"I see the way you watch her. You hover like a mother—or a husband. You're more worried about that baby than she is. If I didn't know better, I'd think you were the father."

Edward's jaw pinched. "I'm not."

Pavel lifted a hand. "Of course not. But the baby needs one."

Edward could only close his eyes, feeling Pavel's words. "I know." He dug his hands through his hair, feeling the grime and crust of the past few days, and wished he could have stayed behind with Magda. He'd give a clean bed and a shower to have this mission over, to see her safe in Schenectady. Frustration clogged his throat. "I have a plan."

"A plan?"

He met Pavel's curious gaze. "I'm going to bring her out. After this mission, I'm going home. I want to bring Magda with me."

Pavel nodded, suddenly serious. "Why do you call her that?"

"Magda? I thought she needed a different name. Mara only makes her cling to bitterness. Magda means strength. She needs that image right now."

"You're a wise man, American Edward."

"Not wise. Never wise." Edward couldn't look at him. If Pavel only knew. He wondered if Pavel ever thought with his emotions, ever made mistakes that cost lives. Pavel was a healer, a man who offered life through his hands. What did Edward offer? Death.

He stared at his hands, seeing stain. Guilt rose in his throat. What good could God do with a man committed to war? *Edward, do you love Me?*

The voice rumbled through him, like the motion of the

195

train. He felt it more than heard it, but answered with a nod. *You know I do, Lord.*

Then feed My lambs.

He frowned and looked out past the fields and the scrape of forest to the azure sky, where his heavenly Father watched. He put a hand over his chest and rubbed.

"I'm a noodle. I gotta get some sleep." Pavel curled into a ball, his rucksack beneath his head. "When we have to jump, just drag my carcass off, *pashalysta.*"

His eyes closed, but a smile tweaked his whiskered face.

Edward watched the terrain skim by and prayed for Madga, God's lamb.

<hr>

Marina felt like a snowman, dressed as she was in three layers of sweaters, the ratty coat lined with sheep's wool, and two pairs of pants under a brown woolen skirt. But at least she was warm. She stood at the corner of a chipped cement building, watching a clump of German soldiers jostle each other as they lined up in front of a milk cart. Behind them in the yard of a kindergarten, more Germans, some in officers' uniforms, lounged on seesaws and swings like overgrown children. Her gaze traveled farther down the main street to the rubble of the administration building and the charred remains of the cultural center.

"Over there, behind the milk cart." The old woman beside her pointed with a fat finger. "Peek in the door, offer them this." She handed over the baked *peroshke,* filled with dried prunes and wrapped in a dingy white cloth. "Maybe the woman is inside."

Marina took the bread in her knit-gloved hands. The babushka placed her calloused hands on Marina's cheeks.

Her brown eyes seemed to reach out and embrace her.

"Baba Nina, how can I thank you?"

The old woman had more guts than her entire partisan unit, and Marina could hardly believe her good fortune. Perhaps Edick's prayer for her was taking effect.

"It's you we must thank, *Devochka*. Your bravery will save Russia." Baba Nina pulled her face down and gave her a wet kiss. Warmth ran through Marina's spirit at the kind gesture. First breakfast—Baba Nina had shoved nearly an entire pot of mashed potatoes down her throat, along with a goodly amount of canned tomatoes—then the woman had filled Marina to her ears with spicy tea that chipped the chill out of her weary bones. Finally, the old woman had pulled up a rickety stool, took both her hands in her own, and asked, "Why did you come here?"

Marina couldn't lie to eyes that reached into her soul. "I'm not sure. I thought I was here to kill someone. . .but now. . ."

Baba Nina didn't even blink. She patted Marina's hand. "I see." Rising, she'd refilled Marina's cup. "Now, tell me about your baby."

Surrendering to the same magnetic force, Marina unrolled the story of Dmitri, their short marriage, her pregnancy, her new life as a partisan, and finally Edick.

"This Edward—he loves God."

Marina nodded. "How did you know?"

Baba Nina set the pot down on a ratty, knitted hot pad. "Because any man who can love another man's child as his own must be a man after God's heart. God knows all about adoption."

Marina bit her lip, mentally tracing Edick's strong face, feeling his tender touch on her stomach. She nodded.

"So, you must find this Raina?"

"I have a bad feeling about her."

Baba Nina nodded. "So do I. Now, come with me. My husband's clothes will make you warm again. That baby is liable to freeze inside you with this winter coming. I can feel it in my joints—we're in for cold."

Baba Nina waddled through her tiny house, clucking to the small child who peeked from the door. Marina followed, then paused, enraptured by the wide brown eyes. She crouched and eased the door open. *"Privyet."*

The child shrank from her, eyeing the gun propped against the table. Marina grimaced, then reached out and took the child's hand. She placed it on her stomach. A slow smile broke across her face. "Do you have a name?" Marina asked.

"Nadezhda." Hope.

"That's a beautiful name for a beautiful little girl." Marina ran a hand down the chubby, soft cheek, giving into a foreign, tender impulse.

"This is my daughter's child." Baba Nina set a hand on her shoulder. "My Sveta was murdered by the Germans only a month ago." She squeezed Marina's shoulder, and Marina couldn't help but notice the slight tremble and tears that rimmed her eyes. "This is the first word Nadia has spoken since her mother's death."

Oh. Betrayed of words, Marina could only cup Nadezhda's cheek. *What a sweet, innocent child. At least she had a grandmother.* A sharp grief nipped at her heart. If she died, who would watch over her child?

Her throat thick, she rose and followed Baba Nina. The old woman opened a tiny hatch in her floor and descended into the cellar. Marina climbed down behind her into the darkness, lit only by the glow through uneven floorboards.

The damp, earthy smell and the gentle humming of the elderly woman yanked Marina back in time. She felt, for a shallow moment, she was with her mother, hauling potatoes from the cellar for supper. Tears pricked her eyes. Yulia knew just what to say, how to say it. And she had the faith of a saint. Why didn't some of that steadfast faith trickle down to her daughter? Why was Marina's soul so bereft?

On the street, the cold wind chilling tears on her cheeks, she stared into Baba Nina's face and longed to borrow some of the babushka's calm. Nina squeezed her face between her field-strong hands. "Now you go quickly, and don't let on to those Germans that you've got a gun under that skirt." Her brown eyes misted. "Go with God, my *lapichka*."

Marina's throat felt wooly as she nodded. "Thank you, again."

"Shoo!" the old woman admonished, but her face creased into a smile.

Marina turned and strode out into the street, keeping her head down but searching for Raina. A uniformed German leered at her as he smoked a cigarette. Two more surveyed her over tins of milk. She skirted a group of soldiers who sat on the treads of a green Panzer parked with its turret facing north toward Moscow. The high sun glinting off a black, tri-mounted mortar launcher rattled her nerve, but she forced herself past it.

She reached the milk cart and then paused, looking into the shadowed doorway of the kindergarten building. A lanky soldier leaned against the door, a black Lugar on his hip. He surveyed her with a look of disgust. She clenched her jaw and fought for a humble pose. She hoped he thought her a sixty-year-old babushka, with her layers of clothes and the bulky wool stocking cap and scarf. She hunched her shoulders and added a shuffle to her walk, holding out the bread like an offering.

He moved to let her pass, but his eyes burned on her neck. She stepped into the foyer, and a chill filtered through her layers to her bones.

She had played in these halls. Painted pictures of spring flowers—swipes of blue, red, and yellow splotched on dingy paper—hung on the kindergarten walls. A sickly looking spider fern dropped long brown curls around a mosaic planter. The acrid smell of cigarette smoke clung to the high ceiling. She followed the hum of voices and shuffled toward the music room to the right, where she'd learned tunes about Mother Russia and Father Lenin.

The room had been transformed into a war center. Against the wall, the piano had been buried with papers and cardboard folders. A samovar sizzled on a table near the window, steam billowing from the top and spraying the metal surface with water. Muddy footprints splotched the painted wooden floor. The Germans had gathered teachers' desks from the various classrooms and shoved them to the center of the room to hold maps, schedules, and mountains of paper. Officers dressed in riding pants and black boots clumped in groups, their chatter raising the hair on the back of Marina's neck. She started toward a group mingling in front of a grimy window.

How she hoped she wasn't being stupid, walking right into the lions' den for a glimpse of a traitor. But she'd seen Raina march into town without a hint of fear. And the way she'd watched the partisans with a razor gaze, cutting through them to their secrets, well, Marina couldn't abandon Pavel and Edick to an ambush.

Raina was a Nazi. Marina felt it clear through to her soul.

"Haltestelle! A soldier built like a Panzer blocked her path and raised a Lugar to her chin. She froze. The sniper rifle slapped against her leg, and she prayed they didn't see its outline. Thrusting the bread into his face, she smiled weakly. *Please, be hungry.* She ducked her head.

He ran his eyes over her. Finally, he stepped aside. Her breath uncoiled slowly as she strolled the room, offering the freshly baked *peroshke* to the officers while she searched for Raina. She peeked into the yard through the window but saw only soldiers, dressed in wool caps and bulky green jackets. She paused, squinting at one man as he sipped a tin of tea.

"Fräulein!" Marina turned, wide-eyed at the pinched face of a German colonel, the gold bars on his collar glinting like knives. *"Gehen!"* He pointed toward the entrance. She ducked her head and made for the door on legs that didn't seem solid.

Why had she thought Raina had come to this place? War had warped her instincts to believe that a fellow partisan—*someone Edick trusted*—would be in cahoots with the German fascists. She should be counting her blessings—and disappear into Siberia. She tucked the bread under her arm and stalked out of the door.

"Haltestelle!" The command made her stop as it was supposed to, and she whirled, taking a few wisps of spider plant with her. The German soldier by the music room door had his Lugar leveled at her.

Oh. Not good. Not only that, but as she weighed her

future, she watched another soldier, slight and with beautiful high cheekbones and hair tucked into a wool cap, step out from behind him.

"Magda," Raina said and smiled.

CHAPTER SIXTEEN

E dward kicked dirt onto his dying campfire and prayed the evidence of their rough campsite on the outskirts of Tapa, Estonia, wouldn't be easily discovered by a group of scouts. He didn't have time to do better. Worry drove him forward like a cattle driver's whip. He had to get to Tallinn. Today.

"Pavel, let's go." Edward shouldered his pack, two roasted potatoes still warm in the bottom, and pulled out his compass. Comparing it to his folded map, he turned his body northeast. "Hopefully, we'll run into the tracks just north of Tapa."

"More train jumping?" Pavel's tired face broke into a wry smile. "I'm getting pretty good."

Edward snapped his compass shut and flipped up the collar on his jacket. Looking up, he strained to make out the sun through the haze of fog that layered the forest and crept around birch and pine trees like a spirit of gloom.

Pavel tied his rucksack and shoved his Russian pistol in his belt. "Have you gotten through to your colonel yet?"

Edward shook his head, frustration knotting his neck muscles. His radio seemed to be working. . .but he'd yet to receive an answer to his attempts to contact Stone or the partisan group he'd left behind. Precious time edged away as he tromped through these woods. Winter stalked the eastern front in Russia, and if he wanted to sharpen its bite, the Velikaya Bridge had to go.

The sun climbed higher, eating off the fog and licking warmth into his bones as they hiked toward Tapa. Few words passed between them. Fatigue and hunger warred with their reserves of energy. Edward chose a path around Tapa that intersected with the railroad tracks northeast of the city, where they cut through a patch of thick balsam and spruce forest. He stopped under the branches of a wide pine and dug into his pack until he pulled out a soggy, yet still warm potato. He and Pavel ate in silence, their ears straining for an approaching train.

"I'm not going back to Pskov with you, Edward," Pavel announced in a low tone. He rolled his potato between two grimy fingers. "I'm going straight to Voru."

"No." Edward took a long swig of river water from his canteen, then wiped his mouth with his sleeve. "I can't contact you that way. How will I know when the train's coming?"

"I've been studying the map. The Pechory station is the last stop before the Velikaya Bridge. They'll be looking for trouble there. But the bomb could be planted at Voru. I was there once for a medical conference. I know the town and the station. I think I even know a place where I can jump on." He grinned at Edward. "Learned from a pro."

Edward didn't return the smile. "I don't want you on that train when it goes up."

"I'll get off at Pechory."

Edward ran the back of his hand under his jaw. A week's growth of whiskers scraped at his cold skin. "I should be the one hopping the train and planting the bomb. It's my mission."

Pavel popped the last bite of potato in his mouth.

"Well, I've been praying about that. I'm not so sure."

"You've been talking with Colonel Stone?"

"Nope, God. I think you need to go back for Magda."

Edward watched the doctor study his dirty fingernails and weighed his words. "I've been praying about that, too."

"And?"

Edward shook his head. "Pavel, the thing is, I've got a history of not using my head when it comes to women. These past few days, I've been thinking. Perhaps her situation simply sucked me in and made me think I could help." He traced her image in his mind, her burnished blond hair blowing in the wind, the glow in her beautiful eyes as the baby grew inside her. His throat thickened.

"I can't do anything to help her. My mission isn't to drag a pregnant woman out of Russia. I have to stay focused on the goal." The words tasted like steel in his mouth. Magda had gouged a place into his heart, and the thought of leaving her behind made him hurt right in the center of his chest. But five days skirting German troops like a rabbit had helped clear his mind. Magda was better off in Russia than with an OSS agent committed to victory. Besides, he had penance to pay for his mistakes, and Edward would serve his time behind enemy lines until a German bullet sent him home.

Pavel continued to study his hands. "Maybe you have the wrong goal, Edick."

A crunch of pine needles behind them sent Edward to his feet. Grabbing his Colt, he backed into the shelter of the wide fir. A low-hanging branch brushed at his cap and spread sap along his neck. The forest seemed clear—filled with furry pine and the whisper of ocean wind from the north. Edward held his breath.

Like shadows, figures moved out from behind the

trees, men dressed in brown suede coats and stocking caps drawn low over their ears. Edward two-handed his gun and leveled it at a burly Estonian who had pointed an American Tommy at Pavel's chest.

Marina awoke for the fifth day to the dim light shafting through a gutter window into the storage cellar of the kindergarten. She rubbed her hands over her upper arms, thankful for the layers they'd allowed her to keep, even if Raina did steal her sniper rifle.

She should probably be doing some sort of jig that she still lived and hadn't been shot at dusk in the middle of the very schoolyard where she'd learned to play hopscotch.

The sharp odor of coal saturated the room and seeped into her pores. Hunger gnawed at her, and she longed for some of Baba Nina's bread. During the past five days, scraps of food had been tossed in, and someone had left a bowl of murky water for her to drink like a dog. Oddly, however, they hadn't interrogated her. Raina probably already knew everything, anyway. Still, why hadn't they killed her?

Perhaps they'd forgotten about her.

God certainly had.

The Lord heals the brokenhearted and binds up their wounds. Pavel's voice hummed in the back of her mind. She shook free of it before she shook her fist at the Almighty.

It wasn't that she didn't believe. It was just. . .well, God hadn't necessarily been on her side. Ever. Forsaken at birth, she'd grown up without a father, been abandoned by her husband, and now even Edick, the man who claimed to love her, had left her for the wolves, preferring his mission over her safety.

Yeah, God had been pretty clear in communicating just how He felt about her.

She moved toward the wooden door and banged on it with a gloved hand. "I'm hungry!" The only reply was the thump of movement inside her womb. She covered her stomach with her hand. "Sorry, baby. I know you're hungry, too." She banged again. Sooner or later they'd have to remember they had a hostage in the basement. And sooner rather than later, she was going to have this baby. She went cold at the thought. She still had a month left—but her body felt odd, as if the baby had shifted and lodged lower. And wouldn't that just be wonderful. Or poetically poignant. Giving birth alone on the floor of a coal cellar.

She slapped the door with an open palm. "Please!"

The sound of a key clicking in the lock made her freeze. She backed away, eyes wide, as the door opened. A Panzer-sized guard stood in the entry. Eyeing her with menace, he stepped back, and Raina swept in past him. Her hair, clean and bright, was slicked back in a harsh bun. Dressed in a pair of green wool trousers and a gray wool sweater, she carried a cup of tea. Steam snaked from the surface, and the spicy aroma reached out and clawed at Marina's hunger. Raina's cold blue eyes raked Marina up and down, settling on her stomach. Marina hugged her womb and stepped back. She fought to find her voice, summoning anger to do so.

"Traitor!" she spat.

Raina smiled.

"What do you want?"

Raina held out the cup of tea. Marina stared at it in disbelief. Her own body betrayed her as she reached out and took it. Eyes on Raina, she drank it, feeling like Judas but gulping it down despite the burn in her throat.

"Feel better?" Raina's Russian had improved. Marina narrowed her eyes and slowly nodded.

"Good. Now, tell me how Edward is going to blow up the bridge."

Marina stiffened.

Raina rolled her eyes. "Don't tell me you don't know. I spent a month with you. I know Edward thinks he is in love with you. And he just doesn't know his own weakness when it comes to love." She smiled slyly. "He loves to share his deepest secrets when he is holding a woman in his arms."

Marina felt sick. She backed away and felt the scrub of the wall on her neck. "He didn't tell me anything."

"Nothing?" Raina crept up to her, dark gaze locked with Marina's. She put a hand on Marina's enlarged belly. "Not even when you were making his baby?"

Marina slapped her.

Fury engulfed Raina's eyes. Her face twisted as she palmed her cheek. "Too bad he won't live to see it."

"What?"

Raina backed away. "He'll come back for you." She gave a slight smile. "I'll be waiting for him."

"Why didn't you just kill us all when you invaded our camp?" Tears burned in Marina's eyes, and she hated herself for them.

Raina smiled. "Because I had to know how extensive your partisan unit was. Unfortunately, I think Natasha was the only one left." She folded her hands. "And she claimed not to know Edward's plans, either. What a pity."

Marina's jaw trembled. "Your own daughter died at the hands of the Nazis!"

Raina laughed. "Irina was never my daughter. She was

a very useful pawn, the peasant child of two stupid Poles. My husband is a commander in the Third Reich, and my son is a member of the Nazi Children Corps."

"And you're a spy."

"Not a spy—a partisan, from Germany. I'm fighting Germany's war against traitors like Edward Neumann. Men who organize resistance against the Führer and the glorious Third Reich." She rubbed her hand over her smooth hair. "I've been tracking Edward since Berlin."

"You knew Edward in Berlin?"

"I was part of the SS unit that tracked him to his traitorous Katrina. I watched him run when the SS descended, and I knew then I was tracking a coward."

"Edick's no coward. He loved her."

Raina shrugged. "He should have died with her. Instead, she faced the firing squad—alone."

"He grieves her still."

"Good. Cowards should suffer."

Marina flinched. The cold gleam in Raina's eyes filtered to her bones. "So, why kill him now? You've been tracking him so long. . . ."

Raina smiled. "He's outlived his usefulness. We almost had him in Poland, and he eluded us. Before, he was an easy way to track down partisan units and other OSS soldiers. But the partisan force in Poland is destroyed and your force. . ." She shrugged.

Marina closed her eyes, and faces traveled through her mind—Lydia, Lev, Sasha. . .

When she opened her eyes, Raina was backing away. "You weren't even a worthy adversary, Russian scum." She spit on Marina. "Time to die." Raina whirled and stalked out the door.

"Drop the gun, Neumann." Colonel Stone stepped out of the blur of forest, his gun panning away from its aim on Pavel.

Edward nearly collapsed with relief. "Colonel." He sheathed his weapon, saluted, then closed the gap between them in three quick strides. Stone met him halfway with a firm handshake. "You're a sight for sore eyes."

Like apparitions, partisans materialized from the forest. Edward locked hands with Ravik, a dark-featured Russian built like a boar. "Keeping everyone alive?"

Ravik laughed and hit him hard on the back. Edward nearly toppled to his knees.

A dark-haired Pole set a shiny black Thompson SMG on his shoulder and held out a bony hand. *"Privyet,* Captain."

Edward took Marek's grip. "Good to see you back on your feet."

The unit had grown, from the count of the gaunt, fierce faces. "I see you've been busy behind the lines, Colonel," Edward said, indicating the armory of the assembled crowd. "We could use some of those Tommies on the eastern front."

Stone nodded, his lips a thin line on his wide face. "We're working on that." He shot a look at Pavel, standing slightly behind Edward.

Edward followed his gaze. "This is Pavel. He's helping me with a few details." He ran a hand behind his neck, kneading a tense muscle. "How'd you find us?"

"For pity's sake, Neumann, you're calling the entire countryside on your little walkie-talkie." Stone shook his head. "My transmitter's busted, and I had to stop you before you had a chat with the Krauts."

Edward made a wry face. "Sorry."

Stone lifted a hand. "Tell me what you know."

Edward hauled up his pack and slung it over his shoulder. "How far are we from some grub?"

The colonel led him northeast. As the day wore on, the sun began to drop into the western sky and gilded the clouds, frosting the horizon with crimson. A strange uneasiness pricked Edward's spirit. It became physical and churned his stomach. Pavel marched quietly behind him as if he, too, sensed it. Even when they came upon the partisan encampment, secreted deep under a canopy of pines, Edward felt little relief.

"Not hungry, Captain?"

Edward pushed his squirrel stew around in his tin. "Famished, actually, but I think food is just going to rot in my gut."

Stone steepled his fingers, setting his elbows on his knees. Dressed in camouflage-green parka pants, a matching coat, and wool hat with the flaps dangling down like a lop-eared rabbit, he looked the part of retired general on site to survey the lines. "Shell-shocked, Captain?" He tapped his fingers together in rhythm. "I could send Richards in. He's down in Byelorussia."

The idea of Bull Bill Richards taking over his plans, walking into his group, making friends with Natasha, holding Magda's baby— "No. I don't have combat fatigue."

Stone raised his gray-streaked eyebrows.

Edward rubbed his fingers under his eyes, concealing the twitch under his left eye with his thumb. "I'm just worried about someone."

Stone pursed his lips. "So, how are the Russians holding up? We've had some recruits here—soldiers caught behind the lines when the Germans stormed through

Estonia. Even some Poles made it up."

"Yeah, Raina said she tracked you. She's been with us a couple weeks."

"Raina?" Stone stared at his palm as if reading it. "That Pole with the daughter? I thought she never made it back."

Edward watched Stone rub his palm with his thumb. "I thought so, too. She said she checked in here—and you told her what I was up to."

Stone shook his head. "Never saw her. But then again, I've been in and out. Got a sub patrolling the coast, keeping tabs of Finnish mines."

Edward chewed his lower lip. "Well, she's helping. And I have two more women—Russians—eager to help send the Jerries packing."

"So, is this person you're worried about one of the partisan women?"

Edward winced and looked out toward the forest, where the firelight dissolved into night. "She saved my life. Now she's about to have a baby."

Stone hummed.

Around them, men and women had collected the dishes. Without caves, they'd dug bunkers in the cold ground and would pull blankets of bushy branches over the top, concealing their beds with fir. Edward didn't relish crawling into a hole. Even a damp stone cave seemed a better sleeping pad than a dirty foxhole.

The soft darkness of dusk layered the forest. Stone's face took on an angular boldness in the erratic glow of the fire. A cold, salty wind filled the silence. Edward saw Pavel rise and tuck himself under the arms of an ancient pine. So he didn't like the holes, either.

"I don't want to pry about what happened in Berlin,

Edward. You have your demons, I know, over Katrina's death. But it wasn't your fault."

In the darkness, Edward winced. Regret speared him, remembering her steely gray expression in front of the firing squad. He'd wished, at that moment, he'd been captured with her. Why had he left? The mission. He had papers, information to deliver. But even worse, why had he gone to her in the first place? Couldn't he guess the SS would be following him? He had only his impulsive, untamed emotions to blame. He'd missed her so much that desperation drove him to her hiding place, intending to beg her to leave immediately. He had wanted to save her. He'd killed her instead. He dug his hands into his grimy hair, feeling dirty down to his soul.

"I am to blame."

Stone blew out a breath. "Sometimes, when we are so close to a situation, it is hard to see it clearly. You were followed, yes. But Katrina loved you. Do you think she was sorry to see you?"

"If she'd only known the consequences—"

"She knew. She wanted to see you. She'd already begged me to send you."

Edward shot him a look. "She wouldn't have if she knew it meant her death." He squinted at Stone in the dim light.

"Katrina was a patriot, willing to give her life for her country. But she also loved you enough to risk her freedom, her life, for that love."

"No," Edward groaned, unable to hear the truth. "It wasn't worth it."

"What wasn't worth it? The risk? The love?"

"The grief." Edward's eyes burned. "Love isn't worth the grief."

Stone began to twirl his ring around his finger, staring into the fire. "I know you're a religious man, Edward. Me, I'm a good Catholic, but Mrs. Stone does the praying for us. You remind me of St. Peter. Headstrong, sometimes impulsive, passionate." He reached out and clamped his hand on Edward's knee. "According to my Bible, God used such a man to build a great faith."

He rose, slapping his hands on his thighs. "I think I'm going to sleep under the stars. I'm with Pavel. . .I just can't abide those holes. Makes me feel like a mole."

Edward watched him disappear into the envelope of night, then scrubbed a weary hand over his face. Was love worth the price? And how could God use a man stirred by his heart instead of his head? He slid down to the ground, leaned his head back on a log, and watched the stars pierce a velvet sky. *God, please protect Magda and her baby.* The thought of losing them cut a swath so wide in his heart, he gasped. With a shudder, he closed his eyes and let his memory run over the image of Magda. Her blond hair the color of polished oak running like silk between his fingers; the smell of her skin, earthy, spicy with a hint of pine drawing through him like a fragrance; her stormy blue eyes that loosed all the anchors holding down his heart. Her courage, despite the burden in her body. She'd reached out beyond her loss to trust him.

He didn't deserve her trust. Yet, for the first time since Katrina's death, he felt alive. Magda made him feel alive. He palmed his chest, pushing against the glorious ache inside.

It was foolishness to think he could leave her behind. Whether or not it was God's plan, he would bring her out of Russia. Or die trying.

CHAPTER SEVENTEEN

Marina shivered in the filmy darkness of her cell, unable to break free of the cold fist clutching her soul. Raina's words echoed though her mind, and every footstep she heard above her, every dent in the shadow streaming through the tiny cellar window turned her blood cold. Her stomach ached, and the baby hadn't moved for so long, she knew something must be wrong.

She stretched her legs and closed her eyes, willing her heart to stop the relentless pounding. Why hadn't they come for her? Why didn't they simply shoot her in the cell? What were they waiting for? Dawn?

She clenched her teeth and tasted tears. She didn't bother to wipe them away. Instead, she surrendered to them, bowing her head and letting sobs shake her body. The tears dripped off her chin. She felt shredded from the inside out. She grieved for her child, yet it was the emptiness in her own soul that terrified her. Dmitri and God would welcome her baby—but who would welcome her?

She pressed her fingertips to her eyelids. "Go with God," Baba Nina had said. And Pavel, the soft voice of faith in her head—*The Lord delights in those who fear Him, who put their hope in His unfailing love.* Marina reached inside her coat to a place next to her skin and tugged out her bent photograph. Her two mothers stared at her, eyes unseeing. She traced her finger across Yulia's face.

Don't forget God loves you. Edick's words wrapped around her like an embrace. She bowed her head, wishing she might have a fragment of his faith.

Yeah, if God didn't love her before, He certainly wasn't going to look her direction now, with the sins embedded in her heart. After all, she'd *killed* people. Willingly.

A thump outside the door stopped her heart in her chest. She tucked away the picture and stiffened as light streamed under the door. Then the door opened, and the light filled her eyes. She flinched and shielded her gaze.

"*Fstavai!*" a low voice said in warped Russian. The guard lowered his flashlight until the stream pooled on the black floor. Marina's gaze riveted to the rifle held at his side.

Please. She wasn't ready. *No.* Her muscles refused to obey. Paralyzed, she watched him stride over and grab her upper arm. Pain streaked into her shoulder as he yanked her to her feet and manhandled her out the door. Her feet were wooden, tripping over themselves, stumbling on the cement stairs, and shuffling as he yanked her through the kindergarten halls she'd played in. She no longer felt her heart beating, just a terrible roar in her ears.

He pulled her out the front door. The cold hit her like a slap and snapped her out of her stupor. She kicked at him, screaming, crying, clawing at the hand that held her arm. He wrestled her down the dark street and past soldiers who regarded her in the pale glow of cigarette embers. When her energy withered, despair sent claws into her heart. She bit her lip, fighting tears, and let the soldier drag her to her death.

He rounded the end of the building and pulled her into

the alley. *This is it. He's going to shoot me and let me die in the dirt.* She curled her free hand over her stomach.

The soldier didn't stop, however, but muscled her through the alley and into the next street, where the burned outlines of houses jutted into the steel blue of the night sky. A thousand stars twinkled at her, and a gust of wind lifted her grimy hair from her sweaty neck.

"Where are we going?"

The guard didn't answer. He summoned her down the street through another alley and another, until they came to the western edge of town. Ahead of her, a barren potato field glistened like an ocean. Weakness rushed through Marina, and her legs threatened to give.

The guard released her. She fell to the ground and crawled away, wondering when the shot would rip through her body. Silence behind her made her glance at the guard.

His dark eyes were on her. His helmet had been pushed back so she could see blond hair poking out like spikes. A muscle pulled in his jaw. He raised the gun to hip level, and the barrel gleamed in the moonlight.

Marina lifted her chin, met his eyes.

"*Gehen,*" he said, but his voice dropped, becoming almost. . .gentle.

She couldn't guess what this final command might be—this last word she would hear.

"*Gehen,*" he said again. This time, he lowered the gun.

She slid back. He pointed at the forest beyond the field. Marina followed his gesture.

Did. . .he want her to run?

"*Gehen.*"

She froze, sickened. Was he going to take target practice? She scrambled to her feet, kicking dirt, her stomach cramping. She turned toward the field.

"*Gehen!*" he repeated and pointed over the fields. She shook her head, afraid that the first step she took, she'd be mowed into the dirt.

His jaw clenched, but his eyes lost their menacing texture. He made a gesture with one hand, rounding it over his stomach. Then he lifted his hand, and moonlight illuminated a gold wedding band. "*Gehen.*"

Run?

Da. Marina took off in a full run through the field. Cramps streamed down her legs. The wind burned her tear-stained cheeks, but she didn't slow or turn back. She half-expected the punch of a bullet, but she reached the woods on the far side without an enemy slug in her back. Scrambling behind an oak tree, she dragged in searing breaths and clung to the bark, peering across the field at the bulk of shadow that was the guard. He seemed to be staring up, watching the sky. Then he turned and peered in her direction. She shrank into the tree.

The German guard raised his gun and fired it into the sky. The shot echoed against the night. Barren.

Freeing.

Marina fell to her knees and sobbed.

A pale moon hung against the western sky, fading as the dawn gilded the east. Edward gripped the sides of his seat, wondering how Stone had ever talked him into this battered World War I relic. The sun polished the canvas wings of the biplane a flame red, which did nothing to ease the tension coiling in his gut.

The wind whipped the leather strap of his flight hood

into his mouth as Edward craned his head. He caught a glimpse of Pavel in the backseat of the second Russian Polikarpov Po-2 biplane. Pavel's mouth flattened into a grim line, both hands clutched the sides of his cockpit, and his gaze was turned heavenward as if beseeching God to save him from Stone's terrible plan.

Yeah, Edward knew exactly how Pavel felt. He shot his own look heavenward. Suddenly, his plane tipped, belly west, and veered eastward, toward Russia. Pavel's plane headed south on a straight course toward the final leg of the mission. Edward fingered the latch on his parachute pack, sending up a fervent prayer that Pavel had actually been listening to the quick course in parachuting and not been as stunned as he looked.

He pulled on his front pack, filled with more C-rations, ammo, and a spanking new radio detonator, set to a frequency to match the device Pavel carried. He had enough supplies to get in, blow the bridge, and escape. Edward mentally marked the location of Stone's pickup off the coast of Estonia in the Gulf of Finland.

Poor Pavel had the brunt of the mission. Drop into Voru, board the train, set the C-3, and jump off near Pechory without being shot. All Edward had to do was detonate the bomb once the train mounted the Velikaya Bridge.

Edward also carried an American passport with the name Margaret Neumann. He needed pictures, but Stone would obtain those once on board a US destroyer heading toward the base in England. There would be plenty of time to get into port, marry Magda, and settle her in a clean, safe English hospital for delivery.

A buoyant smile touched his lips. Good old Stone had

read right into his heart, abandoned his rigid code, and granted Edward his only request in three years. He prayed this time the foray that followed his emotions would lead to happiness rather than tragedy.

"Almost there, sir! Get ready!" The words were screamed over the propeller noise. He had to admit to a moment of worry when he'd climbed in behind the woman pilot, but when Stone introduced her as Lieutenant Tupolov in the Russian 588th Women's Night Bomber Regiment, a night pilot with more than a hundred hours of air time who'd been caught behind enemy lines, he forced fear into submission. It was easier than arguing with the square-faced woman who looked like she could tie him around her propeller.

He strapped on the front pack, tightening it hard around his waist, and felt for the ripcord on his parachute pack. *Please, O God, no holes, no tangles, no trees!*

The biplane sank low beneath the clouds. Below, fields spread out like a patchwork quilt—lime green, pale yellow, and dirty brown, with a tattered edging of stripped-bare trees.

"Ten kilometers to the east, sir!" Lieutenant Tupolov screamed. Edward could barely make out the Velikaya River cutting a swath through the forest as if God had troughed it out with a lazy finger.

"Right!" His adrenaline buzzed into high gear.

"Go, sir, before we attract flak!"

Edward stood on his seat, his legs suddenly feeling like rubber, and watched the world skim by below.

"Now!" Tupolov yelled.

Edward flung himself out of the plane, falling fast. The wind seared his face, glued his flight suit to his body. He felt his heart rip from the anchors in his chest. Clamping a lid on the first impulse of fear, he reactivated all his West Point training and laid out wide, then arrowed through the air toward a field. Clenching his teeth, he fingered the ripcord and yanked.

The chute tumbled out, opened with a snap, and yanked him up. He clutched the straps, waiting for a give, a hesitation that would tell him to release the silk and pull the second chute.

Nothing. His descent slowed, and he began to float as quietly as a summertime cloud.

⁂

Marina crouched behind a downed, mossy tree, barely breathing as she scoured what remained of the partisan camp. A cold, wet-charred campfire. The hollow cave. No whisper of movement. The air smelled of snow, and beneath her feet, the leaves had become mushy, absorbing sound like a sponge. Even the wind seemed ashamed to murmur.

Marina put a hand over her belly as it tensed. She winced, absorbing the pain. What if Raina had beaten her back and now hid inside the cave?

Nyet. Raina thought she was dead. The miracle of Marina's escape sent a shudder through her. Through the long night and into the first stretch of day, she'd replayed her good fortune over the past week—from warm clothes, still on her back, to a miraculous release by a German who had pity for her child. Despite the days locked in a coal cellar, she'd lived. She didn't have time to ponder the ramifications of this gift. She had precious little time to find Edick before Raina ambushed him.

If she hadn't already.

Sucking in courage, Marina scrambled over the log and crept toward the cave. She smelled the odor trickling from the entrance—blood, old and putrid. Marina steeled her nerve and entered.

Natasha had struggled. She lay in a heap in the dark corner of the cave, her pistol smashed a meter away from her white, stiff grip. Glassy eyes stared at the ceiling, and her tawny brown hair haloed a terrified expression. Gray-black bruises on her face evidenced she'd gone down in a fist-to-fist struggle. Against Raina? Marina clenched her jaw and turned away. Picking up a blanket, she draped it over Natasha's body. The sharp taste of grief filled her mouth, but she swallowed it and stalked out of the cave.

The ammunition and weapons were still safely tucked in a shallow of rock near the entrance. She grabbed Natasha's sniper rifle and a box of shells and tucked them in her pocket. Fighting panic, she lit out for the bridge, hoping Edick was still safely tucked in Estonia. For the first time since he left, she hoped he wouldn't be returning.

<hr/>

Edward landed hard, jamming his hip, but he remembered his training and rolled. The parachute followed in a puff. In seconds, he'd cut off the pack, pulled in the chute, and tucked the silk under his arm. The sun hung over the tree-tops, splashing golden light across the meadow where he landed. He made a painfully easy target should the Germans decide to check into that little white speck in the sky.

He raced for cover at the edge of the field.

He wadded his chute between two thick roots of an aged oak, then switched his pack to his back and buckled it around his waist. Adrenaline quickened his steps as he ran for the river and the partisan hideout. Only when he knew Magda was alive and well, baby in womb, would he resume his perch overlooking the bridge.

A late-season woodpecker, still stalking food, drilled in a far-off tree. The sound echoed through the forest like the *rat-a-tat-tat* of a German Erma. Only a week had passed, yet the anticipation of seeing Magda drove his heart before his steps. A pack of D rations—chocolate bars with vitamins—in the bottom of his bag was a poor but hopefully winning gift. He didn't feel an ounce of the eighty pounds he wore.

A hawk circled overhead, emitting a mournful wail in the chilly air. In its wake, the woodpecker drilled again. Edward smelled the fresh wind off the river to his east. He'd drifted near it, still safely far north of the bridge but with sufficient fear of the Jerries with field glasses he knew guarded the bridge. Antiair flak wasn't only used for planes—more than a few bloomer boys had gotten pipped while hitting the silks over Hun country. Edward had sent up his own barrage of prayers during his agonizing descent.

A cry laced the air. Edward stilled, remembering the night he'd picked up Raina. A lynx, perhaps, stalking him on this cold, wintry day. He laid a hand on his gun, found it trapped inside his flight suit, and cursed his forgetfulness. He should have shed the uniform and buried it with the parachute. Impatience had fogged his training. He wrestled with the zipper, eyes scanning the forest.

"Edward!" Pitched high and frantic, the voice seemed to come from all around him, the frozen trees refusing to absorb sound. He wrenched the zipper down, grabbed his gun, and then froze, wishing his heart would also.

Raina burst from a tangle of brush. Her face was pale and twisted in pain. She fell, then scrabbled toward him on all fours. He shoved his gun into his suit and ran to her, skidding to his knees in the wet leaves. "Raina, what happened?" She looked up and revealed the full extent of her agony. He winced at a dirty gash running from her left ear, down her jaw line. Twigs and leaves twined her hair. She climbed into his lap, clinging to him, weeping into his flight suit with wracking sobs.

"Did the Germans get you?"

She shook her head, leaning into him. His arms circled her, fear drying his mouth. "What?" he rasped.

"She betrayed us all," Raina whimpered into his collar.

"Who?" Dread squeezed the breath from his chest.

She leaned back, tears furrowed down her thin face. "Magda."

CHAPTER EIGHTEEN

The scrubbed-out area along the river where Edick had spent countless hours surveying the bridge still betrayed his lurking. Marina placed her hands into the soft wells where his elbow had dented the leaves and closed her eyes. She willed herself to stay calm, to focus, to figure out a way to intercept him. Her relief at not finding his massacred body in this spot shuddered out of her in a vicious tremble. Her body ached, and she needed food and water like air, but the urge to find Edick and warn him drove her more than physical need. Only a low, dull pain in her lower back made her pause in the damp leaves.

Out of habit, she lifted her gun and sighted the bridge. A squadron of Germans was barricaded on the eastern end. Their recently added tripod-mounted MG-42s peeped out like moles from a mud green metal hole. An impressive-looking twin-mounted *ack-ack* gun had been added to the top of the bunker, its guns sighting the skies for Russian day bombers or even America B-24 Liberators that dared to cross this deep into German occupation.

The Jerries were well stocked. Marina counted four more guards with shiny machine guns milling around the western end of the bridge. One had a cigarette dangling from his mouth. She watched smoke curl toward the cold sky. She exhaled a long, calming breath and nestled her gun down in her lap. *Edick, please, stay in Estonia where it's safe. You'll never blow this bridge.* She leaned her head against the tree. Fatigue settled on her eyelids, and in a moment she surrendered, curling into a ball in the dirt, clutching her rifle like a newborn.

***

Edward flinched at Raina's accusation. He wrapped his hands around her upper arms and eased her away from him. Stress rimmed her blue eyes, and tears trailed down her cheeks.

"Magda did this to you?" He could barely mouth the words, staring at the dirty gash on her face.

She nodded, her lower lip trembling. "She killed Natasha, and when I tried to stop her, she turned on me." She laid a bloody hand across her cheek. He stared at it, feeling ill.

"Is that Magda's blood?"

She stared at it, almost mournfully. "I think so."

He clenched his teeth, betrayal warring with fear. "How did you find me?"

"The plane. I've been watching for it."

If she saw the plane, the Germans had, also. His legs wobbled when he climbed to his feet. "Can you walk, Raina?"

She nodded. He pulled her up beside him. "I need to get you to a safe place." He curled an arm around her shivering shoulders. She slumped against him.

"Where?"

"I'll take you to the monastery. We have friends there who will help."

She leaned heavily against his side as they walked

through the forest. With each step, his chest ached. Magda, the betrayer. Killing Natasha. Attacking Raina? Acid lined his throat. How could Magda have done this? The answer defied comprehension. Was she working for the Germans?

A thousand images flooded into his mind, moments watching Magda taking aim, steel etched in her eyes. No, she hated the Third Reich. She had lost too much to betray them.

So why had she turned on Raina?

He snapped a twig.

The sound of a magazine rattling into a submachine gun made him still. Beside him, Raina froze. He reached inside his flight suit for the Colt and came up empty. He didn't have time to search—from behind a grove of aspen trees emerged the business end of a German Erma and attached to it a man two sizes too big for his uniform. Square jawed, with icy eyes and a firm-set mouth, he hip-aimed his weapon. Raina backed away, hands up, whirled, and ran.

"No!"

The soldier shot, and Raina slammed into the ground, falling into a gully and out of sight.

Fury launched Edward at the soldier. The German swung the weapon and cracked him across the jaw. Pain exploded in his head, and his knees buckled. He tasted blood. Another blow across the back of his head blurred his vision. The forest rushed up at him and sucked him into blackness.

The chatter of gunfire on the bridge brought Marina to consciousness. The sun glinted from the west, still high enough to warm her cheeks and send little shadows across her matted bed. She stretched out and touched the baby. Still no movement. It worried her, and she shook her belly slightly. "C'mon, baby, wake up." Her entire body ached, her lower back screamed, and the muscles in her thighs had turned board stiff.

More shots echoed through the riverbed. Wearily, she lifted her rifle and scoped the bridge. Two Germans were atop the flack gun, firing into the air as if shooting down birds. She cupped a hand over her eyes and scanned the sky. Nothing.

Idiots, using up precious ammo. Let them shoot. She cradled the gun in her arms and leaned against the tree, gazing at the bridge.

The problem of Raina and how to find Edick rushed back to her like a cramp. She blew out a breath and, for the first time in her life, had the sudden impulse to pray. The idea hit her like the caress of the sun, and she leaned into it. *Pray.* She scanned the sky, azure blue streaked with cirrus clouds. Even if God had abandoned her, perhaps He was still watching out for Edward. Edick certainly deserved it. Saving her not once but twice, showing her in simple ways she wasn't forgotten—from rubbing her weary shoulders to promising to look after her. She could even hear the lyrical twist of his Russian accent, the low tenor that sent ripples up and down her spine when he called her Magda.

His tower of strength. Tears pricked her eyes. She'd even memorized his long strides as if digging into the next. But perhaps all men walked that way. Indeed, as she watched the bridge, it seemed that another man had adopted his stride. She could barely make him out, dressed in green, wearing a pack, and surrounded by other soldiers. He strode across the bridge with purpose. Another soldier stalked behind him—

She brought the scope up and zeroed in on the tall German. Square jawed and the size of a tank. . . She scanned to the other man, more slight, with a bounce in his step. . .

Her heart fell through her chest.

Edick.

She followed the duo across the bridge until they became a speck in the road toward Pskov. Fear rattled her fingers on the trigger, and she put the weapon in her lap and folded her hands. She made a desperate attempt to blink back her panic.

Edward had been captured. Another man she loved—

Loved?

She closed her eyes, letting that word find the soft places in her chest, the ones Edward had furrowed with his kindness, his smile, his tender words. Her eyes burned as the thought swept through her. She loved Edick?

Da. She loved him. Loved his courage, his strength, the way his eyes devoured her, the feel of his hands on her stomach, in her hair. She even loved his faith: so rich, so enticing, wild and strong enough to draw her from her darkness toward hope.

She loved Edick. Admitting it felt pure. And whole. And freeing. Dima had been the love of her youth, of her hopes and dreams. Edward was the love of her now. Of this dark time. And just maybe he'd also be her future.

If the Germans didn't destroy it. Again. Bile filled her throat, and pain filmed her eyes as grief swept through her. No. She would not watch as history repeated itself. She could hear Edward's outrage as she climbed to her feet. Yeah, well, he'd just have to yell at her later.

Preferably *after* he kissed her. A few times. *How can a man not love you?* His words filled her, strummed her courage. Covering her womb, she leaned down. "Forgive me, baby, but I have to go and save your new father."

She struggled to her feet, feeling as if the baby had lodged lower and squeezed between the bones of her body. Her lungs, however, felt free for the first time in months. Gulping in fresh breaths of river air, she again felt the impulse to pray.

Edward deserved God's attention. She lifted her eyes heavenward. "God, it's me. I know I haven't talked to You for—well, it doesn't matter. What matters is Edick. Please, help me."

She fisted the rifle and took off in an awkward jog along the familiar path toward Pskov.

Grief knotted in Edward's chest, wrenching tighter with each step as he plodded toward Pskov. Natasha, now Raina. The nightmare of Poland was resurrecting, and with it came the death of his future—and Magda's. Despair clogged his throat as he fought the rope chafing his wrists.

They'd laughed him across the bridge. Germans, their ruddy unshaven faces mocking him. One spat on him. He didn't care and kept walking.

Please, forgive me, Father.

He winced, unable to find words, but inside, his spirit groaned.

Birch trees spiked shadows across the dirt road. On the eastern sky, wispy clouds had turned purple, bruising the sky. "Where are you taking me?" Edward asked in German.

"Silence!"

"Just kill me now!" He whirled, and the soldier cuffed him. Staggering, he fell to his knees. Gravel dug into them. Unbalanced, he toppled, and his chin skidded into the road. He lay there, stunned, waiting for the German to lay the gun to his temple and pull the trigger.

A shot echoed across the purple-gray sky, and Edward jerked, winced, every muscle on fire.

The guard thumped to the ground beside him.

What—?

Edward's heart lodged in his mouth as he rolled away, down into the weeds, and curled into a ball.

The sound dissipated into the winter sky.

Edward's heartbeat drummed in his chest, but all he heard was the hiss of his own breathing. Then reaction ignited all his reflexes. He rolled to his feet, keeping in a crouch, and scanned the road. They weren't so far from the bridge that the other soldiers wouldn't hear the echo. They might think it was their cohort giving Edward lead poisoning.

Or, they might come and check—

He jumped out of the ditch and raced across the road, leaping the blood that trickled down the road like a river. He didn't want to know who the shooter was, not yet. His eyes were on the forest, and beyond that, he was already at the cave, finding Magda and praying Raina had been terribly wrong.

❦

The rifle shook in her hands, and tears streamed down her cheeks and into her mouth. She watched Edick scramble across the road but couldn't feel relief when she'd just killed the man who had saved her life. Her child. The German had freed her because he had a wife and probably a child of his own, and she'd destroyed that with one bullet.

Guilt felt like a knife, and she sat in the tree and sobbed.

Her stomach rippled, and with it came a pain that seemed to seep from the center of her spine. The sensation moved like a wave and crested over her, tightening her toes and widening her eyes. Her breath hiccupped in her chest. The rifle spiraled from her grip.

Marina clutched at a jutting branch and stiffened until the pain moved through her, finally freeing her from its wrenching grip.

Get out of the tree. Gripping the branch, she lowered herself to the next and prayed it wouldn't break. It had been so much easier to climb up than it was to pick her way down. She was nearly to the bottom when another pain swept over her. It ripped the breath from her lungs. Gritting her teeth, she crawled to the forest floor. Pain took possession of her body. She fell to her knees, her head on her forearms, and groaned.

She heard crashing behind her but was helpless to get up, to hide, to save herself. The pain owned her, tore her attention to only one breath after another.

When it finally released her, she dragged in a quivering breath. Sweat peppered her forehead.

The crashing echoed closer. Panic revived her senses and sent her crawling behind the tree in search of her gun. She grabbed it and dragged it to her chest. Fumbling for control, she sat back against the tree, anchored it on her hip, and pointed it toward the tangle of forest.

Fatigue and agony blurred her vision, but it was clear enough to aim at a dark form slinking through the forest shadows. She closed her eyes and pulled the trigger.

A shot screamed over Edward's head and splintered an oak behind him. He dove, face first, into the leaves, breathing hard. Whoever had taken out his German guard was either a terrible shot and after him, or they didn't know it was he tromping through the woods. He gulped in a breath and listened to the pounding of his heart. Inching forward on his knees, he peered through a tangle of brush and sighted a bulky black form, a person the size of a small bear. His legs were drawn up, his rifle held at an odd, untrained angled, and his head hung low. Edward made out a green knit stocking cap.

Edging forward, he fought his bonds, wishing the German hadn't searched him before they tied him up. The soldier hadn't found his gun, which had already mysteriously vanished, but had instead lifted Edward's hunting knife from his boot. Edward ran his mind over his limited options. He could hardly rush the bulky soldier with his hands tied. Still, the man was dressed as a partisan, and the Russian WWI relic looked like something a freedom fighter might use. Especially with the black scope attached.

The man raised his head and groaned with a contorted face.

Magda. Edward scrambled to his feet and burst through the shrubbery.

Magda looked up and blinked at him as if he were out of focus. He fell to his knees, furious that he was unable to hold her, to crush her to his chest, and let his relief surge out of him. "Magda, it was you, wasn't it?"

Her pale hue scared him. She nodded slowly. "I shot him. He saved my life, and I shot him."

Edward frowned at her strange words. "It's okay, honey. I'm fine. You shot the German."

She nodded, then her eyes went wide, and she held her breath.

"Magda?"

She held up a hand. It shook. The other was on her stomach, which appeared as if it had doubled in size since he'd seen her last. She arched her back and dug her head in the tree trunk. Realization moved through him like a groan.

"Magda, are you in labor?"

She didn't answer. Her eyes fluttered closed, and the look on her face told him everything.

Not now. Oh, not now.

"Oh Lord," he said glancing at the darkening sky. "You gotta help me here."

He looked at Magda, counting his heartbeats, his breath, until her face relaxed. She finally opened her eyes, and when she attempted a feeble smile, he nearly lost his composure.

"Magda, can you untie me?" He turned and felt her fumble with the knots. Freedom. He turned and gathered her in his arms. "Magda." He couldn't let go, couldn't stop holding her, half-afraid that he might hurt her, half-terrified that he'd found her too late. "I've been so worried," he said.

"Me, too," she whispered and bit her lip. "You have no idea what happened." She wrapped her gloved hands around his arms, holding tight. "I was taken by the Germans."

"What?" Edward leaned away, searched her face.

"It was Raina. She is one of them. A Nazi."

Raina, a Nazi? He caught his breath, weighing Magda's words. He'd seen Raina's daughter murdered, watched as Raina fought beside him. . .

And what if Magda had been shooting at him. . .and not the German. She had been crying. . .

He felt punched, and the air left him.

"She killed Natasha and ordered my death," Magda said, and he couldn't deny the grief in her eyes.

"I saw them shoot her," he said quietly. "She had your blood on her face."

"Natasha's blood. Raina went into Pskov after you left, and I followed her." Magda leaned out of his arms, her eyes on him, her voice now hinting at defense. "She's a Nazi, Edward. I snuck into the *detski-sod* where they were stationed and she. . .betrayed me."

His body drained of strength. "They caught you?"

Marina nodded, and he saw her flinch. "She told me I would die."

He closed his eyes, feeling for some grip on reality. *Please, Lord.*

"How did you get free?"

"That man. The German in the road, he let me go." Her face crumpled. "I killed the man who saved my life."

She put her gloved hand to her mouth, tears spilling from her eyes. "What have I done, Edward? I shouldn't be here. I should be somewhere safe, waiting for the baby."

Her eyes widened, and she made a face.

He groaned and lowered his forehead to hers as she closed her eyes. "Difficult choices," he mumbled, not sure who he was trying to comfort. Oh, he wanted to believe her. His chest burned with the need. *Please, God, give me wisdom.*

She breathed through her contraction as his fear piled against him. It didn't matter if she'd betrayed them. He had to get her to a doctor.

"She's been tracking you since Berlin, Edick," Magda said softly as the contraction released. "She said she was part of the SS, and she followed you to Katrina's apartment. She called you a coward for not rescuing the woman you loved."

He flinched. Yeah, he'd called himself that a thousand, a million times.

"She's been tracking you, using you to ferret out partisans, betraying your positions to the SS."

I haven't seen her. Stone's words now seared Edward's mind. He backed away from Magda, afraid of the fury coiling in his chest. Raina had betrayed them in Poland. He scrolled back to the moments before the attack, to Raina's disappearance.

She hadn't been hiding. She'd escaped. Because she knew the SS would attack. Jerking to his feet, he stalked the ground, fists tight. "She didn't track me. She was told I was here, after I botched the bridge bombing."

Marina frowned. "How? There are hundreds of bridges between here and Berlin and a thousand partisans to blow them up. How could she pick you?"

He slapped the tree trunk above her with an open palm. "She knew I spoke Russian. And we attacked a number of bridges and supply lines in Poland. Raina did the math and figured out I was the one stirring up the Russian partisans."

But Magda wasn't listening. Her eyes had glazed, staring unseeing past him. Her face turned white as she held her breath, her hands went to her stomach. He fell to his knees beside her and reached out to take her hand.

"Don't touch me!" she rasped. He yanked his hands away.

"What can I do?"

She shook her head.

He wanted to cry, as he watched her stiffen, wishing he understood the pain that made her drive her fingernails into her palms and blanch her lower lip with her teeth. He held his own breath until her pain ceased. "How far apart are they?"

She shook her head. "I don't know. Close. And that one was bad."

"How soon are you going to have this baby?" He rubbed his forehead with his hand, scrambling to sort through options.

"I don't know—I've never had a baby before, Edick." Fear shimmered in her eyes.

Edward stood up, pacing again. "Okay, I have to get you somewhere safe. You can't have this baby in the middle of the woods."

"I can't have this baby at all! It's a month too early!"

Her words stopped him cold. "Are you sure?"

Fear outlined her expression. "I—I don't know."

He crouched and took her hand. "When were you and Dmitri last. . .together?"

She ducked her head. "We were newlyweds."

Oh. He nodded and pulled a long breath. "When did you get married?"

"February. He left in May."

"You don't remember when you found out you were pregnant?"

She bit her lower lip, looking suddenly incredibly young instead of the wizened, tough partisan who could peg the enemy from a tree. She shook her head. "I lost track. I didn't really realize until after Dima left." Her eyes suddenly filled. "I didn't have a chance to tell him. He never knew."

Edward braced her face between his hands, holding her gently. "It's okay, Magda."

She searched his eyes. Her expression changed. A smile slid up her face, adding a sparkle to the shine of her eyes. She rubbed a finger along the stubble of his jaw. "You came back."

"I did." He tried a smile, but the feel of her tiny face in his hands, the texture of trust in her eyes. He couldn't help himself. "Magda," he said, hoping to ask, but she buried her fist in his coat and pulled him close.

He kissed her. His lips on hers, he felt her fear, her hopes, her relief as she kissed him back. She tasted of tea, sweet, spicy, exactly the woman he'd come to love—

Love.

The thought swept his breath from his chest. Oh, he did love her! He pulled her into his arms and deepened his kiss, delight moving through him as she relaxed in his embrace. He loved her courage, her strength, her trust. She moved through him like the wind, found his cracks, and filled them with hope.

Magda. A woman redeemed.

"I love you," he said against her lips. She gasped, leaned back, her eyes wide.

"Is it another pain?"

She smiled, a new expression that spoke of mischief, even teasing. "*Nyet. Da.* Sorta."

He frowned.

"Edick," she whispered. "I love you, too. But. . ."

238

She kissed him again, this time laying her hand on his face, pulling him gently to her.

Perfect. Sweet. Surrender. He wanted to cry with the feelings that burst to life in his chest.

It was indeed worth the grief to love Magda Vasileva.

Abruptly, she reeled away from him, her face pale.

He swallowed the Russia-sized lump in his throat. Another contraction.

"I don't think you're supposed to hold your breath," he said softly.

"What. . .do. . .you. . .know?" Her eyes closed. He tucked wisps of sweaty hair into her hat, panic turning him inside out. *God, please don't let her have this baby here.*

The contraction released her, and she slumped into his arms.

"I gotta get you out of here." Slinging her rifle over his shoulder, he slid one arm under her knees and the other behind her shoulders. She groaned as he lifted her to his chest. "You've gained some weight since the last time we did this."

However, she still packed a fairly solid wallop.

CHAPTER NINETEEN

The crisp, clear, early rising moon laid a path of pale luminance through the forest as Edward carried Magda toward the monastery. With each contraction, he crouched low, holding her tight, urging her to breathe. The fear that edged her expression began to dissipate as she stared into his eyes.

What kind of guts did it take to trust a foreigner when her entire world had shattered?

A cold November wind snaked into his collar, chilling the sweat that ran down his back. The faintest aroma of baking bread drifting from the far-off monastery kitchen sent his stomach into spasms and powered his pace. Magda groaned in his arms.

"Hang on, *doragaya*. We're almost there."

Her eyes were closed, her hand knotted into his jacket, her face screwed up in a knot of pain.

The monastery doors were shut tight, but as his boots scraped on the rocky path, the noise alerted the bulldogs. Their throaty growls hung on the wind. Magda stiffened. Edward kicked at the door. The bulldogs erupted, their barks menacing enough to frighten, but instead they provided Edward a sense of peace. The monastery was obviously still unsuspected. He kicked the door again. "Brothers! I come in peace!"

The small peep door opened. Two eyes blinked at him in the backlighting of a lantern. The door was slammed, and a moment later, while two brothers held back the lunging bulldogs, the doors swung open.

Edward marched through. "Please, I need Brother Timofea."

"Here, Edward." The monk emerged from the darkness. "What is the matter?"

"Magda is in labor."

Brother Timofea's face slacked. "She needs a hospital."

"There's no time." Edward stalked past him. "And Pavel is already wiring the train. I need help."

Brother Timofea ran to catch up with him and opened the door to his cell. A lone candle, its white wax spilling onto the metal holder, flicked orange across the stone walls. The familiar scent of dampness and wool surrounded him like an embrace.

"Put her here." The monk smoothed his bedclothes. Edward lowered her onto the hard cot.

Magda's eyes fluttered open. "Thank you, Edick."

He took off her hat and smoothed back her hair, wet from sweat. "You're going to be okay." The white hue of her face had him scared.

Her fingers dug into his jacket. "Stay with me, please."

"Of course." He took her hand and squeezed. "But I'm not much good. I've never delivered a baby." He hung his head, hopelessly out of options. The nearest doctor was on a train somewhere on the Russian/Estonian border planting a bomb. Brother Timofea, for all his wisdom, most likely had little experience with delivering babies. "Do you know any midwives in the village?" His gaze scanned between Magda and Timofea.

Timofea shook his head. "Lydia had a litter of puppies last year."

Edward groaned and ran a hand behind the screaming muscles in his neck. "What can we do?"

Timofea knelt beside him. "I'm going to pray."

Edward saw Magda's face tighten. "Breathe, Magda. Breathe deep and try and relax."

"I'm ripping in half, and you're telling me to relax?" Agony pitched her voice high. Edward and Timofea exchanged a look.

"I think I'll wait outside," Timofea said. Edward sent daggers at him as the monk left.

Edward rubbed Magda's hand, then leaned his forehead onto it. "Lord, I'm in big trouble here. I need help. Please, send Magda someone who can help her." He met her gaze and ran his hand across her forehead.

"Oh!" Magda's blue eyes went wide.

"What?"

Magda pushed herself up on her elbows. "Something. . . popped. Inside me." Her mouth opened into an astonished O.

Uh oh. His mother had given birth to four other children after him, but he'd only remembered the last. "Maybe your water broke?" *Oh Lord, I am in way over my head!*

She licked her lips and groaned as another contraction swept over her. Edward tensed, helplessness digging a trench through him.

"Edward, are you there?" The voice came from inside his rucksack. "Edward?"

Edward ripped open the pack and dug out the two-way. "Pavel! I'm here." He held the radio to his ear, years of practice weeding through the static to make out Pavel's words.

"The package is on board and heading your way."

Edward's gaze locked on Magda's strained expression. "Where are you?" His hands had gone sweaty.

"On board. I'm going to ditch right before the bridge." Edward shook his head. He needed Pavel here, now.

"Pavel! Magda's in labor." He kept his voice dull, praying the panic didn't surface.

Static on the end of the line made him repeat his statement.

"*Da, da!* I'm thinking!" Pavel came back. "Where are you?"

"The monastery."

Edward pushed the radio against his forehead. *Lord, help!*

"Okay, I know a place." Pavel's voice had tensed. "I can get off and cut north. It's about two kilometers, and I'll have to cross the river, but I can probably make it in less than an hour. You go to the bridge."

The bridge! Edward winced. He glanced at Magda, her pain-filled eyes ripping his heart out of his chest. "I can't leave Magda."

"You have to. Go! I'll be there."

Edward shook his head, but Magda reached out and clamped her hand around his wrist.

"Go, Edward. That's why you're here."

His chest constricted. He wiped his forehead with the back of his sleeve. "I'll be there," he confirmed. "Out."

Static echoed on the line, and despair filled his heart. "Magda—" he started.

She slid a hand along his cheek. "You've done all you can do. Now you have to go. You have a job."

He shook his head. "I don't want to leave you."

She smiled. "You'll come back."

He pushed her hair back from her face. He trembled at her words, knowing what it cost her to say that, to let him go in the face of her fears. She'd lost Dmitri to war, and now, when she needed him most, she had told him to go. He pressed a kiss to her forehead. "I love you, you know."

She cupped her hands around his face. "I know." Tears glazed her eyes. "I've always known."

He pressed a kiss to her lips, desperate to communicate every feeling that layered his heart. He pulled away with a groan. "You'll be in my prayers."

She folded her grip into his jacket. Her eyes went to his and searched them. He saw her expression change from fear to determination. "And you'll be in mine."

❧

As Edick stood by the door, Marina fought the contraction, knowing it might be the last time she saw him alive. Pain pushed against her, but she kept her focus on Edick's worried gaze.

He loved her.

The thought made her soar. She'd felt her emotions at the edge of his kiss, and it was all she could do to keep herself from clinging to him, to beg him to stay.

Still, she couldn't help the feeling of déjà vu. *Please, please come back.*

He threw his field glasses around his neck and pocketed the detonator. She felt raw and emptied as his eyes stared into hers one final time. "I'll be back," he repeated hoarsely. She noticed the tic under his eye, and it made her want to cry.

"I know."

The door hung ajar slightly when he left. The cold lick

of November washed over her face. She bit her lip and surrendered to the contraction garroting her body. *What had
he said? Relax. Oh sure.* She white-fisted the sides of the cot
and focused on the dim ceiling. Her toes curled. Tears
blurred her eyes.

Brother Timofea entered, stress puckering the lines on
his face. He knelt beside her and pressed a cool cloth to her
head. The contractions flexed and tightened across her
body, and between pains, exhaustion tugged her into a
drowsy stupor.

Wave after wave of pain crested over her, the intensity
gradually increasing. She found herself reaching for
Timofea's support. The touch of his calloused, bony hand
in hers gave her something to squeeze when the contraction took possession. Her proffered apologies fell on deaf
ears. The monk simply continued to dab her forehead and
murmur fervent prayers.

***

Edward raced toward the bridge, his feet landing loud and
hard in the dark forest. He hated the war, hated himself,
hated the ache in his heart that nearly made him turn and
run back to Magda. It was Berlin all over again, and again
he was choosing the mission over the lady. His insides
twisted in frustration.

He cut toward the river, toward the gray-blue light illuminated through the trees. Skidding to a halt, he raised his
field glasses and scanned for the bridge. No activity. He
judged the bridge's distance at less than a half mile, but
he'd have to cut that distance in half to be in range for det-
onation. His pulse thundered in his head as he dropped the
glasses and ran along the river toward the bridge. The

glasses smacked him in the ribs with each step.

Twigs splintered, branches whipped his face, and he sounded like a boar charging through the forest. He lifted a prayer that there weren't any scouts about and ran with one hand extended, although his eyes had long adjusted to the hues of the night.

The familiar sound of a freight train lumbering toward the bridge thundered in the night sky. His jaw clenched. He stopped and floundered for the swinging glasses.

No train. Still, he had precious distance to cross. Dropping the glasses, he pulled out the radio detonator and took off, careful to keep his thumb off the trigger. Predetonation would take out the train, but obliterate his chances at ever destroying the bridge.

The thick arm of an elm skimmed across his forehead, taking skin with it. He stumbled, and his ankle screamed in response. The roar of the train seeped right into his soul. He could see the bridge with his naked eye, and still no train.

Then he saw the specks in the sky, eclipsing the moonlight. His breath seized. Messerschmitts. Searching for the partisan supply center. *Oh Lord, not tonight. Don't let them find the monastery.*

How could they guess a group of monks were supplying the Russian resistance with food, clothing, guns from Moscow, and information?

Unless, of course, Magda or Natasha or Pavel had told Raina. Suddenly, every conversation he'd had with the woman played in his brain.

The planes arrowed north, the direction he'd just come, dropping as they searched.

Edward braced a hand against a tree, watching them. His mouth dried. The monastery. He'd told Raina where she could hide. Behind his eyes, he saw her shot, rolling into the gully. . .and knew in his gut that it had been a ruse. To trick him into betraying his compatriots.

Edward felt nauseous. Leaning over, he gulped in deep, razor breaths. If she truly were a German SS agent, it wouldn't be hard for her to connect the dots. He always knew Timofea was courting death with his partisan escapades. If they lived through this night, they'd have to move operations.

If. . .

His cry of agony merged with the far-off whistle of an eastern-bound train.

"Brother, please, help me!" Marina folded her hands into Brother Timofea's robe and pulled him toward her. Her entire body trembled, and another contraction wrung her out. The monk's eyes widened. "I'll get the father."

"He'd better know how to deliver babies because I think this one is about to make an entrance!" She collapsed into the bed, her back arching.

The door slammed open. "Magda!"

Marina focused on the wind-blown man, his brown eyes filled with worry. Pavel had aged a decade since she'd seen him last. Breathing hard, he marched into the cell. "How close are the contractions?"

She shook her head, unable to speak as another pain gripped her. Pavel's expression told her everything.

"I need boiled water, a clean sheet, and a blanket." He instructed Brother Timofea, then turned to her, shedding his coat. Perspiration dotted his forehead and sent his brown hair up in spikes. "Sorry I'm late."

"You're. . .just. . .in. . .time."

He smiled and touched her forehead. "Can I take a look?"

Oh. She felt her face heat and cut her eyes away.

"I'm a doctor, remember?"

Sure. Except, well, she didn't remember him as her doctor, but as the man who had been her friend. A very good friend.

Brother Timofea had already helped her shed her wool coat and one layer of sweaters, as well as the wool trousers. Pavel washed his hands in a basin on the table, then sat down on the cot next to her. His demeanor had changed, and she wondered suddenly if she knew him at all, this man who felt comfortable around a woman's pain, absorbed in the miracle of birth. Peace washed over her at his touch, not unlike the first time they had met. He pulled the blanket over her knees. She watched the expression on his face, and when he frowned, fear rippled up her spine.

"What?"

"The baby is sideways." His voice was low, without panic, but Marina felt his concern in the gleam in his eyes and the way he rolled up his sleeves. He positioned above her, pushed the blanket to her hips, and rolled up her sweater. His cool hands on her warm belly made her jump. "Relax, Magda. I'm going to try to turn the baby."

She turned her head away, focusing on a spot on the cave wall while he manipulated the baby in her womb. Her hands dug into the sides of the cot. Tears whisked her eyes, and the agony bubbled up her throat until she cried out.

"I'm sorry," he said, and she saw the strain on his face. "He's coming out backwards."

She closed her eyes, unable to speak the emotions that bound her chest. "Oh. . .God," she gasped, "please, help me."

Pavel glanced at her. "Good, pray. And hold on, because it's time for you to deliver this baby." Marina held her breath as Pavel moved her to a sitting position. "When I tell you, push."

Brother Timofea entered with the blanket and water. Pavel grabbed the monk's wrist and dragged the shocked man to the cot. "Stand behind her. Hold her up."

Pavel gave her hand a reassuring squeeze. "Push."

Edward watched the bombers disappear behind a dark cluster of clouds. His breath snagged in his chest. The monastery was about to be bombed.

Frustration filled his mouth, tasting like his own blood. "Oh God, help us." His eyes burned as he turned toward the bridge. He heard the whistle and tensed. The drone of the Messerschmitts dissolved into the breath of night. A breeze kicked up and prickled his skin.

Difficult choices. Magda's word rushed at him, her sweet compassion as he'd unlocked his secrets. *You can't be blamed for loving her, Edward.* No, but he couldn't avoid the truth. He'd killed her.

Just like his stupidity was going to cost the lives of Magda and her baby.

Caught between his heart and his duty. He had to choose one.

Not fair.

"God, how can this be Your will? How can I stay here when everything inside me tells me to go back to Magda?"

"Cast the net on the right side of the ship, and ye shall find."

Edward frowned, his hands shaking. "I just don't understand!"

"They cast therefore, and now they were not able to draw it for the multitude of fishes."

Edward shook his head. "I don't know what to do!" His thoughts knotted into a hard ball in his chest. What if it wasn't about what he was supposed to do, but how? What if—he blinked as the words written in the Gospel of John came alive and burned into his soul. The fishermen hadn't changed jobs when they cast their nets to the other side of the boat—they'd changed attitudes. They chose to rely on God, trusting Him even when common sense, their gut instincts, told them it was foolish. After they'd fished an entire night, catching nothing, Jesus told them to throw their nets on the other side of the boat—and the catch had nearly burst the seams, blessings overflowing.

When life didn't make sense, when panic shoved his heart into his teeth, his only choice was to trust God's way. Walk in faith despite the confusion. He clenched his teeth and stilled his erratic heartbeat. He saw Magda's pale face, heard her words: *I'm praying for you.*

Pray, yes, pray, Magda. He recited Pavel's words aloud, disbelief a knife in his chest. "His pleasure is not in the strength of the horse, nor His delight in the legs of a man, the Lord delights in those who fear Him, who put their hope in His unfailing love."

He stumbled toward the bridge, the detonator in his hand. He could see the train barreling toward the river, a hulking black snake creeping along the western dent of sky and forest.

Please, God, help me to trust in Your unfailing love for Magda. For me.

The train rolled onto the bridge.

Edward swallowed hard and pressed the detonator.

"Push, Magda!"

Sweat beaded her face and ran in rivulets off her chin. She felt as if Pavel were ripping her in half.

Pavel shook his head. "She's stuck." His pale expression told her what that meant.

"I'll push more," she gasped. "Just give me a second."

Pavel nodded. "The legs are out, Magda, I just need to get her little head out without breaking her neck."

"Her?" Tears filmed her eyes.

Pavel grabbed Timofea's hand. "When she pushes, you push here." He placed Timofea's hand on Magda's hard stomach. "The baby's life depends on it."

Magda pushed up on her elbows. Raw and ragged, she hauled in a deep breath and nodded.

Pavel pushed the baby's chin down, toward the infant's chest. "Harder, Timofea!"

Magda felt the baby's head inch forward. Then, with a pop, the head slid out, and the baby girl slid into Pavel's arms. Gray-blue, she squirmed in Pavel's grip, then wailed, a sweet cry of relief and life.

Magda gasped. Tears streamed into her ears. "Is she okay?"

Pavel laid her into the sheet, swabbed her mouth, and listened to her breathe. "I think so. She's bigger than I thought."

Marina laughed, a nervous giggle that felt cathartic. *"Da."*

Pavel swaddled the baby, still slick with birth, in the blanket and handed her to Magda. "You have a daughter." His gaze told her how he felt about being a doctor and witnessing this miracle.

"Thank you, Pavel."

He blushed and suddenly reverted to the man she knew.

The baby in her arms wiggled, her tiny mouth turning from blue to pink, her skin from gray to peach. Her eyes blinked even in the dim light of the room. Marina nuzzled her to her cheek and a fullness started at her toes and moved through her. Dmitri's daughter. Her daughter.

O God, perhaps You haven't abandoned me.

"*Maladetz*, Pavel." Timofea clamped Pavel on the shoulder. His eyes gleamed. "You have many gifts."

Pavel shrugged. "I am glad I could be here." He froze. "Did either of you hear the bridge blow?"

Marina shook her head, wrapped up in the way her daughter curled her tiny hand around her pinkie finger.

"Oh, Timofea, I nearly forgot." Pavel picked up his jacket and rummaged through. "This is for you. I met a Russian partisan group in Estonia who asked me to send it your way."

Timofea took it, opened it. He read it, and his jaw slacked. "No. Oh no!"

Marina curled the baby against her chest. "What's wrong?"

Timofea had his eyes closed, his face crumpled in some silent agony. "We have to stop Edward from blowing the bridge!"

"Why?" Pavel grabbed the monk by his spiny shoulders.

Brother Timofea gave Marina a mournful look. "Because Tikhonov and Voloshin are on the train."

The growl of a far-off explosion rumbled against the silence. Timofea went ashen.

In the wake came the low, far-off drone of German Messerschmitts.

CHAPTER TWENTY

Metal and iron shrieked as the bridge crumbled. Edward watched as the engine plunged forward into nothing, dropping sixty feet to the river, pulling its cars into the water one after another in a cacophony of explosions.

Then the plume of smoke from the inferno filled the riverbed. Even from Edward's perch, his eyes watered at the smoke. The stars went out, leaving only the glow of flames.

Above the chaos of the destruction, he heard the low groan of the Messerschmitts, circling high, searching for their target. Fear sent him to his feet. *Please, Lord, make me fast!*

<hr/>

Pavel stared at Magda's face, his own going as white as hers felt. "Who are Tikhonov and Voloshin?"

"Russian generals. Caught behind enemy lines in Estonia. The resistance was smuggling them back to Russia."

Pavel angled him a hard look. "And how were we to know?"

"Didn't they tell you when you met them?"

Pavel shook his head. "I—well, I wasn't thinking. They told me to return it to the resistance in Russia. I just. . .well, nothing at that moment was more important than blowing the bridge." He winced and scrubbed a hand down his face. "Moscow can't blame us for a mistake."

Timofea shook his head. "Yes, they can. This is Russia. It won't matter that we didn't know."

Marina looked down at her beautiful daughter. The baby nuzzled against her, blue eyes unfocused and blinking. "Stalin will hunt us down."

"No!" Pavel stalked the room with the ferocity that made him an effective partisan. "They can't blame us. We took out a bridge—we cut off the German supply line."

Timofea clutched his shoulder. "You need to bury yourself in Siberia, son. Moscow won't know for a couple days. But they *will* know. And I can't hide you forever." His mouth was drawn to a thin line. "I'm afraid you've both become enemies of the State."

<hr />

The thunder of airplanes hummed against the canopy, obscured in the darkness as Edward sprinted toward the monastery. The sky had turned coal black, the smoke from the explosion lassoed by the greedy wind and scattered along the treetops.

Scattered. Making visibility. . .zero. A spasm of disbelief weakened Edward's step. The explosion had blinded the Messerschmitts—and hidden the monastery.

A miracle of God wrought by Edward's obedience. His throat thickened. *"The Lord delights in those who fear Him. . . . "*

Dawn pushed against the eastern sky as he rapped on the monastery gate. The two bulldogs greeted him with throaty growls. He braced a hand on the door and dragged in scorching breaths while he waited for the brother at the gate to restrain the dogs.

He broke into a run as soon as he cleared the entrance and burst into Timofea's cell without knocking.

The sight of Magda holding a small bundle to her chest, cooing into the folds of a worn blanket stopped him short. He stood like a dumb man, every thought deserting him.

She looked up and smiled.

Her hair hung around her face, curling from dried perspiration. A streak of dirt ran up her cheek, and bags dragged under her deep blue eyes. She'd never looked more beautiful.

"Magda?" He crumpled to his knees beside her cot, afraid to touch her. "Are you okay?"

She gave him a crooked frown. "Of course. Women have been having babies for centuries."

His eyes burned. He touched his forehead to her blanketed legs and fisted his hands into the covers. Unable to rein in his emotions, he felt fatigue and relief take control of his muscles. "Oh, Magda, I was so. . ." His voice sounded exactly how he felt.

Raw. Undone.

Only this time, he'd somehow helped to protect the woman he loved.

Her hand wove through his hair. "You came back."

He lifted his gaze, met hers—blue, luminous, reeling him in. "Yes," he said hoarsely. "We did it, Magda. The bridge is out." He cupped his hand on her cheek, and she leaned into it. "I was afraid."

"Me, too." She smiled wryly. "But I prayed for you."

He couldn't swallow the lump in his throat. Reaching out, he moved the folds of the blanket. A tiny face, minute pink lips, long eyelashes. The baby was asleep, moving its mouth in tiny sucking movements while dreaming. "Is it a boy or girl?"

"A daughter." Magda bit her lip behind a delightful smile. Her eyes shone.

"She's beautiful." He touched the baby's cheek with his finger. "Ten fingers and toes?"

"And healthy, although I don't know how after near starvation, being swallowed by a river, and whacked hard by an oak branch."

"God put a shelf of protection around this little one, Magda. He has His plans for you and this baby."

Magda's eyes misted. She rubbed a finger down the baby's delicate nose. "We'll see." Her gaze darkened.

The door creaked open. "I see you finally made it." Pavel entered, his expression as frazzled as his hair.

Edward stood, shaken by the look on Pavel's face. He clamped the Russian on the shoulder. "What's important is that *you* made it. How'd you get here in time?"

"I jumped the train where it jags north, about five kilometers from the bridge. It's just across the river from the monastery."

"I blew the bridge."

"I know." Pavel winced and rubbed his chin with the back of his hand. "We've got problems."

Edward frowned, shot a look at Magda. She ran a finger down her baby's cheek.

"Evidently, the resistance in Estonia was harboring a couple of Russian generals. They stuck them on the train and were sending them home."

Edward closed his eyes. "And I dumped them into the river." His chest constricted.

"*Da.*" Pavel scanned a look to Magda. "And now Magda and I are fugitives."

Edward shook his head. "You didn't know. Blame it on me."

"It won't matter to Stalin. We're as good as dead, if not sentenced to gulag. He's not known for his forgiving nature."

Edward backed away and leaned against the cave wall. "Then I have to get you out." He looked at Magda, at the pained expression on her face, and his resolve hardened. "We'll all go to Estonia. I have transportation arranged and papers for Magda."

Pavel pursed his lips, his eyes on Magda. Edward knew what he was thinking. As a doctor, he was gauging Magda's strength for the journey. Edward didn't like the answer he saw on Pavel's face.

"I'm so tired, I can't think," Pavel said, dodging Edward's questioning gaze. "I'm going to get some sleep, and I suggest you do the same."

Edward watched him go, feeling a sick wrenching in his gut. What wasn't Pavel telling him?

He knelt beside Magda. "Can I hold her?"

Her face broke into a smile. "She's been waiting for you."

The tiny baby yawned, and the small noise that emerged from her lips went right to his heart. She felt so fragile, so helpless in his arms. Tucking her close to his chest, he leaned down and inhaled the smell of baby. "She's perfect. What's her name?"

Magda touched his arm. She was exhausted; he felt it in her grip. "Her name is Nadezhda."

Hope. After all the pain, the bitterness, the grief, she'd

named her baby Hope. His eyes felt gritty. "What a beautiful name."

She smiled, fatigue touching her eyes, but peace filled her expression. "Can you hold her for a bit, Edick? I just need a little sleep. . . ." Her eyes fluttered closed, and she tucked her arm over her chest.

He stared at the baby, at her lopsided mouth and smooth pink face. "It would be a privilege."

<hr/>

Magda woke with a start, a strange ache tensing her body. Like a wave, it came back to her. She'd had her baby. Dmitri's daughter. Nadezhda—her Hope. Her spirit lightened, wrenching free from the grip of grief that had held her captive for months. Hope was alive and had dark blue eyes.

Sunshine seeped under the door, saturating the misty darkness with the pale hues of daylight. The air smelled fresh and crisp, and outside the blankets, her nose tingled. She rolled over onto her side, blinking as her eyes adjusted.

Edick sat against the wall, head lolled to one side, baby Nadezhda propped in his arms. Her daughter's mouth was moving, and she had turned her face into the blanket, rooting for nourishment. The activity called to a nurturing urge inside Marina. Rising quietly and ignoring the sharp pains that rippled through her, she crept over to Edick and lifted Nadezhda from his arms. The baby turned her little head toward her mother.

Marina bit back a grin of joy and returned to her cot. She sat on it, her back to the cold wall, and drew up a blanket. Memories of watching other mothers guided her movements, and in a moment, her daughter was receiving the meal she craved. The sensation sent cramps down to Marina's knees but filled her heart with an unfamiliar delight. She smoothed Nadezhda's feathery brown hair, so much the color of Dmitri's, and Marina's eyes filled. She looked heavenward. "Can you see her, Dima?"

Edick twitched in his sleep, and Marina couldn't help but watch him. The way he'd nestled her child into his arms had spoken volumes to her about his love for her baby. His rich brown hair fell over his eyes, and the copper-colored beard he'd begun to sprout across his strong jaw sent a shiver of delight through her. His hands, now empty, still curled as if unwilling to surrender his precious bundle. They were strong, wide hands, more defined than Dmitri's but still reminiscent of her farmer husband. In those hands, a child could be safe. Those hands would guide and protect.

Longing swept through her to place Nadezhda, and herself, in his hands and never let go. She closed her eyes, willing the image away.

Life had taken a tragic detour with the destruction of the train. Brother Timofea was right. Even though they'd struck a blow against the enemy, they, themselves, were now enemies of the State. Unless they got out of Russia or buried themselves deep inside, Stalin would track them down and order them shot.

It was only a matter of time.

She leaned her head against the wall. Nadezhda sighed, her blue eyes fluttering closed. Marina smiled as she watched her daughter fall into sleep. Fear began a slow stranglehold. The walls of the cave closed in, and suddenly Magda knew she needed air. Sunshine.

Breathing her way through an oppressive doom, she rose and nestled Nadezhda into the covers of the cot. She kissed the baby on the forehead. Then she eased herself to her feet, and despite the wave of feather-headedness and another wave of gripping pain through her body, she shuffled toward the door.

The sun, although climbing a cobalt sky free of clouds, was muted by the chilly breath of winter. Still, the cool air felt good on Magda's sweaty brow. Although Pavel had done his best to assist her in cleaning up after the birth, still she felt dirty and in need of a long, hot bath. The smell of cooking kasha drifted from the kitchen. Chickens pecked and squawked in the dirt by the barn. Marina stood in the courtyard and watched the monks carrying water, feeding livestock, and hurrying about the compound; and she suddenly felt like a scarecrow in the middle of a field. Turning, she shuffled toward the chapel, aiming for privacy.

The tiny cave had been whitewashed and spoke of orderliness. Icons of saints hung on the walls. Their mournful gold and brown faces depicted the ideas of a holy and sanctified life of the twelfth and thirteenth centuries. Circular holders on tall metal stands held thin orange candles, their flames flickering shadows across the faces of each icon. At the front of the chapel, a molded bronze Jesus hung on an ornately carved wooden cross. Two candleholders held an array of yellow candles with thin flames sending spirals of smoke heavenward and gilding the statue with licks of gold and amber.

Marina stared at Christ's face, drawn toward the expression of peace. After all He suffered, she somehow expected to see a shadow of grief, a twist of despair etched into the sculpture. Of course, this was only one artist's view of the Savior Jesus, but still, it puzzled her.

Feeling another rush of weakness, she hobbled toward a bench along the wall, behind the statue.

The chapel had been built into the cave, and hidden behind the display of Christ, an array of pockets had been etched into the stone walls. Inside the wells, jeweled crosses, a leather-bound book, a tarnished challis, and a jewelry chest gleamed in the dim light.

Marina leaned her head against the wall, fatigue washing over her. Oh, how she wished there were easy choices before her. Abandon her country or take her child and try and hide in Siberia. One meant cutting off her roots, the other meant forsaking her heart. The thought of never seeing Edick made her ache. She buried her face in her hands.

"My child, you shouldn't be out of bed." She felt Brother Timofea's hand on her shoulder. Looking up, she swiped her tears with her fingertips and smiled at his kind expression.

"I just needed to think."

He nodded, his mouth drawing into a thin line. "This is a good place to do that."

She took his hand. "Thank you for last night."

She'd never seen a monk blush before. He nodded, then looked away at the treasures lined up on the wall. Uncomfortable at the sight of the monk's embarrassment, Marina followed his gaze.

"What are those?" she asked.

He shrugged. "Various treasures we've found here over the years. Our monastery is the oldest in this part of the country, and over the years, we've harbored many a religious fugitive. Often they leave something in the cells or present gifts to the monastery." He fingered the golden challis. "Interesting what people are willing to part with when they are faced with their own demise." He looked down at her, his brown eyes seeing into her soul. "Or the demise of their loved ones."

Magda's mouth went dry, and her eyes misted. She nodded her head.

He turned and lifted from the display the leather-bound book. "I think you might find this one particularly interesting." He held it out to her, and when she took it, patted her on the shoulder. "I'm praying for you, child. I know God is watching out for you."

She bit her lip as he walked away, aching to believe his words. *God, how can You be watching out for me? I was abandoned as a child, my husband was murdered, my daughter's life hangs in shambles before it's even begun.* So much for her pitiful prayers making a dent in heaven.

She touched the hardened cover. Why had someone left a tattered book behind? She lifted it and carefully opened the front cover.

The name written inside dropped her heart to her knees.

Anton Klassen. She steeled herself against a wave of shock and sat on the bench. Her hand shook as she flipped to a random page. Tiny, choppy printing in black ink.

November 8, 1917

I fear a conflict rivaling that of the Whites and the Reds is brewing between Oksana and my father's wife. I happened to be passing through the hinterhaus *on my way to the barn when I overheard Mother Hilda in the kitchen, tearing into poor Oksana with both claws bared—and for no other reason than she*

had gotten eggshells in the old hag's pljuschky *batter.
Given MH's foul disposition and my own experiences
with her, I knew she would soon seize the blunder as
an opportunity to air a long list of grievances.
Thankfully, I managed to rescue Oksana by soliciting
her help with a phantom project before my wicked
stepmother could engage her young adversary in all-
out war. . . .*

Oksana Klassen? Her mother? Marina trembled. Even
as disbelief fisted her chest, she smiled to think her mother
had her own share of in-law troubles to bear. A wild impulse
made her travel a few pages deeper into the book, until her
skimming stumbled upon the words *untold sorrow*—words
to which she could instantly relate.

November 17, 1917
    *Untold sorrow fills my soul on this day, which
should have been my most joyous ever. No sooner had
I found myself adrift in Oksana's sweet love than our
world came crashing in. They died as my wife and I
looked helplessly on from our secret place. Their screams
echo in my heart, torment my every thought, even my
soul. What kind of man am I that my brothers should die
while I live? How can my faith survive such horror?*

Her throat closed as she read the words of this author
whose blood coursed through her own veins. A tear fell on
the page and smeared the ink. With horror, she blotted it
away and held the book out, away from the tears that
dripped from her chin. What screams had Anton and
Oksana endured? However, his question found the most

bruised places in her heart. *How can my faith survive such horror?* Hers certainly hadn't. . . .

July 1918

Oh, how I long to go to her, to draw her into my arms, to take her pain upon me and console her grief at the loss of our precious infant, Marina. Our child of promise. Yet I know to do so would endanger us all.

Lord, how much more must my beloved Oksana endure? She has lost all she holds dear. Comfort her with Thy peace that passeth all understanding. Even though I cannot fathom the plan or purpose You have in store for us through all these many tribulations, still I will pray the words of Your suffering servant Job, as Brother Timofea instructed me: "Though Thou slayest me, yet will I serve Thee." In my heart of hearts, I will believe Your hand is ever guiding, and I trust Thee to help me in my unbelief. Today, I claim again the promise I believe Thou didst give me as my own from the pen of the psalmist in the 100th Psalm— that Thou wilt continue Thy faithfulness down through the generations of Klassens yet to come.

She turned the page and sobbed when they were empty. "Oh, Mother, what happened?" Her throat burned. She closed the book, wishing she knew this history. How had he died? And what happened to her that her mother mourned her loss? Anton's words so youthful, so full of hope and faith, swelled through her soul. The impossibility of Timofea knowing this book had been stored among the treasures of the monastery made her skin prickle from head to toe, and in the silence of the chapel, she heard the whisper of memory. *"For the LORD is good and his love endures forever; his faithfulness continues through all generations."*

She closed her eyes. Of course. Psalm 100. How many times had Yulia quoted it to her as they settled down to sleep in the wide straw bed? The verse had been imprinted on her soul, and now she knew why. She was a Klassen, and this was their verse. Her father's, her mother's. And now hers.

Could it have been Timofea who'd scratched the reference into her husband's grave? Obviously, he'd known her father and known about the book. . . . She held it to her chest and sobbed, undone by the awesome love of God. Her thoughts found the moment Dmitri had left her, so many months ago. She'd told him she had no one.

He told her she had God. That He would bind their family together, no matter what happened.

And God hadn't abandoned her. He'd given her two mothers, both of whom loved her more than life, a husband she would see again, a child who healed her wounded heart. God had saved her life countless times, from a fall from a tree, from a plunge into a raging river, and from execution. He'd given her a man to walk by her side—a man who earned her love and gently brought her from grief to hope.

"Oh, God, forgive me for my earthly perspective. Your hand has been upon me this entire time. Forgive me for not having eyes to see it!" She closed her eyes. "You haven't abandoned me. You've loved me through it all and protected our family, just as You promised my father."

She drew out the warm and slightly bent picture of her mothers and smoothed it on the journal. She traced the outline of Oksana's creamy, almost regal face, then Yulia's. Finally, she pressed a dry kiss to the image of Anton's gravestone. "Thank You, Lord, for allowing me to meet him."

She tucked the picture inside the journal and curled the book against her chest. She would take the book with her when she escaped to America, just as Edward had planned. Just as her father had believed in God's love, so would she.

A rush of warmth swept through her at the thought of Nadezhda growing up in his arms, sheltered by those capable hands. . .perhaps having a son, Edward's son. . . .

She stood, and her head spun. Then she fell hard, hitting the chapel floor with a cry.

Her legs seemed not to work. She lay there, feeling strangely light-headed, weak. A feeling of fatigue like she'd never known passed over her. She closed her eyes and relaxed into the embrace of darkness.

TWENTY-ONE

M arina felt hands under her, lifting her, and for a moment she resisted. Then familiar smells—wool, the scents of the forest, made her curl toward the warmth of the embrace.

"Edick," she murmured.

"No."

She opened her eyes, and Pavel's concerned gaze met hers. "You're bleeding, Magda. Badly. I need to get you to a hospital where I can get supplies and stop the bleeding."

She felt so very tired, her eyes must have weights on them, and she could barely make out his words. "Hospital?"

"Yes. Pskov's the nearest one."

She fought to clear her confusion, took a deep breath, and pushed herself up.

She lay on the floor of the chapel in a pool of blood. Pavel crouched beside her; Brother Timofea loomed over her, worry in his brown eyes. "The baby. Where's Nadezhda?"

Timofea pocketed his hands in his sleeves. "I just checked on her. She is sleeping soundly. As is Edward."

Edward. She glanced at Pavel, who had his arm behind her shoulders, helping hold her. "I'm dying, aren't I?"

Pavel flinched. "We need to get you to a hospital. Now."

She took a deep breath and fought the wave of pain, of

crushing exhaustion. "I know someone in Pskov who might help." Her thoughts tracked back to Baba Nina and her cellar. Maybe. . .

Only, what then? If she lived, she would live as a fugitive. Running from Stalin until he found her and Nadezhda, executed her, and sent her daughter to a state orphanage. "Pavel. What if I go with Edward. . .what if. . ."

He swallowed; his face twitched.

"I'm not going to make it that long, am I?"

He shot a look at Timofea. "Maybe if we can get you help, stop the bleeding, let you rest—"

"It's okay." She closed her eyes. *"Though Thou slayest me, yet will I serve Thee."* She opened her eyes and looked at Timofea. "My father loved me, didn't he?"

"Very, very much, my child. He was willing to lose his life to save yours."

She nodded, then took Pavel's hand and squeezed, very aware of the fear on his face. "I'm a Klassen. And I'm going to follow my father's footsteps of courage."

⚜

He saw her as he imagined her. So many times he'd watched her as she sat in the sunlight, a slight smile of tease on her face, as if she knew what he might be thinking. Only, as he watched, he knew it couldn't be her. Magda didn't smile so freely, didn't laugh aloud, a sweet giggle of joy. Not, at least, the Magda he'd first met. But this Magda might be the one he'd seen blossoming, becoming life and joy despite the grief around her.

He knew it must be a dream, also, because she sat on his porch in Schenectady, rocking a baby, its downy head covered with brown curly hair. She hummed and again cast him a sly look. "I love you, Edick."

Then she stood, came toward him, the bundle in her arms. She transferred the baby, then leaned close and ran a feather touch across his mouth, like the softest of summer breezes. He smiled in his dreams, seeing Magda's hair rustled by a warm wind, her blue eyes in his, reaching to his heart, her lips full and smiling. A rich and earthy smell with a hint of pine drew through him. He put his arms out, as if to hold her.

She dissolved through his fingers.

"No!" He jerked awake, wrung by the sense that something was wrong. Across from him, the baby lay in the folds of Magda's cot, quietly sucking her fist, banging herself occasionally in the face. She'd begun to wiggle and fuss, upset by a twinge of hunger, perhaps. Edward blinked, his eyes adjusting to the pale light. The candle had snuffed out, but sunlight streamed under the door.

Magda was nowhere to be found.

The baby whimpered. Edward crawled over to her, picked her up, and cradled her in his arms. "Where's your mamma?"

"Gone."

Timofea stood in the shadows against the wall. His face was drawn, and Edward's jaw pulsed at the sadness in the man's eyes. "I don't understand."

Timofea leaned down and peered into the baby's eyes. "She is hungry."

"Yes. And I can't feed her. She needs her mother. Where is she?"

Timofea rubbed his chin with two fingers. "I think the cook will boil some milk."

Edward shuffled to his feet, a hollow feeling constricting

his chest. "Where is Magda, Brother?"

"We'll have to find a bottle. But a baby this size won't take much." He turned, shuffling toward the door.

"Timofea!" Edward held the baby tighter than he meant, and she let out a wail. Her tiny fists punched the air. "Where is Magda?"

Timofea hung his head.

No. Oh no. "She's not. . .I mean, that's not what Pavel wasn't telling me, was it. . . ?" He felt weak and sat down hard on the cot. "No, Brother, she can't be—"

"She left with Pavel. About an hour ago."

Edward gasped as if sucker-punched.

Timofea's wizened eyes glistened. "Magda is very ill. Pavel will take her to a hospital, try and stop the bleeding. From there, I don't know." He wrung his hands and tore his gaze from Edward.

Edward opened his mouth, gulping in air, or maybe just trying to get a sense of sanity. "No, Timofea. She's supposed to come to America. With me. I love her."

He tried to catch his breath, but it seemed as if something hard had slammed into his chest, leaving him unable to take a full breath. He closed his eyes, aware that he was holding a baby, wanting very much to scream or maybe just hit something very, very hard. He purposely blew out a calming breath. Something to keep him from trembling. "Why would she do this?"

Timofea sat next to him. He held the baby's fist to her mouth, and she sucked at it greedily. "For Nadezhda. For her family." His tone turned solemn. "She knew she couldn't make it to Estonia with you. Even now as a fugitive, if she lives, she will forever live in hiding. That is no life for her baby."

Edward stared at the baby, clenching his jaw and fighting the burn in his eyes. "No, this can't be happening. Why didn't she wake me before she left?"

Timofea shook his head. "Because she knew you would never let her go. That you would follow her. And she needed you to stay with Nadezhda." Timofea drew a folded paper from his sleeve. "You have earned a great responsibility, my son. I'd call it a sacred treasure."

Edward took the letter with a weak hand, barely able to comprehend Timofea words. "A sacred treasure?" His mouth dried as he stared at the baby.

Timofea sat next to him, ran a finger down the baby's cheek. "You aren't unlike a young man I once knew, a man full of zeal and passion for right. He wanted to be a hero for the Motherland." Timofea smiled, but his gaze wore the passage of time. " 'Seek ye first the kingdom of God, and all these things will be added unto you.' "

"What?"

Timofea glanced at him, as if reeled back to the present. A slow smile creased his face. "You know, Edward, a hero isn't someone who does great things. But one who lets God do great things through him."

Edward caught the baby's hand, wrapped her tiny fingers around his.

Timofea reached out for the child. "Let me take her to the kitchen and see if we can find something to feed her." He smiled ruefully. "The Nazis haven't found us yet—we still have our cows."

The monk lifted Nadezhda from his arms.

"I can't take the baby, Brother."

Timofea didn't answer but turned away, cooing to the child.

Edward put his hands over his eyes, wiping the moisture that had gathered. *Magda, how could you do this? What were you thinking?* His entire body ached, and he surrendered to the frustration coiling in his gut with a cry.

"No! God, how could You let this happen?" He raised his hand, then closed it into a fist. "I can't lose her, Lord. No, please!" The walls ate his grief and left him nothing but the cold dampness of the cave.

He palmed his chest as if to push back the pain that seemed to be spreading through his body like a flame and then opened the note.

Moy Edick,

I am dying. I can feel it. My strength ebbs from my bones like a river. And if I am gone, there is no one for my daughter. Except you. Perhaps God brought you to Russia for another reason—for my daughter, our daughter. Take her to America, give her a good life. Show her your kindness, your warmth. Love her as if she were your own. In many ways, she already belongs to you. She became yours when you carried me from the flames of the Pskov forest and nursed my bereft soul until it found its true Savior. Do not fear for me. I see now, it is exactly as you said—God has not abandoned me. He loves me, and He's shown it through your love and protection.

I love you, Edick Neumann. I will carry you in my heart, just as you will carry my beloved Nadezhda, the last descendant of the Klassen family, my baby of hope, in your arms. Don't let her forget I love her and that wherever she goes, God is watching over her. Please, give her the enclosed picture. It is of

*her grandmothers. And tell her that God's hand on
our family can be found in the words of Psalm 100.*

Vyechnaya,
Your Magda

He looked at the picture and saw in it two women, one
with the face of Magda. He swallowed hard. He raised his
gaze to the ceiling, to the darkness, and felt it to his soul.
"Lord, no. It's too much to ask. I'm not a father. I can't raise
a child." He curled his hands into his hair, crushing the letter in his grip. "No."

Do you love Me, Edward?

"I do, Lord, but this is too hard. I can't do this."

Feed My lambs.

He grimaced, unable to find words to argue with the
Almighty. An invisible fist gripped his chest in a spasm of
pain. First Katrina, now Magda. He slumped onto the
floor, unable to think past the impossible request. How did
Magda think he could shoulder this responsibility?

*"Cast the net on the right side of the ship, and ye shall find.
They cast therefore, and now they were not able to draw it for
the multitude of fishes."*

The lessons from the night before drummed through
his mind. *"Trust Me even when you don't understand,"* Jesus
said to the disciples, *"one mission at a time, and I will fill your
nets with blessing."*

A thousand moments rushed back to him. Moments
when he'd shielded Magda, when he'd listened to her fears,
when he prayed for her and longed to be the father of her
child. "No," he whispered, his voice broken.

The door opened, and Timofea padded in. If the monk
was surprised to see Edward curled on the floor, sobbing, he

said nothing. He knelt and handed Nadezhda to Edward.

Lord, please, no.

But the moment the baby settled into his arms, his heart begin to swell. Nadezhda blinked at him, her mouth working, her eyes running over him, unable to focus. Then her mouth opened in a lopsided yawn.

Tears ran off Edward's chin.

"In our weakness, and His strength, we are made perfect. When God calls us to a task, He is faithful to equip us for it." Timofea stood and tucked his hands into his sleeves. "She has given you her little lamb, Edward. And He who is the great Shepherd will guide you."

Edward rubbed his finger along Nadezhda's cheek. Her eyes fluttered closed, and she sighed.

He curled her to his chest and sobbed.

***

"Magda, you need some sleep." Pavel crouched beside her. Settled into the soft hay, she felt warm and safe despite the damp aroma of the cellar. Pavel cupped a hand across her forehead. Worry creased his brow. She grabbed his wrist. "It's okay. I know, Pavel."

He shook his head, his face grim. "No, Magda. I'm not losing you." His eyes glistened, and not for the first time, she saw his feelings palpable in his eyes. This time, however, it took her breath away. How had she not seen it before?

Pavel loves you, Magda. Edick's voice. Edick, still protecting her, offering his blessing. Edick, the man who would raise her daughter with his wisdom, calm her fears with his wide embrace, protect her at all costs.

She smiled weakly as Pavel took her hand and traced her veins with his finger. "I'm not Edward, but I'll be here for as long as you need me," Pavel said softly.

She ran a finger down his cheek and along that firm Slavic jaw, so fitting for the partisan she'd come to admire. "You don't need to be Edick." She felt his tears drip onto her hand as he kissed it.

"Don't leave me, Magda." His voice broke, and he looked away as if unwilling for her to see the grief tearing his face.

Fatigue covered her body like a blanket. She summoned her strength and tightened her grip on his hand. "Not as long as you're here." She smiled at him, at his beautiful eyes, the concern on his handsome, ruddy face. "You should probably know, my real name is Marina."

Her eyes fluttered closed, and the last thing she felt was the press of his lips on her forehead.

⚜

Edward emerged from the woods and walked along the bluff. Colonel Stone stood on the beach, the ocean wind flattening his too-long hair and slicking his fatigues to his body. Edward's heart hung heavy in his chest as he shifted his gaze to the inflatable dingy onshore. In an hour, he'd be on board a submarine with all his options severed. He raised his eyes heavenward at the sea blue sky. "I'm taking You at Your word, Lord."

A flock of seagulls screamed into the sky as he scampered down the bluff, keeping his arms tight around his chest. Perspiration dotted his forehead under the wool *shopka*. He had few questions as to what Colonel Stone would say.

"Edward!" The director cut a bold shadow across the pale brown shoreline, crisscrossed with brown seaweed and ocean foam. Edward returned the wave, the vise around his chest tightening with each step. He blew out a labored breath.

"Colonel," he said as he drew closer. He stopped, saluted, then took the proffered hand.

"Didn't know if you were gonna make it, Captain." Stone's smile pushed up bulky cheeks. "Job well done."

Edward shook his head. "Did you hear about the Russian generals?"

Stone's face darkened. "Tikhonov and Voloshin?" He nodded. "Bad piece of luck. But that's war."

Edward swallowed a retort, his thoughts on Magda and Pavel and Brother Timofea dealing with that *bad piece of luck.*

"Where's your lady?" Stone looked past him. "I thought you were bringing someone out."

Edward grimaced. "We had a change of plans."

Stone frowned and clamped him on the shoulder. "Didn't work out, huh, son?" He shook his head. "Sorry about that."

Edward stood still, searching for words. His jacket moved, tiny knees digging into his gut. Nadezhda had grown fat and healthy in the month since her birth. Still, every time she cried, a ripple of panic wove through Edward.

Stone's eyes widened as he stared at Edward's movements. "Don't tell me, Neumann."

Edward unzipped his coat. "She's hungry."

Stone's expression hardened. "We're not an adoption service. This is the US Navy. We don't carry babies on submarines."

Edward caressed Nadezhda's cheek. He could hardly believe that she'd come to know his touch and to calm to his voice. The pleasure it gave him at her response balmed the ache in his heart. "Cast your net on the right side of the boat, Colonel."

"Huh?" Stone's eyebrows pinched into a wrinkled line. His eyes held no humor.

"It's obedience to God even when we don't understand that often leads to the greatest blessings." He smiled at his daughter, the fruition of more than he could hope or ask for. "Colonel Stone, I'd like you to meet my daughter, Hope."

SUSAN K. DOWNS

Susan served as the Russian adoption program coordinator for one of America's oldest adoption agencies prior to her decision to leave the social work field and devote herself full-time to writing and editing fiction. Through her adoption work, however, she developed a love for all things Russian and an unquenchable curiosity of Russian history and culture.

A series of miraculous events led Susan and her minister-husband to adopt from Korea two of their five children. The adoptions of their daughters precipitated a five-year mission assignment in South Korea, which, in turn, paved the way for Susan's work in international adoption and her Russian experiences. The Downses currently reside in Canton, Ohio. Read more about Susan's writing/editing ministry and her family at www.susankdowns.com.

SUSAN MAY WARREN

Susan and her family recently returned home after working for eight years in Khabarovsk, far east Russia. Deeply influenced and blessed by the faith of the Russian Christians, she longed to write a story that revealed their faith during their dark years of persecution and a story of their impact on today's generation. *The Heirs of Anton* is the fruition of these hopes. Now writing full-time in northern Minnesota while her husband, Andrew, manages a lodge, Susan is the author of both novels and novellas. She draws upon her rich experience on both sides of the ocean to write stories that stir the Christian soul. Find out more about Susan and her writing at www.susanmaywarren.com.

Don't miss the next book in the

HEIRS of ANTON

family saga.

OKSANA

By Susan K. Downs and Susan May Warren

ISBN 1-59310-349-2

COMING AUGUST 2005

Wherever Christian books are sold

"For the LORD is good and his love endures forever;
his faithfulness continues through all generations."
—PSALM 100

ALEXANDER PALACE, TSARSKOE SELO,
SOUTH OF PETROGRAD, RUSSIA,
FEBRUARY 27, 1917

From the outside looking in, she lived the fairy tale—
a peasant caught up in a princess life. But regardless
of what the Bolshevik rabble thought about those
who served the royal family, Oksana Nikolaevna Terekhova
had endured her fair share of suffering in her twenty-plus
years. She possessed no immunity from heartbreak, no
royal dispensation of never-ending bliss. In fact, from the
inside looking out, the fairy tale was fast turning into a
tragedy before her very eyes.

Starting with her hair.

She still couldn't bear to look in the mirror. True, the
pinned damask drapes allowed in only the barest of light,
but she could trace her appearance in her thoughts. Crude,
barren. Oksana ran her fingertips along her now-naked
scalp, stripped of its crowning glory. A bad case of the
measles had caused her hair to fall out in clumps, and the
mantle of sores that covered her had made it necessary for
Yulia to shave Oksana's head to keep the gooey discharge

from caking what little of her hair remained. In the grand scheme of things, her humiliation should be of no consequence, she knew. She was only an orphan, raised to serve the needs of the Romanov royalty. Still, she couldn't help but think she'd die of embarrassment before her hair returned.

If the measles or the revolutionists didn't kill her first.

Revolutionists.

This morning's news from Petrograd brought the bleak report that the capital city had fallen into rebel hands. The insurgent horde that fought to bring down the monarchy had already seized control of the village of Tsarskoe Selo. They now pushed toward the Alexander Palace grounds, intent on attacking the tsar's residence. Had anyone bothered to tell the revolutionaries that Tsar Nikolai wasn't at home?

As if the threat of an imminent hostile coup wasn't stress enough to bear, an outbreak of measles had erupted among the tsar's children and confined them to bed. For over a week now, Oksana, too, had suffered with the disease, quarantined from all human contact save that of Yulia Petrova, her fellow servant and best friend.

If she closed her eyes, she could pretend away the humiliation and instead find herself cruising the Gulf of Finland on summer holiday.

The gentle scent of lilacs and lilies woke her, and though she struggled to open her eyes, Oksana knew before looking that Her Royal Majesty, the Tsarina Aleksandra herself stood by her bedside. Terror balled in Oksana's throat. A midnight visitation from the tsarina to an infectious servant's bedchamber did not portend good news.

Even the dim glow from the tsarina's candle hurt

Oksana's eyes, but she swiped at her tears and struggled to rise.

"Don't get up, child. I know you're ill." She spoke in English, her voice as soft as the candle's radiance. Both the tsarina's choice of language and her tone added fresh credence to Oksana's fears. "Poor thing. You look just like my girls."

Oksana eased back on her pillow. That her misery held such esteemed company served to ease Oksana's embarrassment at her wretched appearance.

Dressed in her invariable Red Cross uniform, the tsarina didn't look well herself. The accumulated political stresses both at home and abroad made her look more apparition than human—pallid in color, cadaverous in form. She set her candle on the nightstand, then perched herself on the bedside chair.

"I regret having to disturb you when you're so sick. . . ."

Oksana recoiled beneath the royal's scrutiny, and she felt her fever rising until she realized that Her Majesty stared not at her, but through her.

The tsarina shook off her trance and reclaimed her thought. "But our present circumstance dictates that I speak with you." She sighed and looked away. "I'll try to be brief."

The flickering candlelight sent the tsarina's silhouette on a nightmarish dance across the ceiling and plaster walls. "We all pray this season of rebellion is soon suppressed and order restored to our land, but in the event such is not ordained. . ."

Oksana's pulse, fueled by panic, roared in her ears. Did the tsarina truly believe this rebellion, this affront to everything noble and just might overtake, even overthrow so many centuries of holy rule? She swallowed hard.

Tsarina Aleksandra's gaze fixed on her hands as she smoothed and picked at the folds of her uniform. "Well— as you know, the tsar is a thorough and deliberate man, and although he, as do I, place our full trust in our troops' strength and abilities to protect us, he feels we should prepare for any eventuality. I'm certain, as always, I can trust your discretion concerning any matter we discuss."

"Of course, Your Majesty." Oksana's reply came out wobbly and weak. She cleared her throat and started to reiterate, but the tsarina continued.

"Child, I've come to extend an offer to release you from service to our family." The statement seemed to drain the royal mother of all remaining color in her face other than the deep maroon circles that ringed her eyes. "You must flee to safety while the opportunity for such action still exists."

"No—" Oksana's protest barely made it past her lips before the tsarina silenced her with a stay of her hand.

"Hear me out." Empress Aleksandra patted Oksana's quilt-covered arm with the same gentle touch Oksana had seen the tsarina extend time and again to the injured soldiers she tended to in her hospital work.

"You've served us well and faithfully from the first day the nuns brought you to us as a child," the tsarina said. "You have fulfilled all we've asked of you. Our girls see you more as another sister than a subservient. However, in your position of personal service to the grand duchesses, you've been made privy to information that, if it should fall into the wrong hands, would bring disaster to the crown."

Fall into the wrong hands? Nausea forced Oksana to close her eyes.

"I fear a day is fast approaching—is, in fact, now upon us, when a decision of loyalty to the crown will put your life at grave risk. Think about my offer before you respond. Weigh the gravity of this decision. Already, other servants have chosen to leave. I bear them no malice. On the contrary, I understand their fear. But, I believe I know you well enough to surmise you will insist on staying with us. Both due to your station as an orphan and your adherence to that which is noble."

Oksana nodded in agreement before she realized her response was not received with the enthusiasm she expected. The tsarina shook her head, her lips pinched. "I need to warn you, Oksana Nikolaevna, if you choose to remain here, you will likely face whatever sentence is imposed on the nobility. The result may include imprisonment or, God forbid, death." The tsarina's speech faltered, but she regained her composure with a quick shake of her head.

"I need to know, should you make your choice to remain loyal to our cause, are you willing to accept whatever direction your sovereign deems best?"

Oksana didn't need to deliberate on her answer. To live outside the circle of the only family she'd ever known, such would be a fate worse than death. Regardless, Oksana knew she had but one answer to give. "Your Majesty, now, as always, whatever you require, I will do."

If you enjoyed the

family saga

MARINA

then read:

EKATERINA

ISBN 1-59310-161-9

& NADIA

ISBN 1-59310-163-5

By Susan K. Downs and Susan May Warren

Wherever Christian books are sold